DEDICATION

To Heather

Our introduction was something of a rom-com meet cute, but in a way that I found a collaborator, cheerleader, and friend. Thank you for pushing me to and through this book, even when you barely had the strength to stand yourself.

Chapter 1: Gloria

My first love was Broadway. My second was a man named Aaron John Michaels.

Both broke my heart.

Aaron also broke my soul and my mind.

And I'm on a journey to reclaim them all. When people say they're on a journey, they usually mean a metaphorical or figurative one. Not me. This quest has me covering so many miles I feel like a Hobbit.

I'd say I'd walked five hundred miles but I drove it. And I can't afford to have that earworm going. Everyone knows the only way to get rid of an earworm is to sing it out, and right now that just can't happen. Won't happen. But maybe again someday.

I open my mouth to sing—to see if by some miracle I'm already better and words come out—but silence fills the car. My throat dries and my chest constricts. The blood pounds in my ears as the mere *thought* of singing incites panic.

Singing used to be my mood regulator, always making me feel good. No wonder I've been such a mess since I lost the ability.

If this works, maybe it can happen again. I cross my fingers on the steering wheel.

But still, I did drive five hundred miles. Well, actually six-hundred and twenty-eight, to be exact. Ohio to New York with a smidge of Pennsylvania in between. Alone. That never would have happened ten years ago, or even five. This is progress.

Despite my accomplishment with the drive, I realize how rough it's been. The last decade has been a string of "the worst day ever" on endless repeat, like my own personal *Groundhog Day* movie. Starring me.

Quite literally.

Get over it. That's what I've been told, by well-meaning people who think it's so long ago it shouldn't matter. Or that it wasn't even a big deal in the first place. You know, ten years ago, I wouldn't have thought this would paralyze me the way it has. If I had a nickel for every time someone told me to get over it, I wouldn't have decided to sell all of my belongings to move to the middle of nowhere to work with the only therapist this side of the Mississippi who can possibly fix me.

But I don't have the nickels; all I have left is hope. The last of the settlement money from the college will be used to pay for my treatment, without leaving me much to live on when I'm better. Initially, though the money was a poor consolation for losing my education, my degree, and my career, I'm glad I've had it to live on. I'm sure it was hard for them to put a dollar amount on the damage caused by betrayal and faulty online security practices. Though my parents have never made me feel guilty, I can't go on living in their house forever. Finding a job while I'm here is priority number one.

Number two if you count finding a bathroom.

I should have stopped at least an hour ago. Maybe two. I probably should have stopped for gas as well. I was riding high on this now unfamiliar feeling of anticipation and didn't want to delay the finish line even for a few moments. My car is practically on fumes as I coast into town, down the main road, and across the tiny bridge that leads to Chapel Street, where my apartment should be. Instructions direct me to on-street parking. I timed this well, as there's only one last sad clump of snow leftover from a relatively mild winter.

Maybe if this treatment works and my brain gets fixed, I'll enjoy the rolling hills and colorful main street. It seems like a charming little town, nestled on the eastern-most border of New York state. According to the map of the state, it looks like I'm about a hundred or so miles north of New York City.

There was a time— the time before it all happened— that I'd dreamed of living in New York City. It was the only thing I'd ever wanted. Now the mere thought of all that hustle and bustle and *all those people* is enough to send me running back home and into bed for a week.

No. I pound on the steering wheel. I've done too much work to run and hide. I can do this. I look up at my new residence. It's go time.

My apartment—or flat, as the landlord calls it—is on the second-floor in an old brick brownstone-ish type of house. You can tell this place has seen a lot.

Much like me.

When I'm in my low points and overwhelmed, all I can think of is that I've wasted ten years. A third of my life. I have nothing to show for the past decade other than pain and anguish and a pitiful savings account almost emptied by therapy bills. My hopes, my dreams vanished with the click of the 'send' button.

I can't let myself stay in that deep, dark place for long. If I do, I'll never get out. I haven't come all this way to be perpetually trapped. I was never a negative person. Not until the panic attacks and anxiety that accompany my PTSD took over. And you can only live in fear for so long before actual depression sets in. No more. I'm here to get my life back.

To be able to work. To somehow repay my family for taking care of me. To sing again.

I shake my head, trying to clear it. That last one—the dream to be on stage again—seems like the impossible dream. Better to focus on my mental health. That's much more achievable. If I can leave Hicklam with that intact, I will have had success. That will be a reward in and of itself, one I will not take for granted.

The key is on top of the doorframe, as promised, which seemed like a good idea at the time. Mostly because in my mind I'm larger than life. In reality, I'm five-foot-two and am not able to reach the key. At least not without some kind of jumping and wiggling, all of which my bladder is strongly urging me not to do. I'm almost positive that wetting my pants on my doorstep would not be a good omen for this adventure.

I stare up at the key on the doorframe. Should I throw something at it? Should I jump up and try to knock it off? I bend my knees in a crouch to jump, but the increased pressure on my bladder is an automatic nope.

I do the only thing I can think of.

I run down the stairs, out the door, down one block, and across the street to what looks like a coffee shop. I push open the door, my gaze frantically searching the back of the store for a restroom. The kitschy sign hangs, off-kilter I might add, in plain view.

Score.

My urge to go is so strong that I don't even stop to look for a hidden camera. You know I am desperate when I don't do that. The feeling that I'm always being watched, especially when I'm in such a vulnerable position, is something I haven't been able to shake since the betrayal that sent me on this downward spiral. This is one behavior I can't wait to extinguish.

Ah sweet relief.

Sometimes I'm glad that my biological needs can short circuit my brain, even if for a small little moment.

As I'm washing my hands, feeling worlds better with an empty bladder, it occurs to me that I should probably buy something, considering I used the bathroom. It's basic courtesy. I think I have fifteen dollars in my wallet. That's not going to go far. Maybe they'll let me clean the bathroom here in exchange for coffee. I look at my watch.

Shit. I'm going to be late. No. No. No.

I can't be late for the first therapy appointment. Malachi said he was a stickler for promptness.

Maybe they won't notice that I snuck in and out without buying anything. Maybe the three people at the counter are distracted enough and I can slip out and—

"Hey! Can we help you with something?" the barista shouts out to me.

I need to do this right. "Um, yeah. Um, can I get a coffee?"

The barista smiles. "I'm gonna need a little more information. What size? How do you want it?"

I glance up at the chalkboard menus hanging above the coffee bar. I'm surprised at the variety and number of choices. Things are looking up—at least I won't die of caffeine withdrawal while I'm here. I'll take this as sign that everything will be okay.

Fingers crossed.

"Medium. Plain. I mean just a plain coffee but with cream and sugar. Not a fancy coffee."

"Fixin's are behind you." She nods swiftly. "Two-ten."

The price is reasonable enough. I scrounge in my pockets for change, but come up empty handed. I hand her three crumpled dollar bills and dump the change into the tip jar. I now have twelve dollars to last me until I find a job.

I wonder if they're hiring here? It means I'll have to talk to people, but my options are going to be limited based on the size of the town. I look around. The cash register is old school and I don't see any surveillance equipment. No computer, no cameras. Two of my biggest triggers. I could probably deal with people if those two things weren't an issue.

"Um, are you hiring? I'm new here and need to find a job." The words tumble out of my mouth before I lose my nerve.

The barista shakes her head. "No, sorry. We're on a skeleton crew until the summer as it is. Maybe then?" She offers sympathetically.

"It's okay. I'll ... I'll figure something out. Thanks."

I try not to start running the numbers in my head right here on the spot, willing my anxiety to stay subdued. Of course, if I had any control over this, I wouldn't be here. And now the numbers start rolling through my brain. Food, car insurance, gas. I wish I qualified for disability but since I don't, my settlement money will pay for visits to this specialist at two-hundred bucks a pop. Two hours a day, three times a week for a minimum of three months.

That number alone is enough to make me vomit.

For those of you not good with math, it's almost fifteen grand.

My broken brain is going to cost me fifteen grand to fix.

Maybe.

Hopefully.

And that's not even to put me back to where I was before Aaron sailed in and ruined me. Betrayed me. *Humiliated me*. Not back up on stage for sure. All I'm hoping for is enough to be able to function in society. To possibly use a computer or smartphone without a panic attack. To talk to people without the dread and fear that they *know* and that they've *seen* the video.

Yes, *that* video.

When you put it that way, fifteen grand doesn't seem like a lot. I've probably spent that on medication and co-pays and lost work over the past ten years. Hell, my college scholarship that I forfeited was about twenty grand.

All because of Aaron John Michaels.

I wish I could sue the SOB for pain and hardship so that I could afford a fancy coffee.

"You looking for work?" the voice behind me asks.

Great. The cliché that in small towns, everyone's up in everyone else's business and people like to talk to each other is true. I've totally lost the art of small talk. Add that to the list of things I'm here to reclaim.

No time like the present.

I nod and slowly turn around.

I don't want to though, because I know without even looking, based on the melodious timbre of his voice, that I want nothing to do with him.

Seeing him only confirms it. I could tell by the voice he has dashing good looks. That's how I'd describe him. Dashing. Hell, I think Merriam-Webster's probably has a picture of him.

Square jaw. Clear ivory skin with a ruddy undertone. Green eyes that twinkle. A dimple.

For the love of God, he has a dimple.

Ten years ago, he would have made me weak in the knees, just as Aaron did.

Now I'm willing the panic not to rear its ugly head.

Add that to my list of triggers. Computers, cell phones, cameras, performing on the stage, and now charismatic, confident men. As if I needed another trigger for my PTSD.

I will not be conned by another good-looking man. I will not be conned by another good-looking man. I will not be conned by another good-looking man.

"Are you new here? I don't remember seeing you before." He is still talking.

I nod again. It's about all I can manage. *Please stop talking to me before I have a full on panic attack right here and now*.

"Grayson, honey, are you picking up the usual?" the barista asks.

He leans around me. "Sure thing. You know we're up much too late to be any good without Dean's Beans to get us going." He laughs and his gaze swivels back to me. "I like my coffee. You could say I like it *a latte*."

Inwardly I groan at his pun but outwardly, my gaze darts to the door. One side of my brain wants to talk and be normal. I've missed that part of my brain. That part of my personality. That part of *me*.

The other side is telling me to run. Guess which side wins?

I have to get out of here before I start to freak out.

Reflexively, my right hand seeks out the beads on my left wrist. I don't need to look at them to see the numbers, reminding me to breathe in and out slowly. The guy steps around me to hand over his credit card to pay for his standing drink order.

"You know your money is no good here," I hear the barista say. I use this distraction as my chance to make a break for the door. I don't even stop to put cream or sugar in my coffee. Within seconds I'm out the door and crossing the street back to my new apartment, gulping for air faster than I should.

Once upstairs, I put my coffee cup on the floor and jump up and down until I manage to knock the key down. I'm afraid of what I'll find when I open the door but am pleasantly surprised by the cleanliness of the apartment. I'm not sure if the shabby chic is intentional or cost effective, but it's clean and pleasant.

I begin to search for cameras, my ritualistic behavior that I can't wait to leave behind. My eyes immediately see the paper on the floor, obviously slid under the door. It's a note from my therapist, Malachi Andrews, postponing our session because one of his clients is in crisis.

It would have been easier if he could have texted or called me, but since I can't handle owning a cell phone yet, this will have to do. I fold the note and put it on the counter. Time to resume my search.

****

I survived my first night. Nothing crawled out of the mattress and ate my face. I probably shouldn't have watched that episode of *The Big Bang Theory* before bed where Sheldon is convinced that a used chair contains vermin and critters. Spoiler alert, it did.

A thorough and somewhat obsessive scouring of the place revealed no recording devices. I knew in my rational brain that there wouldn't be any here, but my rational brain is very rarely in charge these days. I didn't wake up to anyone weird staring at me. The bedroom appears to be a safe place, as bedrooms should be. A place to relax. A place where you can let your innermost self out and no one can see. Where no one should be able to see.

There's heat and electricity and even cable TV in this place. I shouldn't have expected less, as this is what the agreement stated, but sometimes I don't have a lot of faith in humanity.

Betrayal does that to a person.

But it's not in Malachi's best interest to do a bait and switch on me. After all, his brother and sister are the owners of this building. The three siblings truly have a sweet deal. Malachi brings the patients to town, Marvin and Malyia put them up.

It's super convenient as well.

I only have to walk next door to get to therapy. And home again.

There's no place like it.

It's not like I'm agoraphobic. Not technically anyway. It's more that going outside where someone could be recording me or where people might have seen the video triggers my anxiety, so staying inside feels better.

But after a while, those walls close in and the only place that has been safe becomes a prison. I want to be able to leave my house without feeling the panic. The fear. I want to be able to leave the shelter my parents have provided.

"Ria, so nice to meet you in person. I hope you got settled in sufficiently and got my note yesterday. Malyia said it was in plain sight. I'm so sorry to cancel on you like that. I apologize for the inconvenience." Malachi Andrews stands as I enter his office. There was no receptionist out front. It looks more like his house than an office.

Probably because it is his house.

I feel like he's about to whip out a bowl of popcorn and ask me to watch a movie or something. I'd be okay with that, in this warm, safe space. It's completely different than what I'm used to. I've only improved so much with the conventional therapies and medications. They've helped me enough that I was able to get into my car and come here. I mean, it took me two years, but I'm here. I need something different to change the way I'm living.

To fully heal.

"Um, yeah. It was fine. Gave me time to settle in. No worries." Reflexively, I look around, trying to find the exits and where I'm supposed to sit. I need to find a chair where I can keep my eyes on the doors and windows.

Another behavior I'll be happy to extinguish.

Malachi must be used to this as there is a perfect spot that he gestures toward. "Please, have a seat. Anywhere is fine."

Okay, so we're getting right into it. I'm ready. I sit down on the front edge of the chair. My hands grip the armrests. Partially to hold me up, but partially in case I need to launch myself out of the chair and toward the door.

You never know when you'll need a quick getaway.

Malachi opens a folder, which I assume is my chart. I'm surprised he doesn't have it all on a computer. Now that I look around, there's not even a computer in here. At least not that I can see.

Good. I wonder if he removes it for me. Is he hiding it? What else could he be hiding? Nervously, I look around, trying to see if I'm being watched.

You may think I'm crazy. I'm not. At least I never was. I used to be confident. I thought I was invincible. I was fearless up on a stage. But that all changed the moment I was recorded without my knowledge. Now I'm a fractured, damaged shell of who I was. Afraid of the world. Afraid of computers and cell phones and technology.

Malachi is my last hope of living a normal life.

Unless I'm going to become Amish. But black's never been my color.

Chapter 2: Grayson

"I have news."

First off, news from my mother is never good. Especially when she calls me when she knows I'm out for my run.

You didn't get a call back for Waitress.

We can't cover your rent in New York plus our mortgage here. If you don't get a show, you have to move back home.

Your father has pancreatic cancer.

"Mom, I haven't had my coffee yet. I'm on my way to Dean's Beans now. Can it wait until I get back?"

"The crew isn't coming."

I want to think she means something different. Like there were more words that she has to say. The crew isn't coming in *this morning*. Or the crew isn't coming in *today*. The dread creeping up my spine tells me it's not that.

I let out a sigh. "Why?"

"Um, I maybe had a little disagreement with Dave about the direction he was taking us."

I look both ways before crossing the street. One more lap around Van Buren Park and then I'll be off to the coffee shop. At least that had been my plan before the latest bomb that Mom is currently dropping.

"Maybe?"

"He's robbing us blind. I looked up the supplies he's ordering. He's padding the cost and the labor fees are through the roof."

I stop jogging. "Mom, please tell me you aren't saying what I think you're saying."

"Grayson, I had no choice. I can't afford to get ripped off."

The actual statement should be *we can't afford to get ripped off* since it's both of us working our tails off for The Edison. When Dad died, I was appointed as Co-Executive Producer with Mom. We're supposed to run this together, though some days, I feel like managing her is more of what I do.

"Mom, you can't afford not to finish. Where will the cast live? Where will the audience sit? Where are people going to take a shit?"

"Language, young man."

It doesn't matter that I'm in my mid-thirties. It doesn't matter that I've been in shows—shows which she purchased—that had simulated sex and foul language. I'll always be ten years old to her. This tends to be problematic in her being able to see me as an equal business partner.

"Mom," I plead. "You can't fire Dave."

"Don't worry. I have a plan."

I start jogging again. I need to do something so I don't punch the next thing I see. Lucky for most residents of Hicklam, there aren't a lot of people out in the park at ten a.m. My teeth are gritted so hard I can't even speak.

"Come back as soon as you're done working out. We're going to have to talk about that too. You might need to make some schedule adjustments. And we're going to need bodies." That's her solution. Schedule adjustments and bodies.

She never has been a planner. That was Dad's specialty. I never wanted to be a planner, but one of us has to step up.

"Bodies? Are we opening a mortuary?"

"Warm bodies. Competent bodies. Bodies who can work."

Oh God. She wants to foreman this herself. Which means it will be on me. The woman has never been able to plan her way out of a paper bag. She must have lost her mind.

"Ma, are you nuts? I can't take this on too."

There's no way I can manually do the renovations we've started, in addition to the day to day running of my family's theater company, the lodging and accommodations for the cast and crew, getting directors and choreographers to drive almost two hours up from the city to bring some culture, and then acting in most of the shows, which are all already on me.

No big deal.

I need to enjoy this run. It might be my last for a very long time.

"Grayson, you know I don't have much of a choice. This could be it for us."

What she means is that *we* don't have much of a choice. She—we—have put everything into The Edison. This renovation, though much needed, is a massive financial risk, and we need a successful season and a packed house to be able to keep the property when we close in September. I can't even begin to tally the sacrifices we've made to keep this theater company open and running summer after summer, like my grandparents and great-grandparents did. Hell, my grandparents insisted my parents include The Edison in their wedding vows.

Which they did.

It was only fitting, seeing as how they met when Dad was cast in a show and Mom was on set design. If it weren't for The Edison, I wouldn't be here.

As I'm circling to the far side of the park, I notice a woman doing ... yoga? It's unusual, seeing as how it's a balmy fifty degrees. But no, there she is. I don't think I've seen her out here before.

I would have noticed.

I look away as she stretches back, hands on the ground and her ass high in the air. I should not be looking. The she presses forward, her stomach on the ground with her back arching up and her face tilted toward the sky. I focus on her movements. It looks as if she's moving through choreography.

Oh wait, it's the girl from the coffee shop yesterday. The one who I apparently scared off with my terrible pun.

It wasn't that bad. Not bad enough to run from, certainly.

Oh screw this. I'm done running for the day. I turn and head toward Dean's Beans.

"Grayson, honey. The usual?"

I love that Heidi asks every day. Usually it is. But now, since there apparently is no longer a crew working at The Edison, I can downsize considerably.

"Um, no. Just mine today."

"One latte made with love coming right up."

While I wait, all I can think about is how screwed we are. Where am I going to find a competent work crew? Anyone in Hicklam this time of year who isn't working doesn't want to work. It's a small town that's relatively dead during the winter, but there aren't tons of residents. Most construction people head down south for the winter where they can work without freezing their asses off or getting buried in three feet of snow. With it being March, we could still get hit with at least one more snow storm, so none of the snowbirds have returned home yet.

Smart people.

"Heidi, do you know anyone looking for work?"

"What kind?" The steam rises from her metal pitcher as she pours my milk into the cup.

"Contracting. Home renovations. Well, business renovations. For The Edison."

"Don't you have a whole crew up there working? Who've you been buying coffee for? That's a lot of caffeine for you and your mom, especially when I know for a fact that with her heart, she can't handle it."

Sigh.

Small towns. Where if you sneeze at one end of town, someone on the other side says, "God bless you."

Heidi continues. "What happened to the crew? You can't afford to lose them. You start auditions and rehearsals in four weeks. Where will the cast stay if you don't finish? Your mama can't handle this kind of stress. You know her heart."

The woman has one episode of palpitations and the whole town has her on her deathbed. I wonder who the real actor in the family is. What I wouldn't give for the anonymity of a Starbucks in the heart of Manhattan right about now.

"Well, that would be why I asked if you know of anyone looking. What about the guy who painted this place last year?"

"Nah, he's wintering in Georgia. Not sure if he's coming back."

Damn.

Heidi hands me my coffee. "Thanks. If you hear of anyone looking, can you send them to The Edison? I'll take literally anyone."

She stops and cocks her head. "What about Plain Coffee?"

Confused, I look at the cup in my hand. "Um, I'm fine with my latte, and you're right about my mom not having caffeine. But thanks."

Heidi laughs. "No, the gal who was in here yesterday. She ran in like her pants were on fire, used the bathroom, and then reluctantly ordered a coffee. She kept calling it plain coffee. You talked to her. She asked if we were hiring. I've never seen her before, but maybe she's staying if she was asking about a job? Don't know where you can find her though." Heidi shrugs.

I put my coffee down, "Heidi, you're brilliant. I could kiss you right now."

Her face darkens and I realize my mistake. Heidi's flirted with me for years. I've worked very hard not to lead her on.

"Sorry, I didn't mean ... I ... shit."

She waves me away and turns around hastily. "You don't need to apologize, Grayson. But you do need to tell me why I'm so brilliant."

"Because I literally need every warm body and hand on deck if we have any hope of getting the work done at The Edison. And I know where to find Plain Coffee. At least I think I do. Now can I have a plain coffee to go?" I pause to look at the bakery case. "And one of your killer ginger scones."

"Are you sure, Gray? You can't go giving these out willy-nilly. You know they are very powerful. Almost as powerful as that one-hundred watt smile of yours."

I go to pull out my wallet only to realize I'm in my jogging pants and that I didn't bring any money with me. "Shit, Heidi, I don't have my wallet."

She waves me away. "You know your money is no good here. Mostly because I keep a tab of your expenses. Hell, I won't even add these to it. All the business you generate for me during the season almost covers your tab for the rest of the year." She winks at me. "Almost."

We're back in the friend zone again. Phew.

"I promise I'll get you later." Heidi hands me the bag and the black coffee. I turn to the condiment counter where I add cream and sugar. I don't know how exactly she likes it, so I do my best. Once I replace the top, I put both cups in one hand and carry the bag in the other. Those years of waiting tables in New York City are finally paying off.

Now to hope she's still doing yoga in the park.

Chapter 3: Gloria

"You look like you could use a cup of coffee."

I squeeze my eyes shut, trying to close out the voice, but wondering who could be bringing me coffee. I've only been here a day. Other than Malachi and Malyia, no one even knows I'm here. My parents aren't even sure exactly where I am, though I promised them I'd tell them when I got settled.

I was afraid to tell them what I was going to do here in Hicklam. They've worried so much for me. Because of me. I want to get better so that I don't cause them any more pain.

I look up from my child's pose to see the latte guy from the coffee shop yesterday standing over me holding out two cups of coffee and a small brown bakery bag. The way he's standing, with the sun behind him, makes him look as if he was backlit in heavenly light.

Like he needs any help.

I will not fall for a charming smile. I will not fall for a charming smile. I will not ... my stomach rumbles in response, betraying my plan to deny the fact that I'm starving, as well as jonesing for caffeine.

"You like it a latte?" My hands fly to my mouth. Oh God, please tell me I didn't actually say that out loud.

He places the bag down next to me and then transfers one of the coffees from his left hand and puts it down as well. "I got these for you. I didn't think my joke was that bad."

"It was." I can't help but smile at him. Just a little.

He sits down on the ground next to me. He's wearing joggers and a sweatshirt and has got to be freezing. Now that I've stopped moving, I'm getting cold.

"Not bad enough for you to go running out of the shop."

I start to tell him that it's not why I ran, but it seems like too much to get into right now.

Or ever, for that matter.

I stand up and roll up my yoga mat. I tuck it under my arm and then reach down for the coffee and bag. The coffee yesterday was amazing. So much better than the chain shop which shall remain nameless at home. A quick peak in the bag reveals a scone. Instantly, my mouth begins to water.

"Heidi makes the best ginger scones. Trust me, once you have it, your life will be changed."

Maybe it's full of Xanax or something. That would certainly help.

"Well, um, thanks. That was nice of you." I don't know what else to say and if I stay any longer, I'll either have a freak out or fall in love. Neither seems like a good option at this point.

I start to walk away.

"Um, wait!" he calls. "I have a favor to ask."

There's no such thing as a free coffee.

The urge to freak out is winning the battle. I want to run. Not figuratively but literally. I want to get the hell away from him and hide in my bed for a week.

Would it be rude to take the coffee before I sprint off?

"Don't look so scared. It's not bad. I promise I'm not a sexual deviant or anything. I don't even have a sketchy van to lure you to. I ran here. Well, I was out for a run. I live up there."

He points up the hill to a large ... building. It's not a house but not an office either. It looks like a dorm or something. I don't think there's a college around here. The town doesn't seem big enough for a college.

And he looks way too old to still be in school. Either that or he parties too hard and it's catching up with him.

Though I doubt that because it's only ten a.m. and he's already been out for a morning run. When I was in college, after a night of partying, the next day didn't start until after noon.

But that of course was a different time in a different life.

"Look, I've got to run. I have a place I need to be." That is, perhaps, the most lame thing I've ever said. But at least I didn't run away. See? I'm totally making progress here.

I look at the coffee in my hand. Is it rude to take it? Or more rude to give it back? What will he think—

STOP.

I square my shoulders and take a deep breath. This is how my downward spirals always start. Questioning and second guessing myself. Wondering what everyone else will think of me.

I need it not to matter.

"Thank you for the coffee and scone. It was really nice. See you around."

I turn and walk away. I don't think this guy's a creeper, but obviously I'm not the best judge of character, so I walk the opposite direction of my apartment. Then I walk some more and when I've finally drained the last remnants of the coffee, I make the turn that will bring me back to my house.

I can't believe I have to wait until tomorrow to talk to Malachi about this. I will definitely be bringing this up. Though let's face it, I've had enough therapy to know what he's going to say. Trust issues, trust your instinct, blah, blah, blah.

What he can't—what nobody can—understand is that the trust issues aren't with other people. I mean, they are, obviously, but they're more with myself. I can't trust my gut. It doesn't know the difference between friend or foe. It doesn't know when someone wants to love me or hurt me.

I probably shouldn't have eaten that scone either. What if he laced it with something? What if he's trying to poison me? What if he put hallucinogens in it to make me think I'm going crazy?

Not that it's a stretch.

Hell, I packed up moved across the country for some super expensive, alternative psychotherapy treatment for my PTSD.

Perhaps the hallucinogens would help.

I pass Dean's Beans. Maybe I should do some reconnaissance work, instead of falling down my normal spiral. Find out who this guy is. Find out what he wants. Find out if they have more scones and if they all taste that good.

I walk in, yoga mat still slung over my shoulder. The same barista from yesterday is here.

"Hey honey, did Grayson find you? How was your scone?"

I have to remind myself that this is how small towns work. She doesn't have a camera. She isn't spying on me. God, just talking to that guy has me even more on edge than normal. I rub the beads on my bracelet, trying to calm down.

"Um, the scone was delicious. Thank you."

"What can I help you with then? You need another cup?"

I shake my head. "Um, no. I was just ... well, the guy who bought my coffee ..." I don't know how to finish without sounding weirder than I already am.

"Grayson?"

I nod. "I think?" I try to remember yesterday, hearing this woman talk to him. Maybe that's what she called him. My memory is shit. Another nice bonus of anxiety. It's not bad enough that you freak out and obsess all the time. Not being able to remember anything doesn't help.

"Yes, Grayson Keene."

"Do you know him? Well, I mean, because obviously you know him. At least his name. And that he bought me coffee and a scone. I mean, how well do you know him?" My words tumble out like a raging river.

So much for hiding my weirdness.

The barista sighs. "Oh yes, I've only been in love with him since that boy hit puberty." She actually leans on the counter with her chin on her hands and a wistful expression on her face.

Crap. I'm barely in town a day and am already sticking my foot in it.

I squint a little at her. I could be off—way off—but she looks older than him.

"I'm sorry, I don't even know your name," I offer. If I'm going to pry about her age and the man she loves, I should at least know that.

"Heidi Dean. Welcome to Hicklam." She extends her hand over the counter toward me. Now the name of the place makes sense.

I shake her hand. "G ... I'm Ria." I stumble over my name, reminding myself of my resolve to go by this new nickname. It's a layer of protection. No one can look me up and find *the video* this way. Ria Benedetti brings up zero hits. Gloria Benedetti ... that's another story. "So Grayson is—" I break off. I was going to ask if he was off the market, but that makes no sense because I'm not shopping. "—your significant other?" I finish lamely.

Heidi's head tips back in a laugh. "Oh God no, honey. He dated my kid sister for a while. I don't think I'll ever get out of that friend zone with him. Which is fine. I mean, it's only been twenty years. But he's got that charisma that when you see it, you can't help but go a little weak in the knees. Like one of those big Hollywood stars. That's him. A total star."

"Oh." Sometimes, there's nothing else to say. Dashing good looks. Tons of charisma. A dimple. There's a churning in my stomach, a battle between the innate attraction I feel for that type of man and the damage done by one such type.

He's my kryptonite. I'd better stay far, far away.

"It's fine. I don't think he's actually my type or anything. He's dreamy. And he makes you feel like you're the only one in the world when he talks to you. Know what I mean?"

Unfortunately, all too well. Exactly my type. The desire hard-wired into my brain wins the battle over the trauma caused by Aaron. I cannot let myself be stupid enough to get caught up ever again.

I really need to stay far, far, *far* away.

"Okay, then. Um thanks. The scones are really good. If you ever need someone to work here, let me know."

I don't know why I say this again. I doubt circumstances have changed since yesterday. It's not like there's a sudden influx of people. Heidi mentioned that they wouldn't be busy until summer. But it would be nice to be around someone so happy.

"You don't want to work with Grayson? He's in dire need. I can't believe his mama did that to him." Heidi shakes her head. "Well, actually I can," she mutters. "That woman has been a hot mess since ... well for the last few years. And poor Grayson spends his life picking up after her."

"Huh?" Sounds like there's a story here. If I wasn't staying far away, maybe I'd want to know what it is.

"Didn't he ask you about doing some work for him? I mean, it's probably not what you want to do, but trust me, Grayson Keene is a good man, and he needs the help. I was even thinking about going up there after work."

"Up where?" I'm not even sure I'm really following this conversation. Again, I'm terribly out of practice.

"The Edison. They'll never get the rooms ready at this rate."

Ugh, another thing to hate about being stuck in this small town. Not only does everybody make it their business to be all up in your business, but everybody knows everything. And if you're new, you have no idea what they're talking about. I try to process what Heidi just said. The Edison. It sounds like a resort or hotel or something. And then she mentioned not getting the rooms ready in time.

I bet it's a hotel.

Sounds perfect.

While most people would shy away from cleaning hotel rooms, it's right up my alley. I wouldn't have to deal with people that much. I bet I could move my therapy sessions with Malachi to the late afternoon, since most rooms have to be made up by mid-day. This sounds promising, as long as they don't rent rooms by the hour. Or quarter-hour.

I'm almost hopeful.

"So where is The Edison?"

"It's up the hill." She jerks her head toward the back of the store. If I have my bearings right, it seems to be the general direction of those dormitory looking buildings that Grayson was referring to earlier.

I hope his hotel looks better from the front than it does the back.

That is, if I even get the job. My resume looks like a ghost town, and I'm not ready to get into all the reasons why. No one needs to know. Not to mention, while it's illegal to discriminate against people with mental illness, it doesn't mean it doesn't happen.

Frequently.

"I don't have a lot of references or experience, but I can work hard."

"You don't need to sell yourself to me, honey. Sell yourself to Grayson."

Heat fills my face at her suggestion. The rising color must clue her into my embarrassment.

"That's not what I meant, honey. I mean tell this to Grayson. I'm pretty sure if you have a pulse and will show up, he can use your help. And trust me, he needs the help right now. He'd be the first to help any of us out, if he could. He's already given up his career to stay up at The Edison."

I smile and thank Heidi for the information.

As I walk out of Dean's Beans, I stand in the street for a moment. If I turn left, I can go back to my apartment. If I turn right, I can head up to The Edison and get a job.

Going home is infinitely more appealing.

But that's not why I'm here in Hicklam. I'm here to get better and reclaim my life. And if cleaning toilets and picking up other people's towels is the key to doing it, then so be it. Not to mention, Heidi said Grayson needed the help. Maybe he's not the only one who's had some loss in life. He did buy me a coffee and scone after all ...

I turn right.

Chapter 4: Grayson

This is bad. Like so not good, it's not even funny.

The dorms are in shambles after tearing out all the walls to address the mold issues. About half of the rooms have drywall up but have yet to be taped and mudded. They're not even ready to be primed, let alone painted and trimmed.

At least the electrical and plumbing is mostly done.

I may kill my mother.

And you thought only patricide was popular in the theater.

I mean, that was ancient Greece, but I'm willing to draw upon my stage ancestors at this time.

I've texted the entire stage crew to ask them to come into town early to help. The problem is now they have nowhere to stay once they get here. I've got to get at least four rooms done so the gang can come back.

Though many of them are working with other theater companies until the end of April. That's just under four weeks away.

It sounds like a lot of time, and it's none at the same time.

I was supposed to be using this next month to set up auditions and schedules and firm up choreographers and directors and costume designers. To work on press and social media and all that jazz.

See what I did there? Musical joke.

Yet none of this seems like a joke. It's the most opposite of funny as you can get.

I'm not even supposed to be here. Three seasons ago was supposed to be my last. I'd booked the national tour of Elder Price in *The Book of Mormon*. It was going to be my big break.

And then Dad's miraculous recovery was no longer so miraculous and all bets were off. As was the tour.

I couldn't leave Mom.

Especially not when she'd shown a complete and total lack of capability on the business front. Though, based on the condition of the finances, Dad hadn't done that much better himself. Actually, he had done a great job until he got sick and thousands of dollars of medical bills erased all his hard work.

So here I am. Doing all the things that Dad used to.

God, I miss him.

I only hope I can get things back in the black for Mom to take over so I can go back to the life I'd planned on having.

That's a lot of hope that I don't really feel in this moment, surrounded by buckets of spackle and ladders and wires hanging out of holes in the walls and ceilings.

It won't be much of a theater season if we have no cast and crew because they have nowhere to stay.

Rent, a one-man show.

I guess I'm doing it myself. Sleep is overrated anyhow. You know what they say; the show must go on.

I don't even know where to get started. Give me a show that's a book and score, and I can make it come to life with sets and costumes and choreography. Give me a song and I'll sing the hell out of it. That's what I can do. This ... not so much.

I walk through the rooms, making a list. After a few arrows here and there, crossing one item out and moving it up, I copy everything onto a new list and feel ready to begin.

I think.

I know some of my buddies from high school would come up when they get off their day jobs, if I asked, but I hate to do that. I need to get going on my own. Taping it is.

I think. Maybe you mud first?

Oh shit, I don't even know how to start.

"Hello?"

The voice startles me, as it's not Mom and no one else should be here.

"Back here." That's probably stupid. What if it's a band of roving thieves and they sent in a young female to lure me out and ...

I live in the theater world a bit too much. I should get out more.

"Um, I'm sorry to ... I wanted to thank ... do you ... are you hiring?"

It's Plain Coffee.

"Hey, what are you doing here?" I wipe my hands on my pants, hoping I don't smell too bad. I'm not holding out much hope though.

"Heidi said you need help up here." She's looking around, the color draining from her face. She's still in her leggings and sweatshirt from the park, her dark hair still contained in the messy bun atop her head. "But I think I misunderstood."

"No, she was right. Obviously." I look around again. I'm pretty sure a natural disaster could hit and you wouldn't be able to tell the difference.

Now she's looking around. "Um, I think I made a mistake. This isn't what I was expecting. I don't think I'm qualified."

I laugh. "I know I'm not qualified. In no way shape or form. But I'm desperate. Do you have a pulse?"

She shrugs.

"You are moving so I will take that as a yes. You are, in fact, a warm body. Yes?"

She nods.

"Will you show up?"

She looks around the room before eventually coming back to me. Her brown eyes are wary and it's like she's measuring her words carefully. "I have some obligations a few hours a week. Can you be flexible?"

"I'll take whatever you can give, as long as you're willing to put in fourteen to sixteen hour days and never take a day off."

Her face pales, making her brown eyes look large. "Um, maybe I should go."

I put my hands up and step forward. She steps back. Wow. That message is loud and clear. Okay, I'll maintain my distance. "I was kidding. I'm not going to lie. I'm desperate. Totally desperate. I've got staff and everyone coming in four weeks. *Four weeks*!" The panic rises. "I will literally lose everything if we can't open and run. I need this summer to even have a chance at saving this place. It's been in my family for fifty years. So I will take whatever you can give me."

It's a Tony-worthy monologue.

I mean, every word of it is true, but still ...

"Okay." She looks around again. "But I'm not sure what exactly it is you want me to do."

Relief floods me and I want to kiss her.

Her.

I don't even know her name. I can't call her Plain Coffee forever.

I extend my hand. "I'm Grayson Keene."

She looks from my hand to my face and back again, but her hand doesn't reach out. She's gripping her left wrist with her right hand and appears to be playing with a bracelet. In any case, she makes no effort to complete the hand shake.

"Ria," she says, barely audible.

Immediately, I want to know more. What's her last name? Is Ria short for something? Maria? I knew a Ryah in college who was Indian. I don't think this Ria is Indian. Maybe Mexican or Italian or even a hint of Asian. Definitely not Indian though.

This girl is a mystery.

I realize I've stared at her a bit too long. Oops. "Okay, Ria, we have to tape. Then we have to mud. I think that's how it goes. Do you know how to do either?"

She shakes her head.

"Good. Me neither. I mean, I've watched a handful of home improvement shows, and my dad was a big Bob Villa fan, so there's that. There's also YouTube. Let's see what we can find."

She stands there, unmoving. I pat my backside, but my phone's not there. "I don't know where my phone is. Can we use yours?"

Ria shakes her head. "I don't have a phone."

What? "Did you break it?"

She shakes her head again. Her gaze darts toward the door and then around the room. "I don't have one. Maybe I should leave."

"No, don't go. A phone isn't a requirement for here. Mine is around here somewhere. Give me a second. I promise."

I've never met anyone, besides old people, who don't own a phone. And even then, a lot of the senior set in Hicklam are as glued to their devices as their younger counterparts. There are some ferocious online Scrabble games, from what I hear.

I glance around and spy my black case peeking out from behind a bucket of spackle. I quickly grab it and Google "how to tape and mud drywall." Within an instant, I'm redirected to a video that promises how to have smooth walls with minimal need for sanding, which the host, Phil, insures us, is the pits.

I gesture for Ria to sit on a bucket and then pull one over next to her so we can watch my phone together. Her arms are pulled tightly around her, and it's more than clear that she's trying really hard not to be too close to me. Also, she seems to be looking anywhere but at my phone. I inch away. I have a tendency to be a close talker so I should try to give her some distance.

After nine minutes of watching Phil swipe and press, I think I might have an idea of where to start. I look at Ria, still holding onto herself for dear life. "Do you think we can do it?"

She nods. "I think. It sounded okay. I've done some painting and used scrapers and wedges. It's probably like that, right?" Ria looks at me, hopeful.

For the record, it's not like that, and it is hard, and there is a steep learning curve. Our second wall looked better than our first and the third even better. We're so busy concentrating, I forget to wonder about Ria's background. Normally, I want to hear everyone's story. No one lands in Hicklam by accident.

But hours have gone by and there's barely any light left in the sky. I haven't thought about Ria. I haven't even thought about food. In related news, I'm starving. And we only have one room done.

At this rate, we'll never be done with the dorms.

Forget about finishing the theater itself.

"I'm sorry," I say, dejected. "This took all day and we barely have anything to show for it. I didn't think it would be this tedious. I understand if it's not what you envisioned."

Let's face it, I wouldn't be here if I didn't have to.

Ria's face breaks into a smile. It's small and cautious, but it's still a smile. "Are you kidding? Of course I have to come back. I am determined to see this through and become a master mudder."

I return her smile, relieved that I won't have to do this on my own. "I bet you will. And then you can make your own video and become internet famous."

The light drains from her face, and it looks as if a fast-moving storm has rolled in. Her mouth is pale— almost white.

"I ... I've got to run."

And faster than you can say jackrabbit, Ria is out the door. It takes me a minute to realize that she really left. I look out the window and see her running down the hill toward town in a dead run. It wouldn't surprise me if she wiped out, going fast like that.

But seriously, what got into her? I know it's late, but it's not as if the clock is about to strike midnight and she's going to turn back into a pumpkin. I want to look out and see if there's a glass slipper on the hill.

I know there's not.

But there doesn't seem to be any other logical explanation for her behavior.

Chapter 5: Gloria

Shit. Shit. Shit.

My breaths are short and staccato. I need to slow them down before I pass out.

In other words, I'm hyperventilating.

I haven't officially hyperventilated in almost six months. Great. I feel like I should have one of those signs: Days since last full panic attack: zero.

Here I am, twelve hours later and still freaked out. Still unable to regulate my breathing or my heart rate. Still triggered. Panic coming in waves throughout the night. Mom, as always, talked me through, her voice calming on the other end of the phone.

Here I am, the next morning, and still barely holding on. I only hope my session with Malachi helps me finally regulate.

"So, are you getting settled in?"

Malachi looks comfortable in his chair. Comfortable in his office. Comfortable in his skin. It must be nice.

"Um, no. I mean yes. I guess."

"You look off."

I hate that he can tell, but it probably means he's sort of good. He should be with what this is costing me. "I am off. I had a panic attack yesterday. I still feel shaky. I keep hyperventilating."

"Okay, well, that's why you're here. Let's get back to your history. We should finish that up today and then I'll have your treatment plan for you and we can start the preparation the next session."

"Aren't we going to talk about yesterday? Why I had a panic attack?"

Malachi folds his hands in his lap and suddenly I get the impression that I'm going to be scolded like a schoolgirl. "Do you know what the trigger was?"

Of course I know. The mere *idea* of making a video to go on the internet ... it makes my skin crawl. The one video that's out there is enough to make me want nothing to do with the world wide web ever again.

I nod.

"Is it related to the trauma for which you are seeking treatment?"

I nod again.

"Then it's irrelevant. You're here to deal with that trauma and be desensitized to it. Yesterday happened. You experienced an episode of trauma related to your initial trauma. Once we fix the precipitating event, hopefully your panic attacks will be much less frequent and much less severe. Now, where did we leave off with your history?" He looks at a notebook on his desk. "Oh right, college."

"So that's when it happened. My senior year."

Malachi nods.

This is where he gives me the space I need to relive the worst time in my life. Should be fun.

"You can be as detailed as you like. I know the time frame. That's all I need. You can tell me more, but it's not necessary."

Huh? Where is the probing? The examination of conscience. The deep penetration that makes me want to wilt into a ball and never get up again. I mean, we are in therapy here.

"Do you want me to talk about it?"

"I'll leave that up to you."

This has me confused. Speechless. Well, almost.

"Don't you want to know what happened to me?"

Malachi smiles a little. "Do you want the answer you want to hear, or the truth?"

It's never occurred to me that those are two different things. "Um, the truth, I guess."

"It doesn't matter what happened. It only matters that it did happen. I don't care what it is. The point of this is to get you to work through it so that you can better process the trauma and not have it constantly sabotaging your life. You've tried pulling it apart in more traditional therapy prior to this, I assume. How did that work for you?"

My mouth opens and then closes. "Not great. I mean, I made progress. I can leave my house now. I even drove all the way here, by myself. I didn't check your office for a camera today. In fact, I didn't check The Edison either." I think on that for a minute. Maybe it was because there was nothing in the rooms. "But I'm not where I want to be yet. I'm not totally healthy."

Malachi's smiles widens. "Right. I'm happy to listen if you want to tell me. We don't need to unpack it right now though. All I really need to know about is how you were functioning before and after. That'll give me a better idea of what you need."

His bluntness is refreshing. I've had enough smooth-talking to last me a lifetime.

Full of anticipation for something else besides traditional cognitive behavior therapy to help me, I watch as Malachi shifts in his chair, ready to start my journey with Eye Movement Desensitization and Reprocessing.

Let's get down to business.

****

"Sorry I'm late. I have a ... commitment in the morning a few days a week. I'll be up as soon as I can on those days," I say, walking through the back door of the hotel as I did yesterday. I glance around the room quickly, but don't feel the need to scour and examine every surface. Grayson's in the room next to where we worked, squatting on the floor and trying to work mud into the corner seam.

His phone sits on an upturned bucket, the screen black and non-threatening. At least in theory, it's non-threatening.

I've decided I'm just going to pretend that I didn't freak out and run away yesterday. Maybe Grayson has short-term memory problems and won't remember either.

"I didn't think you were coming back!"

Sugar balls. No such luck.

"Yeah, I don't want to talk about that. I'd say it won't happen again, but it's not something I can guarantee. But today is a good day so far, and I'm here, if you want me."

"Oh, I definitely want you."

My face feels hot. I hope I'm not blushing. I—

"You know what I mean." Grayson jumps up. "All I can say is thank God you're here. You are so much better at this than I am. I can do straight lines and screw holes. Corners, for some reason, are beyond my skill set."

He extends his arm toward me, handing me the drywall knife.

I take it and drop my bag on the floor. I don't have much—just a few snacks for later. I don't have a huge food budget right now, and I'm not sure how—or if—I'm getting paid. Let alone when.

I should ask about payment, even though Grayson never specifically said. It's implied with asking me to work, but you never know. I can't just *hope* everything turns out the way it's supposed to.

I shouldn't have to be shown yet *again* that people cannot be trusted. That good faith is as real as unicorns and kale that tastes like potato chips.

"So, I don't want to make things weird, but I need something from you."

"A kidney?"

I shake my head quickly, trying not to laugh. "God no."

"You can't have any of my other vital organs because I'm pretty sure I'm using them."

"I don't want your organs."

"Blood? Sperm? Saliva?"

"No and yuck." I wrinkle my nose. "I wanted to know if I can get paid for helping you. I need a job that pays in money. Not bodily fluids."

Grayson laughs, wiping his hands on the front of his thighs. "Of course. I'm going to be honest; we're on a budget. A tight one, but we can swing a hundred."

"A hundred what?" Cents? Dollars? Free cheeseburgers?

I could go for a cheeseburger right about now.

"Dollars a day, assuming it's a full day's work. You can't go pulling one of these, 'I was here for an hour so it counts' deals."

"I would never!" I'm offended that he'd think that about me, but it's not like he knows anything about me. Like that I value integrity. "I'm not like that."

"That's what they all say." He laughs. "Can I give you a check at the end of the week? There's some paperwork for you to fill out. My mom said she'd bring it up later on."

"Your mom?" I don't know why this surprises me. Maybe because he's never mentioned her. Or because I ... well, I don't know what I thought.

"Yeah, she's down in the front office in the main building. I can take you down there later or tomorrow or whenever. She's working on fundraising and corporate donations, so that's a full-time job right now. This is when she does all that stuff."

"Is it just the two of you?"

He looks down. "Yeah, my dad died two years ago. It's ... it's been rough since. She's had a tough time working during all of this."

I certainly understand not being able to work. I've tried—and failed—to hold down jobs more times than I can count. Poor woman. "Makes sense."

Now I see Grayson staring off. "This isn't how we thought things would be, you know?"

Oh I know.

He continues, "This is going to sound terrible, but some days I'm torn between wanting my old life in the city back and being here. But this ... means everything to my mom. She's already lost so much. I can't be the reason she loses any more." He closes his eyes for a second before turning to look at me. It's as if he's flipped a switch and that emotional piece is gone. "Now are you going to fix my mess in this corner or what?"

Even though I'm slightly shocked at his sudden turn about, I smile and get to work, unsure of how else to respond. It seems like he needs me to continue. Or at least his mom does.

After about an hour, Grayson asks if he can turn on the radio. It'd certainly help with the silence that stretches between us. And I wouldn't feel pressured to make conversation.

"Sure."

He goes out into the hall and pulls in an old radio, covered in paint splatters. "The work crew left it behind. Their loss is our gain."

"What happened to them? How could they leave you in the middle of a project like this?" I ask.

So much for not making conversation. It's almost like I want these walls to come down with this incredibly attractive and outgoing guy.

Which I don't.

Shouldn't.

Can't.

"My mom is what happened, God love her. She's a little too impulsive for her own good. Make that a lot too impulsive. She thought Dave was charging too much, which he probably was. But on the other hand, Mom isn't necessarily the best at this sort of thing, so I don't know if she was right or wrong. It doesn't matter. All that matters is she fired him so now we have to get all the work done in time for the crew to arrive in about four weeks."

Four weeks? Wait, did we have this conversation yesterday?

Damn, I hate anxiety. I hate how it's robbed me of the person I used to be.

Here's a fun fact: when in moments of panic or anxiety, did you know your working memory shuts down? It means you can't make new memories *and* you can't always access what's already in your brain. Nothing compounds feeling anxious like not remembering any of what happened and not knowing what the hell is going on most of the time.

"Okay, then let's get to it. I bet we can get three rooms totally done today."

"I was thinking about finishing this room and then going back and sanding. Maybe to make sure we're doing it okay. You know, tweak the process before we do too many more. There are twelve rooms to do."

I consider his plan. It would work too. "Sounds reasonable and logical."

"Crap. I don't ever want to be reasonable and logical. How dare you insult me so?"

I think he's kidding. He must be kidding. He's clutching his chest in an overly dramatic fashion.

Ten years ago, I would have made a comment about him being a drama queen or something to that effect. I would have been funny and clever and witty, all with a smile on my face.

I say nothing.

Damn, I hope this therapy works and I can get back to my funny and clever self.

Grayson fiddles with the radio for a minute. There's not great reception in here and only about two stations come in clear.

"Oldies or country?" Grayson asks.

"Oldies."

Grayson immediately starts humming along to the song that's on. And the next. And the one after that. I swear, he knows every word to every song.

And man, can he sing.

Shit. Crap. Fuck.

Why does he have to have a direct line to my Achilles heel?

Inhaling deeply through my nose, it takes everything I have not to scream at him to stop singing. There's no way I can say it without either sounding offensive or opening myself up for questions.

No way I can let that happen. Not now. Not ever again.

Chapter 6: Grayson

This woman is an enigma.

I mean, she's obviously got some serious stuff going on. I'm not sure how stable she is with the way she took off yesterday. But she showed up again today and appears to be working hard.

It's a start.

And hell, I'm used to dating actresses, so it's not like I go for the stable, conservative type anyway. My mind immediately wonders what Julianna is up to. Who she's hooking up with now. And if she's really going to come back to The Edison or leave me in the lurch. It could go either way. And either way, she'd be sticking it to me.

At least that one aspect of her is predictable.

I glance over at Ria and thoughts of Julianna drift away.

I'm sanding our work from yesterday, and the guy on the video was right. It's terrible. And we used way too much mud. Consider it corrected in the next room. The mask is making me claustrophobic, but it's better than breathing in all that dust.

I hated wearing a mask when I did *Phantom*. I've been accused of selecting shows for The Edison that won't require me to wear anything on my face. I don't deny these accusations.

It's the perks of being the boss.

Well, the boss's son.

And before you cry nepotism, remember the fact that I gave up traveling to be here for my mom and dad. I gave away my big break.

A voice pulls me out of my own head.

"Um, Grayson?"

Shit.

"Sorry, I was in my head a bit. Did you say something?" I pull the mask down.

Ria burst out in laughter. For a second, her face is totally transformed. It's like a veil has dropped, and I can see her for the first time. Holy shit.

She's beautiful.

"Your face!"

I pull my phone out of my pocket and flip the camera on. The top half of my face looks like I wrestled with a bag of flour—and lost.

"You know, I heard this is the next big fashion style coming off the runways in ..." I draw a blank. "The European cities where fashion matters."

Ria raises an eyebrow. "Paris? Milan?"

"Yes, and Hamburg." I don't know why I add this.

"Hamburg? Like Germany? Last I checked, the Germans are not known for their fashion."

"Oh, yes. You add a pair of lederhosen and the half-flour face and voila!" I raise my hands in a flourish. "It's all the rage."

She laughs again. I will do anything to keep her laughing.

"Now I know that voila is French, not German."

"But my entire extent of the German knowledge comes from *Cabaret*, so unless it's *Wilkkomen* or *Mein Heir*, I don't know it."

Her face falls a bit. Maybe she's not a fan of musical theater. I'll convert her.

"Well, I was going to ask if you minded if I took a break to grab a bite to eat," she says quietly, looking down at her feet. She's rubbing that bracelet again.

"No, of course not. Let me get cleaned up, and I'll join you."

Since there's no running water back here in the bunks, I have to run down to the house to get cleaned up. I debate changing my clothes, which are likewise covered in drywall dust. I decide against it, as I'll be covered as soon as the break is over. I settle for washing my face and arms and even run some water through my hair.

Mental note: tomorrow put a hat on when I'm sanding.

Mom's left a plate for me in the fridge. Yes, I'm thirty-five years old and my mom still makes my sandwich. It's not like she has to. I don't even ask her to.

But I'm not going to complain either.

I love coming in from rehearsal and finding a plate ready. Once I discovered theater, rehearsals and vocal lessons and dance classes seemed to overtake most weeknights. I got used to doing my homework in the car and while sitting on the floor backstage. I also got used to reheating a plate of whatever Mom and Dad had already eaten at a much more reasonable hour.

When I lived in the city, I missed coming home to that. It was quite an adjustment of having to forage for my own food. So it's one benefit of being home.

I transfer the food to a paper plate so I don't ruin Mom's matching set up at the bunks and walk back up the hill. I love the bunks. The entire building is set up at the very top of a hill, and looks down on the town and surrounding area, including The Edison itself. The location was used as a lookout during the Revolutionary War. I can see why. Perfect leverage.

In a few weeks, the entire valley will be exploding in every shade of green as spring bursts forth. For now, it's still covered in the drab grays and browns that winter has left, but at least there's no more snow.

Ria is sitting on the back stoop. It's almost sixty degrees today, which is warmer than expected for this last week in March. I guess it's going out like a lamb this year. The bag at her feet is open, but doesn't show much. A sleeve of saltines. An apple. A jar of peanut butter and a knife are at her feet.

"Eating light?"

She shrugs.

It seems like there's a lot she's saying with this shrug. I want to ask, but then think about her desperation to get a job. I bet she doesn't have much money. I really need Mom to get her paperwork in order. Maybe we can pay her cash for the first few days or something.

"What brings you to Hicklam?" I decide to pry in a more subtle way. No that anyone's ever accused me of being subtle.

Ria stares intently ahead, leaving the question hanging unanswered in the air.

"Okay, how are you liking Hicklam so far?"

A small smile hints at the corners of her mouth. "It's fine. I guess."

She is certainly working in the right field right now, because she's an expert at putting up walls.

"I hear the people are super nice and push you into manual labor totally outside your skill set."

The smile widens by a millimeter. "It's not outside my skill set. Remember, I'm the one who can do corners."

I nudge her with my shoulder. "But how are you with the other tools?"

"I'm familiar with a hammer, and of course I know how to screw."

She did not just say that. But she did and suddenly, thoughts I should not be thinking flood my mind. I don't know this girl from a bum on the street. Like literally. And the last thing I need is something—or someone—complicating my life more than it is.

"Oh God, I can't believe I just said that."

I nudge her again. "It's fine. Don't worry. I'd never think you meant anything other than using tools. Of course." I can't keep the grin off my face.

"You're a terrible actor. Your thoughts are written all over your face." She nudges me back and for the first time, I feel like the invisible wall between us has come down.

I hop up. "I take great offense to that. I'm an award-winning actor! Destined for greatness. And you can say you knew me when."

She takes a bite of her apple, her eyes downcast. "Sure, I'll do that, Olivier."

"So what's your story?" I know it's a risk, coming out and asking her like this. But that's me. I'm a risk taker. As is my mom, obviously. I come by it honestly.

Ria chews slowly. If I didn't know better, I'd swear she was doing some sort of deep breathing while chewing. Finally, she swallows hard. "I don't have a story."

I might be a risk taker, but I'm not stupid. If she were any more guarded, she'd be bearing her teeth and growling at me. She'll tell me when she's ready. Though I do often wonder what would bring someone here, to this small town about two hours from anywhere. Maybe she's on the run from an ex or something and doesn't want to be found.

That would explain the phone thing.

I look down at her and see that her arms are wrapped tightly around her body, like she's holding herself together.

Whatever her story is, I don't think it's a happy one. I feel badly for pressing her into manual labor, but it's all I can do. Maybe when The Edison is done, I can find something for her to do in the theater.

That is, right after I convince her to love it as much as I do.

"Okay, so let's get back to it. These walls aren't going to fix themselves. And despite our fancy construction lamps, it's better to work while there's a little daylight. I'm glad the days are getting longer." I prattle on about everything and nothing, trying to fill the void that seems to surround her.

Whatever it is, it's got to be quite the story.

Ria stands slowly, popping one more cracker into her mouth. I feel guilty for having eaten my sandwich without offering her any. "So, after we finish for the day, let's go down the hill and grab a bite to eat. I need to feed you something more substantial if I plan on taking advantage of your labor skills over the next few weeks."

"Um ... I'm not sure." Her voice is hesitant, soft.

"Okay, well think about it. Biff's has the best burgers and Plaza is the place if you want pizza."

She stops moving. "This place actually has a restaurant called Biff's? Have I landed on the set of a sitcom or something? What has my life come to?"

I sling my arm around her shoulder and give her a little squeeze. "Drywall, sandpaper, and listening to me sing. Most people would pay good money for that."

She mutters something, but I can't make it out. "What was that?"

Ria pulls away from me slightly so she can look at me. Her eyes are wide and introspective. "I said, it must be nice to have that kind of confidence. To feel so certain about things."

I step back, letting my arm fall down to my side. Tilting my head to the side, I study her. There are shadows under her eyes and her skin is pale. Not fair, but pale, like she's not well. She's petite. There's an air of fragility about her. Like if I move too quickly or say the wrong thing, she might shatter into a million pieces.

I'd never want that to happen.

I freely admit there are a lot of things I don't know, I do know one thing—this woman needs to be protected.

"It's an act, mostly. My whole life is an act. Fake it 'til you make it. Well, obviously I'm here so I haven't made it yet. I can't even seem to get out of my childhood home. And from the looks of it ..." I take in the shambled state of construction, "I never will."

The weight sits on my chest and suddenly it's hard to take a breath.

I force myself to inhale deeply. "But if I focus on that, I can't move forward. So I keep moving, keep faking, and maybe someday, it'll happen for me."

Now Ria tilts her head, looking at me. "Is it nice?"

I squint. "Is what nice?"

"Having this much hope." The longing in her voice is thick and palpable.

"Some days, it's the only thing I have."

Chapter 7: Gloria

What the hell am I doing here? What am I thinking?

I'm not thinking, that's what.

The thing is, when you lose the ability to trust yourself, you lose so much more. Sleep. Hours in the day spent second-guessing every thought, action and desire. Years.

I've spent years agonizing over every decision, paralyzed into inaction. Hell, I found out about Malachi over two years ago after seeing a story on ESPN about a catcher with the worst case of the yips in sports history. You wouldn't think my problem is in any way, shape, or form related to a baseball player who can't throw the ball without a weird hesitation, but it is.

Trauma is a fun thing.

Other than paid mental health professionals, this is the most I've talked to a non-family member since the incident. And I know barely anything about this man, other than his dedication to his mother, which is impressive.

Of course, that's if it's what he makes it out to be. There's always the chance he's playing me by trying to make me feel empathetic. It wouldn't be the first time it's happened.

But he's here, covered in dust and sweat, doing something that's obviously outside his comfort zone. That makes two of us. He takes his phone out of his pocket and pulls up another video.

I could do without that. It's occurred to me to tell him that it makes me uncomfortable—alright, downright panicky—but I also know he needs access to it. I'm here, after all, to learn how to be functional in this type of situation. Grayson and his YouTube will be a good litmus test to see if my therapy with Malachi is working.

"Yo, man! Where you at?" A deep voice calls out from the front of the dorm, several rooms away.

"We're back here," Grayson returns.

My eyes widen, not sure what to make of this new development. I'm not ready to people yet. I'm stuck in the crouch position where I'd been, sanding a small patch in the corner. Maybe I can escape before anyone else gets here. Or if I make myself small enough, they won't see me.

Suddenly, whether I like it or not, there are three other men in the room. I freeze. They're dressed in grubby work clothes. One in honest-to-god coveralls with the name patch reading, "Joe." They all do that guy-hug thing where it's more of a slap on the arm or back. Joe says, "Heidi said your mom fired Dave."

"Heidi is not wrong. Unfortunately." Grayson's voice drops to a mumble.

"Good," Guy Number Two says. "Dave is a dick and no doubt he was ripping you off. He does good work, but based on the few jobs he does a year, there's no way he should be driving an Escalade if he's on the up and up."

My leg starts to cramp, so I shift. The movement catches the eye of Guy Number Three (seriously, why can't they all wear name tags like Joe?). "Well, hey there. I don't think I've seen you before. I think I'd remember."

I stand up, my shoulders tight and my hands fisted at my side. Breathe. Breathe. *Breathe*.

"No, I'd definitely remember." Number Three looks me up and down.

I don't know if it's a leering look. I don't know if he's trying to place me. I don't know if he's looking at my outfit. I can't tell. It all feels like I'm standing in front of him naked. That he *knows* what every inch of my flesh looks like.

He's probably not leering.

But I don't know that for certain.

There's always that possibility.

I need to get out of here.

"Drew, Kyle, Joe, this is Ria. She's new in town, and Heidi also sent her up here. I'm going to have to start paying her a headhunting fee."

"Or you have to just fu—" Kyle, aka Guy Number Two, breaks off. "Date her. Get it out of her system."

"Heidi and I are friends. Always have been and it'll never be anything more."

"That's because you tapped Kelsey," Joe adds helpfully.

Heidi did mention that Grayson dated her kid sister. It would explain a lot. I guess he really did *date* her. And sisters? That would be a hard pass for me. I have to say, Grayson's stock rose a bit with his limit. Though, somehow, it's not surprising. He seems like a kind soul.

But I've thought that before.

"No, I mean yes, but it's not that. Heidi and I are friends. I'm not her type." Grayson defends himself.

"She doesn't seem to think so." The voice providing this information is mine, which is ... surprising. Grayson gives me a quizzical look.

"Oh really? Were you two talking about me?" A sly grin spreads over his face, coaxing his dimple out.

"No. I mean yeah. I asked about you because of the scone and coffee, and Heidi said she was in love with you."

I probably shouldn't have said that out loud. Shit.

Grayson shrugs. "She doesn't really love me. We're not right for each other. Our personalities wouldn't go together. You can't have two people in the spotlight at the same time."

"And we all know, you won't give up your spot," Joe says quietly.

Ouch.

What kind of friends are these?

Not like I'm one to be questioning the caliber of friends one has, but Grayson's been so kind to me. I'm mad that his so-called friends treat him like this.

Grayson laughs, unruffled by the dig. "Joe, my man, you are right. And don't worry, one of these days, Heidi will see that I'd make her miserable and that someone else is right for her. Probably someone who has been right under her nose all along."

Joe's face reddens a bit and he clears his throat. Is there a story there?

"So what are we doing here? You have us for three hours or a case of beer, whichever passes by first."

Grayson starts assigning work, passing the sanding onto his friends. He grabs me by the hand. I tense, unused to physical touch. Part of my mind screams for him to let me go, but a larger portion revels in the human contact.

"Let's go mud. We know what we're doing, and I can't trust these yahoos not to muck it up." He leads me to the next room, where I promptly get to work.

With Grayson by my side, I feel safe. Almost safe enough to forget that there are other people here.

The next time I look up, it's dark outside. For once, the voices and the laughter and the music kept my internal darkness at bay. I didn't even notice the passing hours.

My stomach has, however.

I stop and place a hand on my midsection. It's definitely rumbling. Thankfully it's loud enough in here so that no one can hear the noises my body is making. My God, I'm so hungry that I'm hallucinating about smelling pizza. Can you hallucinate a smell? Is this another sign of my mental health issues? Because the scent fills my nostrils.

"Gray, Ree, food's here. Time to take a break." Drew sticks his head in the room.

We're almost done with our fifth room. Close to half-way there. At least for these rooms. I don't know what the scope of the rest of the project entails.

"Sweet. Tell Tina that I love her."

Drew laughs. "You can't have all the women in town. Tina said yes to me, and she brought us dinner."

"Sounds like she's the perfect woman." Again my voice, my boldness, surprises me. Maybe I'm delusional from low blood sugar or something. It doesn't even grate that he calls me "Ree," like he's known me for years rather than minutes.

Drew sighs. Like, with that dreamy look on his face and everything. "She is. We got engaged last week. You have to ask to see her ring."

Grayson elbows me, leaning in to whisper in my ear. "Please, don't ask about the ring or proposal. It's all he's talked about for months on end. We all thought now that it was a done deal that he'd stop talking. Please don't bring it up. I'll be your best friend forever."

"Yo man, I thought I was your best friend." Kyle says, knocking into Grayson.

Grayson shakes his head. "No, your mom just pays me to hang out with you."

I don't know what to do. This is obviously a close-knit group. People who care. People who know everything about each other.

It reminds me of the theater groups I used to belong to. People so close that you lived a lifetime together through the course of a six-week show.

Not my kind of situation. At least not anymore.

I don't need anyone being that familiar with me ever again. At least that's what I tell myself, the best offense being a good defense and all.

"Hey! I'm Tina. I didn't bring much to drink, 'cause I knew they brought beer. Do you want me to go get something else?" A woman with sandy-blonde hair is suddenly standing before me.

I'm parched and my water bottle was empty hours ago. The guys have been drinking the beer, but that's not an option for me either. I gave up alcohol when I realized I was using it to cope with everything. I haven't had a drop in over six years.

But I really am thirsty. "I'm fine, thanks."

"Are you here with the company?" Tina plops down on an overturned milk crate next to me.

Company? What company? "Um, no. I'm ... just ... here. I was looking for work and well..." I shrug.

I'm so going to make friends because of my articulation skills.

"But, like, no one comes here until May at least. Why would you come to Hicklam? I mean, it's a great place but there's not much here." It's Tina's turn to shrug.

My own mother had asked me this question once I told her where I was and what I was doing. Or rather, she'd asked me what I'd tell people if they asked me. It was a good thing to plan out. My canned, rehearsed response is ready.

"I'm writing a book about this area."

"Oh, a book!" Tina claps her hands. "What kind?"

"Um, it's, um, historical fiction about the early textile industry in this area." Mom researched what this section of New York was known for. I also wanted to come up with something bland enough that no one would want to talk about it. Thank you, Mom.

"Oh, wow. That sounds ... interesting. Can't wait to read it." Tina smiles.

If I was looking for a friend, Hicklam seems to have more than its fair share of worthy candidates. And I always thought people in New York weren't friendly. But it seems my *friends* in Ohio weren't the candidates I thought them to be either.

I also thought I could trust Aaron.

And Marissa.

I think wrong a lot.

By the time the pizza and the beer are consumed, it's fairly apparent that we won't be getting much else done tonight.

I stand up, stretching my back. I may have to do some yoga before bed to loosen up so I'm not sore in the morning. It'd be the first time in a long time that I wasn't doing yoga to calm my mind.

It seems like Hicklam might be good for me in more ways than one. Will wonders never cease?

Chapter 8: Grayson

I'm being a creeper. I know I am and there's nothing I can do to stop it. I'm using all my best acting tricks so she doesn't see, but I can't stop watching her.

There is a lot Ria doesn't want people to see or know.

Like, for starters, her last name.

She isn't drinking the beer and refused Tina's offer to go and get her something to drink. Frankly, she was reticent to even take a slice of pizza until I plopped a plate on her lap. I saw what she had for lunch. It wasn't much.

Either she doesn't trust us or she doesn't know how to accept help from others. I suspect a little of both.

I stand up and run to the kitchen area of the dorms, grabbing some water out of a cooler that Mom must have dropped off at some point during the day. It's not super cold anymore, but it's wet. With all the dust in here, Ria's throat has got to be parched and raw, as mine is.

I put the bottle down at her feet. She glances around before her hand sneaks down and clutches the bottle. The contents of the bottle disappear in several consecutive gulps.

I text Mom that we need some petty cash to pay Ria for hours already worked. I can't have her starving and dehydrating here. I should see if I can get her a phone too. I remember a local group collecting used cellphones for a domestic violence organization. I've got to think about who that was so I can look them up. Ria needs a phone.

And I'm guessing she needs a ride home. Shit. I've had a few beers. I wonder if my mom is around to drive her. She shouldn't be walking in the dark.

I don't even know where she lives. I mean, I'm guessing it's somewhere in the downtown area, by the park or Dean's Beans.

Tina and Drew are packing up, trying to clean up the pizza boxes and paper towels. "I've got it guys. You don't need to do that."

Ria stands up. "Thank you for the pizza. I should be going."

"Wait!" I call out, not sure what I'm going to say next.

Ria turns to look at me.

"Do you need a ride home?"

She looks me up and down. "Not from you." Her words are sharp.

Ouch.

Quickly, she realizes her faux pas. "I mean, you've been drinking. I'd rather walk. No offense." She purses her lips tightly. She didn't drink at all. I wonder if her ex was a drinker. Could be.

I wonder if there's even an ex. Maybe she's just weird.

It would be more plausible.

But something nags at my gut that there's a story there. One that will take a long time to tell.

"What time should I be here tomorrow?" She's looking at the ground, instead of me, as she's inching toward the door.

"Hang, on, we can figure that out in a sec. You need to get home safely."

I wish I'd thought of this before Tina and Drew left. I won't suggest she go with Kyle or Joe, though I know she'd be safe. I get the distinct impression that she wouldn't feel the same. Ria gives off the impression of a caged animal. You know, the kind that would gnaw off their own leg to get out of a trap.

I whip out my phone and text my mom, who replies immediately with a thumbs up emoji. I swear, ever since she discovered those on her phone, she barely writes words. If she can't say it with an emoji, she says it with a gif. She's so proud of herself.

"My mom will give you a ride."

Ria shakes her head. "She doesn't have to do that."

"Yes she does. I mean, I should, but you're right. I shouldn't be driving. And we owe you. Both literally and figuratively. She's going to bring your pay for the past two days, as well as the paperwork to fill out so we can get you on the books."

"You don't want to pay me under the table?" She tilts her head.

"Um, no. We need to account for where our money goes. You're still a lot cheaper than the contractor who was in here previously, but we need to be careful of what we're spending."

"So what you're saying is I should ask for more money then." A smile hints at her lips.

The caged animal is gone for a minute as the sense of humor peeks out.

"Dave didn't have to watch a video for each step of what he was doing."

"Touché. But still, I can walk. It's late and dark and she—"

"Is capable of driving you home and that's all there is to that." Mom walks in, tone set and a large envelope in her hands. "I take it you're Ria?"

"Yes, ma'am." Ria looks at her feet. "I'm sorry to bother you."

Mom waves the concern away. "No bother. I'd rather talk to you than this one. He's mad at me for all this, and he hasn't been good company the last few days. And by days, I mean the last several hundred in a row."

Guilt fills me as I know Mom's right. I haven't wanted to be here, and I haven't made any secret about it.

I mean, I do want to be here. I want The Edison to be here.

But I want Dad to be the one here, running it.

But mostly, I want Mom's heart to be unbroken.

I always thought I'd do one show here a summer, and stay for a week or two between shows. That it'd always be my home, but not where I'd actually hang my hat every day or anything.

It's the least I could do after Mom and Dad helped me out all those years when I lived in New York City. It wasn't that I felt entitled. It was that as a struggling actor, New York City, where you need to live to find jobs, isn't affordable. I was guaranteed a little over a thousand dollars per week when I was doing a show. Sometimes as much as twelve-hundred, if I was working on Sundays. I always offered to help move set pieces, which gave me an extra eight dollars per week.

Every little bit helped.

But after my parent's aid ceased, I was truly falling into the starving artist category. When the chance to sublet my room came up because I'd be on tour, I felt like I'd won the lottery. No rooming expenses for the duration of the tour. I'd be able to get ahead and ...

That's when the bottom fell out. Dad's treatments kept him alive but unable to work. And someone had to do it.

Of course, that someone was me. It's always me.

I have to get this place back on its feet so hopefully someday, I can leave. If I can just make it work for Mom, then she can focus on The Edison and remember how much she loves it and she'll be happy again.

It's got to make her happy again.

An hour later, after I've showered and had another bite to eat, I sit down in the office and work on our social media. Mom's been working hard on our corporate donors and sponsors, securing the donations that account for at least twenty-percent of our annual expenses. This year, she needs to cover more than thirty percent so we can pay our construction loans back. I schedule posts about the construction, the upcoming shows, the upcoming auditions, and what talent we already have booked.

Julianna Rickey, for one.

Ugh.

But she was born to play Roxie Hart. It's her signature role, and The Edison is frankly too small of a theater to host talent like hers. We're anticipating a sellout for all eighteen shows. People who would pay three-hundred bucks a seat to see Julianna at the Wintergarden Theater will drive the ninety miles to Hicklam for an eighty-dollar ticket.

I need Julianna.

And all my connections.

I schedule an Instagram post of one of Jules's pictures from when we did *Chicago* off-Broadway. Back when we were a *we*. I need to get Julianna to put it on her website as a scheduled stop so we can start selling tickets.

I sit back, running my fingers through my hair. I've about three more hours of work to do tonight, and I want to do none of it.

I hear Mom calling my name as she walks in from the garage.

"In the office."

Her keys clink in the bowl I made when I was in fifth grade. She opens the fridge and closes it. I know she's thinking about having a drink.

She thinks about it a lot.

Sometimes, she doesn't just think about it.

She's been making an effort lately to do better, but while Dad was sick and the first year after ... not a good scene.

It's been tough.

I don't hear anything else and don't see her holding a drink when she enters the office.

"You'll never guess where she lives." Mom's flair for the dramatic is nothing to be underestimated. I've often wondered why she didn't pursue a career on stage.

"Somewhere off Chapel or Main?"

"Not off Chapel. Right on it. As in one of the buildings that the Andrews's own. She's a *tenant*." Mom whispers the word, like she's cursing and doesn't want to get in trouble.

I'm surprised Mom hasn't made herself a bowl of popcorn to tell me this story.

You see, when it's not summer, not a lot happens here in Hicklam. During the summer, there are all these theater people around. They tend to live up to their reputations of drama and show, and there's plenty to talk about. After Labor Day, fodder for the gossip mill dries up and the biddies in the town need something to keep themselves entertained.

Enter the Andrews siblings.

Malachi, Marvin, and Malyia are undoubtedly three of the nicest people I've ever met. There's not a soul in Hicklam who can tell you any different. Their only fault is that no one knows them. At all.

They own a few buildings. Rental units. But this is the weird thing. They don't rent them out. Not to residents of Hicklam.

But they have tenants in them. A lot of the time, we don't see these tenants out and about. Maybe running into a store here and there or picking up food. But not hanging out at Dean's Beans. Not catching a show at The Edison. Not doing yoga in the park in the middle of the day during the middle of the week.

But the tenants go into the Andrews's house. They're there for a little while and then they leave. Then someone else goes in.

It's all a bit odd.

I'm sure, if I spent any real time thinking about it, I could come up with a logical explanation.

I have neither the time nor the inclination to do that. I can honestly say that before now, it's never really concerned me.

"Okay. Those are nice places. The refurbished flats that once housed the mill workers?" The textile mills were here a hundred years before The Edison. The prosperity and job security created by those mills were what allowed my great grandparents to build something so frivolous as a theater in this otherwise small community. The mill workers were doing well, but not well enough to travel to Manhattan or Albany to see a show.

"Grayson, do you know what this means? She's one of *them*."

"Who them?"

"One of the people who goes into the Andrews's place."

I look up. Mom's leaning in, staring at me hard. "Okay."

Mom flops back. "Grayson, how can you say it's okay? We don't know what's going on in there!"

And the Tony goes to ...

"Mom, what do you even think it is? I heard Ria tell Tina she's writing a book or something, so maybe it's about that."

"Or maybe it's not."

I want to slap my head. Or hers.

I sigh. "What? Do you think she's a member of a weird sex cult or something?"

"Well how else do you explain it? I was watching *Discovery ID* the other day and ..."

My earlier thoughts about Ria being on the run from someone return. It certainly would explain things. Maybe the Andrews help people escape domestic violence.

Makes more sense than a sex cult.

"To each their own, Ma."

She stands. "That's all you have to say?"

I stand as well. I can't think anymore tonight. Not to mention, Mom's a little worked up. I don't want to leave her roaming the house by herself. "Let's go watch some TV, as long as it's not one of your true crime shows."

"But what are we going to do about this girl? She's supposed to be filling out the paperwork and returning it tomorrow."

"Then we submit it and pay her. Unless she wants to have an orgy here, I think what she does on her own time is up to her. Although, maybe I'd be okay with an orgy."

"Grayson!" Mom slaps me lightly upside the head. She's smiling again.

Mission accomplished.

Chapter 9: Gloria

She thinks I'm in a sex cult.

It's written all over her face, and I don't know whether to laugh or cry.

There is no doubt about it, Grayson's mom thinks I'm up to no good. As soon as she pulled up and saw the building, her demeanor changed. And this time, maybe for the first time, it's not my anxiety lying to me that there are other forces working against me here.

It didn't help that she said, "Oh, this is one of the Andrews's buildings. Lots of people coming and going, but no one knows why." And then she arched an eyebrow at me.

I wanted to reassure her right then and there that I wouldn't be stealing her son away to participate in some weird sexual rituals, but I don't because how do you even broach that topic?

Plus, it would open a whole suitcase that I'm not ready to unpack yet.

But at least I didn't freak out. I didn't have a panic attack. I think my heart rate went up slightly, but that's small potatoes in terms of my system.

I wonder if the truth would be any more acceptable.

I don't want to find out. I don't want them to know. I'm sticking with my writing story and pray to God no one asks me any questions about it. I should probably do some research into the topic, just to be prepared. I feel terrible about lying, but I need to be prepared.

I can see Grayson asking. He seems curious about me. At least who I am and where I come from. You know, the information I don't ever want to share. It'll be bad enough that I have to fill out the paperwork for his mother to get paid. But she doesn't seem like the type to Google a person and find every last thing posted on the internet about them.

It's bad enough I can't face anyone I knew from before. The feeling that everyone I meet knows and has seen ... hell, that's why I'm here.

This is my last chance if I want to have any sort of normal life.

And I want it more than I can ever say.

I'm even inclined to say the work I've done with Malachi the past two sessions has started to help because today I felt pretty good. I was out of the house all day and productive and I even talked to people.

People I didn't know before.

My mom will be so proud. I want to call and tell her, but a quick glance at the clock tells me it's too late. How did it get to be almost eleven already?

Time flies when you're not rocking in a corner sobbing. I look longingly at the apartment phone on the kitchen counter. Writing a quick note will have to do. I pour out the emotions of the last three days before I nod off, the pen leaving a trail off the edge of the paper.

When I awake in the morning, my first thought is that I must be dead, because I don't remember going to bed the night before.

I can't remember the last time I slept this soundly. I'm still on my couch and the note to Mom is crumpled underneath me. Sunlight streams in, filtered slightly by the sheer curtains on the tall front windows.

Oh crap! What time is it?

I stumble off the couch stiffly. I should take time to do yoga before heading up to Grayson's place but I don't want to let him down. Especially not when he showed such good faith in me by having his mom pay me for my first two days in cash. Two-hundred dollars.

Food and gas.

Or one hour of therapy, of which I've already had two.

But even still, if I work five days a week, I can net two-hundred even after paying for my sessions with Malachi. It's not much, not by a long shot, but it would mean I won't have to spend through my meager life savings and go into debt to get well.

I'll have to ask Grayson the extent of the work that needs to be done. Maybe he needs a groundskeeper or housekeeper or whatever once his hotel opens. I was ready to clean toilets going into this. I still could.

I hurry through the shower, anxious to get to work.

And for once, this anxiety isn't the bad kind. Dare I say, I might be excited? It's been a really good two days. Probably the best two days I've had in a long time.

Two days in a row. This calls for a celebratory scone.

Hair still wet, I toss it in a bun on the top of my head and run down the stairs and out the door. A minute later, I'm in Dean's Beans, waiting in a line almost out the door. I hope Heidi doesn't sell out of scones before I get up there. Does everyone know how good they are? Maybe I should bring one to Grayson. He's been so nice to me.

"Aren't you going to be late for work?" A voice whispers in my ear.

Last week I would have jumped. Today, I smile at the familiar voice. "Probably, but since I've decided to get scones and bring them in, I think my boss will forgive me."

Grayson's breath is hot on my neck. It's doing things to me. Things I don't want to be feeling. It's a strange, yet familiar feeling. My mind starts to freak out a little, thinking of other times there was hot breath on my neck. Other parts of my body are responding in a more primal way.

"Do you think so little of your boss that you think he can be bought with a baked good?"

I turn and face him, unable to keep the smile from my face, but needing to put some space between our bodies. "Can't you?"

He's trying to keep a stern expression but the twinkling in his green eyes betrays him. "Fine, you've got me," he says, finally erupting into an easy grin.

Easy grins are his signature expression.

They're also a place that could feel like home.

"Did you have a good night?" he asks, never breaking eye contact. I feel a heat rising in my cheeks from his intensity.

"It was fine. I fell asleep on the couch. When I woke up this morning, I didn't know where I was. I haven't slept that deeply in a while."

"Sometimes when I have nights like that, it takes me all day to shake that initial scare of the morning."

The line moves and we shuffle forward.

The space between us gives my brain a chance to calm, even as my pulse continues to be rapid from the feeling of being close to Grayson. "I'm usually up before the sun. I didn't even have time to do my yoga this morning."

"Do you do it every day?"

I nod. I don't need to tell him sometimes more than once a day. Sometimes it's the only thing that clears my mind and helps me breathe.

"Maybe you can teach me or something. Trainers have tried to show me in the past, but I wasn't interested. I need to stretch out more. My hamstrings have always been tight and now I'm starting to get back pain. I'm too young for that."

"How old are you?" I can't believe I ask. Normally, I wouldn't. Mostly because I don't want that same kind of introspection turned on me.

"Thirty-five."

"In the prime of life. Definitely too young for back pain." Though I know that's not true. My college roommate, before I dropped out, was in physical therapy school. She used to tell me all sorts of interesting facts, including that arthritis starts developing in the early thirties, especially if you're active.

His face darkens, like a quick moving storm cloud has rolled in. "Some may say I'm past my prime."

"Grayson! Ria! The usuals?" Heidi calls. I hadn't even realized the line had moved that quickly. Time has a way of evaporating when I'm with Grayson.

"And two ginger scones, please," I add. "They are the best things ever." I pull out my wallet.

"Honey, your money is no good here. Plain coffee, latte, two scones." She starts passing cups and a bag over the counter.

"But I ..."

Grayson hands me my coffee. "Just say thank you, Ria."

"Thank you, Heidi, but I ..."

"You're welcome. I put it right on Grayson's tab. Any friend of Grayson's is a friend of mine."

"Even Joe?" Grayson asks.

Now it's Heidi's turn to blush. "Well, of course. Joe's great."

"He was asking about you last night. He thinks you're great too." Grayson picks up his latte and the bag of scones. "Come on, Plain Coffee, we have work to do."

I hurry to the condiment counter and fix my coffee before shuffling out after Grayson. He's standing outside, facing the sun, soaking it up like a cat.

"What was that about Joe? He wasn't asking about Heidi. I mean, he was but it was more in relation to you and Heidi."

"She doesn't need to know that. He's had a thing for her for years, but he's too shy to go for her. Plus, he's nervous that she'll shoot him down, and there's nowhere else in town that makes decent coffee. I'm planting the seed. They would be perfect together. We'll see what happens."

"Okay, Emma."

"Emma?"

I shake my head. Not everyone gets the reference to Jane Austen. I've had a lot of time to not leave my room and read over the past decade. "I didn't have you pegged for the matchmaking type."

"I prefer to be called Yenta." He breaks into *Matchmaker, Matchmaker* from *Fiddler on the Roof* because, of course he does. I swear, he can't go more than ten minutes without singing. It's like his entire life is a musical.

Part of me wants to scream at him to stop and part of me wants to join in. It's been a decade since I've sang. Not in the shower. Not in the car. And certainly not on the stage. It's a gaping hole on the inside of me. A void. A vacuum.

And I can never fill it.

In a moment like this, I feel that of all the things I lost that day, singing was the biggest loss.

That, and the ability to trust in people. That's a pretty big loss too.

But in this moment, walking up the hill to the dorms, I don't feel much of a loss at all. Quite the opposite, really.

Chapter 10: Grayson

I jinxed myself.

I made that comment about back pain and now here it is. Every time I bend over, there's a pulling in my lower back.

Ouch.

For years, choreographers have complained about my flexibility. I get it. I'm not, much to the chagrin of all of my dance instructors as well as myself. It automatically eliminated roles for me. Like *A Chorus Line* or *Cats*.

Though with the box office bomb that *Cats* the movie was, I don't think anyone will attempt to revive it anytime soon. It seems to have run through all nine of its lives.

By early afternoon, I can't take it anymore. "So, Ria ... I was wondering ..."

She freezes, mid-motion. I've never seen someone go that ramrod straight. I don't think she's even breathing. I'd better get this out quickly before she turns purple and passes out.

"Can you show me some yoga moves? My back is objecting to something, and I think maybe stretching it would be helpful."

Her body melts as she exhales, the tension draining from her like a balloon. "I'm not certified or anything. I've only taught once or twice. I just do yoga. I don't know if I can help you. I don't want to make you worse by doing the wrong thing."

That's a valid point.

"Well, I know there's a class at the local dance studio. If I went, would you go with me so I don't feel stupid?" I'm going to suck hard at it. And feel stupid.

She shrugs. "Sure. Do you know when it is?" Slowly, she lets a breath out.

I pull out my phone and do a quick search. "Tonight at seven. You want to go?"

"I guess. Since I missed doing it this morning, it's probably not a bad idea."

"Okay, great. It's a date."

She's back to the ramrod posture.

Dammit. That was a stupid thing to say. I can't be so careless with my words. I quickly correct. "I mean, it's a plan."

The rest of the day flies by, our process so much faster than two days ago. On the other hand, the mud only dries so fast, and we have to take the time to do the work properly. Not to mention, I am moving like an eighty-year-old man. But still, by the time we start the tenth dorm room, I'm feeling a bit more confident about our skills. I don't know why

Dave didn't gut the kitchen or bathrooms out here in the dorms, but I'm relieved.

It'll be enough work to get those cleaned up and put back together after we finish painting and trim work. Then it'll be onto the bathrooms and the main theater.

Those projects ... now my head hurts in addition to my back. I'll have about three weeks to get those finished.

I'm going to be buying a lot of pizza and beer for Joe, Kyle, and Drew.

My phone buzzes in my back pocket, and then again. Reflexively, I pull it out to look. Out of the corner of my eye, I see Ria watching me suspiciously.

"It's my friend Henderson. He's sort of my summer manager."

No sort of about it. Henderson produces most of the shows here. He leaves all the grunt work to me, but he's the one Mom and Dad hired to run the stage aspect of things.

Got a problem, mate. Can't get rights for GND. Just sold rights to TriStar.

Shit.

Guys and Dolls was supposed to be a solid gotcha, running as our junior production. Our summer camp in which we teach the kids the show, teach them about the theater, and even give them the chance to work with some of the professionals in town for our other productions. It's a three week commitment, and we have nothing. Now we need to come up with another show. We can't afford to lose the tuition money from camp or the ticket sales.

I text him back.

What do you have in mind?

Let's go in a diff direction... Fresh. Young. New.

Okay. That should be super easy.

Like finishing this renovation, or anything in my life for that matter, is easy.

"You okay?" Ria asks. In light of my newest crisis, I'd totally forgotten she was in the room.

"Yes. No. Business stuff. You know, everything's falling apart."

Ria must think I'm kidding because she smiles. "Then it's a perfect time for yoga."

"Right. I may have to cancel."

She stands up. "No, seriously, you can't. Trust me. Take the hour for yourself."

I start pacing. I don't know how I'm going to fill the hole in the schedule for this. I go to the city the day after next to start auditions. But the keystone of our summer—the camp and production—is leaving a gaping hole. "I don't have an hour."

"Then it's even more important that you take the hour. If there's only one thing I know in this world, it's the importance of self-care."

I consider her words, especially given this is the most she's willingly volunteered to tell me in the three days we've been working together. I've probably spent more time with her than I have with anyone outside a cast lately.

And since I've been stuck here all winter instead of being in a show, it means I've barely been around anyone.

"Fine. But I'm trusting you on this."

Ria nods gravely. "I don't take trust lightly."

The gravity in these words nearly knocks me off my feet. I have no evidence, no proof, no details other than my gut to support this, but I know that she is a deeply wounded creature. "I know. Thank you for the advice."

As the afternoon stretches on, I run through show after show possibility for our junior performance. The cast is usually made up of middle and high school kids. It's a great way to showcase local talent, as well as to scout for future company members. Something fresh. Something new.

Something fresh. Something new.

The words echo in my brain until that's all I can focus on. I probably couldn't even name a show right now because all I can think is fresh and new.

"Um, Grayson?" Ria's tapping me on the shoulder. I was so deep in my head, I forgot I wasn't alone. "You look like you're about to freak out. You're talking to yourself. You keep muttering 'something fresh, something new.'"

I nod.

She shakes her head slightly. "Okay, well, it's a good thing it's time to go to yoga. You need this more than anyone I've ever met. Do you have stuff?"

It's time? How can it be time? It was just two o'clock. I look at my watch. It's just after five. Indeed, time to get changed and head out.

I don't know where the afternoon went. I look around, surprised to see the progress we've made. Man, I was completely in a fog.

As Ria's heading out the door, she yells, "Do you have a mat or block or anything? If so, you might want to bring it."

"Good point! I'll look. See you soon!" I call after her. Lucky for me, my mom's tried every single fitness craze that's walked through Hicklam, so I know there are supplies somewhere. I jog down the hill to the house. A quick search leads me to an unopened yoga starter pack. Bingo.

I do a cursory wash to get the dust off, change my clothes, and throw another coat of deodorant on. I brush my teeth and then double back to the bathroom for some Gas-X. I've heard stories about yoga, and I don't want to be a laughingstock.

One intestinal rumble and it'll be all over town faster than you can say 'excuse me.'

I pull the cellophane off the mat and block. A strap falls out from inside the mat. It must be to carry it. I attempt to wrestle it back on the rolled up mat, but I can't roll the mat tightly enough to get it on correctly. I look at my watch. Shit. I'm going to be late.

I toss the strap on the floor, grab a water bottle, and set off, jogging down the hill toward town. My exercise routines have taken a hit this week since working on The Edison, so I need every chance I can get to work in some cardio.

Ria is pacing in front of the studio when I jog up. "I thought you were going to stand me up."

I throw my arm around her. "I would never."

"I'll try to believe that."

Quickly, she eases out from under my arm as she leans forward to pull the door open. Right. I don't know her that well. In the theater world, I'm used to accelerated levels of comfort, especially in the physical sense. Like when you have to do an intimate dance or kiss someone the first day you meet them. Sometimes I forget that not everyone feels that way.

I'll try to believe that.

Wow. That's a loaded statement. Whatever her issues are, they stem from trust. Or lack thereof.

If I were blocking this scene for the stage, I'd grab her chin in my hand, look deep into her eyes and promise that I would never leave her hanging. Of course, in the way things go in the theater, I'd promptly leave her hanging.

I follow her in, where I'm greeted with a multitude of hellos and hi's and small waves. I'm glad we're almost late so there's no time for small talk. I follow Ria in and mimic her motions as she sets about positioning her mat and water bottle. She glances over as I do the same, holding the block awkwardly.

"Your mom's?" She smiles and nods to the mat.

"Did the pink and hibiscus flowers give it away?" Because of course that's what's printed all over the mat. And coordinating block.

We start in some easy poses, like just standing there, breathing. What's so hard about this? I've heard that some people can't breathe with their diaphragm, but with singing, it comes second nature to me. I've got this yoga thing down.

I'm not even going to be able to log this as a workout.

Twenty minutes later, my attitude has changed dramatically and I want to die. Or vomit. Or maybe a little of both.

"Now, take your straps and put them around the bottom of your feet," Cassidy, the instructor, calmly directs. "Inhale, filling your ribs and deepen your stretch as you exhale."

Shit.

I'm guessing if you're super flexible, you can just fold in half and reach your feet, which is what Ria is doing. I can barely reach my shins. I feel like an idiot. I attempt to exhale and stretch and all that comes out is a strangled groan.

Ria glances over and smiles. I think she's actually laughing but has the decency to hide it. I'm like every bad YouTube video of some jock trying out yoga without a clue of what to do. At least I took the Gas-X first.

She pushes her strap over to me without breaking her pose. I wrestle with the thing, having no more luck getting it around my feet than I did with the yoga mat. Surely I'm more coordinated than this stupid piece of webbing would indicate. Ria quietly reaches over and slides it over the bottom of my feet, handing me one end then the other. She sits up and demonstrates how I should use the strap to pull my body forward.

Oh Mylanta, these are tight muscles, but man this feels good.

"Breathe," I hear Ria whisper and I try, finally feeling the relax into the stretch. I may let out a groan.

Okay, I let out a groan.

A mere thirty minutes later, we're laying on our backs and breathing. There's a mediation component that occupies my mind as I try to feel every hair on every toe or something like that. When we finally stand up, I feel weirdly energized and like something has been freed up in my midsection.

I also feel calm. Super calm. Like I just downed a handful of Valium calm.

I start to ask Ria if this is normal, but Cassidy is there.

"Oh Grayson, I didn't know you were coming. I'd have saved you a spot up front."

"Please don't. I'm terrible at this."

Cassidy playfully slaps my arm. "You're not terrible at anything, are you? Don't be modest."

"Oh no, he's pretty terrible at this," Ria chimes in.

Cassidy turns, as if seeing her for the first time. "And you are ...?" Her eyebrows knit together into a frown.

I jump in, as I see Ria closing down. "Cassidy, this is Ria. Ria, this is Cassidy. Ria's working with me at The Edison. She does a lot of yoga, so she was a good sport to come with me. I'm not very good, but I feel great, so I'll be back."

That replaces the scowl on Cassidy's face with a smile.

We pack up and I try to avoid talking to anyone else. I don't want to answer questions about how things are going. I'm liking this feeling of peace, and talking about The Edison is a surefire way to make that feeling go away.

The night air is chilly, so I shove my hands in my pockets. We're walking down the street toward Ria's place. The least I can do is walk her home. As we walk by Dean's Beans, Ria stops for a minute and then elbows me.

"Look!"

I glance in the window. The shop has a closed sign on its door and the lights are dim, but there's one last lone patron in there as Heidi's cleaning up. Joe.

He glances out and I raise a fist triumphantly at him before turning away. I don't want Heidi to see us out there gawking.

"You did it. You matched them up. Please don't start singing again," she adds in quickly.

I shrug. "Ah, it's been brewing for a while. All they needed was a little push."

"Damn you, Grayson. Now I need to watch Clueless."

I don't get where she's going with this. "Huh?"

"You know, the movie, Clueless? The modern—well at least it was at the time—retelling of Emma. The meddling matchmaker. I love that movie. It's one of my mom's favorites. We ...uh ... we watch a lot of movies together. Now I want to watch it. Tonight."

"I bet you can stream it."

And just like that, her curtains are drawn again, her face dark. "No, I can't. Maybe I'll see if the library has the DVD or something this weekend. Well, here I am." She looks up at her building.

"Thanks for the class. More importantly, thanks for not laughing at me."

She smiles tightly, her discomfort apparent. "I'll be late tomorrow, but I'll see you then." Ria turns and is gone.

As I walk up the hill to The Edison, I replay the conversation in my mind, trying to figure out what I could have said that shut her down again.

I have no idea about a lot of things, and this woman is number one on that list.

Chapter 11: Gloria

"Okay, this is what I don't understand. What I've never been able to understand." I'm talking as I enter Malachi's. This has been running on replay in my brain all night. "I know there's no real threat. Watching a movie online. My mom usually gets the DVDs for me. We go through a lot of movies because it helps when I can't sleep. Though, to be honest, I'm not sure what he means with streaming, like how it works, because, well, you know. I don't do the online thing. But I know the movie and I know there's no threat and I know, I know, I know. So why do I panic when someone mentions it?"

Malachi smiles. "That's why you're here, isn't it?"

"Is it possible to be afraid of the internet? Like Googlephobia or something?"

"The technical term is technophobia."

"That's a thing? I'd look it up but well..." I shrug, the irony not lost on me. "Have you ever met someone with technophobia before? Am I a freak?"

He nods. I'm hoping to the former question rather than the latter. "Watch the light without moving your head." Malachi begins slowly moving a pen light side to side as he continues talking. "Describe to me in one word your inciting incident."

One word. I focus on the little blue light moving left to right and back again. The speed is changing, requiring a bit more concentration. Plus, how do I sum up the worst event in my life with one word?

"Um ... I can't boil it down that much."

"I can."

"How? I haven't told you all the details yet. Just the big picture stuff." My eyes shift to Malachi's for a moment. They're kind and warm.

"Stay on the light. Here's the word I want you to consider. Assault."

Assault?

"But that's when someone attacks someone else. No one touched me."

"Were you not attacked?"

I've never thought of it that way before. My previous therapists have always focused on my need to move past it. "No one put their hands on me or anything. It wasn't a physical thing." My eyes dart back and forth, following the light.

"While one definition of assault deals with a physical attack, Merriam-Webster defines it as a 'threat or intent to inflict offensive physical contact or bodily harm on a person that puts a person in immediate danger or apprehension of such harm or contact.' Considering this, does it fit?"

"Well, I wasn't in physical danger."

"Have you ever contemplated suicide because of this incident?"

Well, duh.

Malachi continues. "Then I would argue that you were in immediate danger because of the contact. Why did you think about ending your life? Keep your eyes on the light."

I blink once, and then twice, and re-focus on the light. "Because I couldn't face anyone. I couldn't bear to know that they had seen. That I couldn't imagine going through one more day of my life."

"And what stopped you?"

"Because I didn't want to die. It was more I couldn't imagine living, but I didn't—don't—want to die." Like an addict on the road to recovery, I acknowledge that every day is a battle. A war that I haven't yet won.

"The law would define this as assault. *I* would define it as assault."

"But it wasn't a physical attack."

"It was your body, your physical being. The assault began when someone hit the record button without your consent. You just didn't become aware of the assault until later. Did you know this became a misdemeanor in Ohio in 2018? It's also referred to as Revenge Porn."

I think about what he's saying, flinching at his use of the 'p' word, while still concentrating on his light. What he's saying makes sense. I always thought that it shouldn't have been a big deal because at the time, it wasn't against the law. "That would be like saying that if someone slips a roofie in someone else's drink, the assault starts then, before they are raped."

"Exactly. So when ..."

"Aaron," I supply without being asked. His name comes out in a whisper. My heart is speeding up, but I stare more intently on the blue light dancing side to side in my line of vision.

"So when Aaron—"

I put my hand up to stop Malachi from talking. "I get your point. You know, when I asked if I was technophobic, this is not where I thought we'd be going."

"I saw the chance to rip the Band-Aid off. The point I was trying to lead you to is you are the victim of a cyber assault. It is only rational and reasonable to be fearful of the vehicle for that assault. I had to get you to acknowledge that you were assaulted." He turns the light off. "Now how do you feel?"

"Anxious." Hell, when do I not feel anxious? "Um, a seven." I give him the rating without being asked. I know it's the next logical question. On a scale of zero to ten, a seven isn't terrible. I've had days—weeks—where a seven was the best I've felt. Anything below it is a really good day.

He clicks the light back on, moving it a little faster now. "Think about what you were doing when you found out. You can say it out loud but you don't have to. Bring it into your mind. Into the present."

It'd started with the silence where applause should have been. I could hear the audience whispering, a low rumble that spread through the theater. I'd nailed all my hard notes. The choreography was precise and on point. I hadn't heard anyone fall or anything like that. That could only mean one thing.

A costume malfunction.

Maybe something had popped out when I did my cartwheel.

I finished the last note of "Hot Honey Rag" and pulled my one arm down as I bent forward into a bow. Nope, the girls were still smashed down into my little black sequin dress where they belonged.

I looked over at Marissa, but she stared straight ahead. Eventually the audience began clapping. We separated to clear the stage for bows.

As I made it to the wings, no one would make eye contact with me. What could I have possibly done wrong? I ran my hands over my backside but everything seemed tucked in there as well. I bent over, looking to see if I got my period or something equally as embarrassing. I waited for my turn to go back out, fear beginning to creep in. What if someone died? Something was definitely wrong.

As Roxie Hart, I had the last bow. I ran to the middle of the stage, where the crowd erupted. Someone yelled, "Looking good, girl!" to which the entire audience burst into laughter.

As the curtain closed for the last time, the cast drifted away. No one hugged me, as they were doing to Marissa. This was not how it was supposed to be on the last night of a show. I looked for Aaron.

Where was he? As our director, he would know what was going on. He would know what went wrong. But as hard as I looked, he was nowhere to be found.

No one approached me. No one said anything to me, but that didn't stop the whispers and pointing. I saw people huddled around a phone and a computer. Someone had an iPad out and there was a crowd around it. Eyes darted from the screen to me and back.

Though I'd spent hours and hours over the past weeks and months rehearsing with this group, it was suddenly apparent to me that I didn't have a friend in the cast. I had to find Aaron. He'd help me.

Except when I turned the corner to go to my dressing room, there he was. With Marissa.

"What's going on?" was all I could say, though it was obvious. They were kissing. I wanted him to shove her off and say she'd thrown herself at him. The bulge in the front of his always-tight pants indicated otherwise.

Aaron didn't make a move toward me. He didn't let go of Marissa. He just looked, that shit-eating smirk on his conceited face. I blinked hard and then turned and ran to my dressing room.

To Malachi I said, as though he'd been present in my memories and knew what I was talking about, "I was heartbroken. I felt used and stupid and betrayed. And that was the tip of the iceberg. That was the beginning. I'd do anything to have it just be that. That he was screwing someone else while pledging to love me. That would be a walk in the park."

The light is moving so rapidly now that it pretty much looks like a continual laser of light. It's hard to follow and requiring more and more focus.

Finally Malachi stops moving, and I slump back, exhausted.

"How are you feeling?" he asks.

"Tired. My eyes feel like they ran a marathon. Doesn't your arm get tired?"

"A little. I keep thinking I should invent a machine to do this for me or something, but I'm not motivated enough." He smiles. "Other than tired, how are you feeling?"

I reflect on it. "I'm not having a panic attack, so that's something."

"That is something. You've brought the incident into your working memory. It's there. It's present, and you're still safe."

"I'm still safe," I repeat. I continue saying it in my head as a mantra. I'm still safe. I'm still safe. But, the dogged determination of my anxiety breaks through. "Of course, I didn't get to the really bad stuff yet."

"Rome wasn't built in a day. You've had—how many years of this?"

"Ten."

"I'm good, but even I can't undo ten years of repeated trauma in one or two sessions. This will take a little time, which is why you're here for a few months."

I nod. It makes sense. I glance up at the clock. It's almost ten. The session time has flown by. "Oh, I've got to get to work."

"Where are you working? How are you getting around not using computers and technology?"

I stand up and arch back a little, stretching. I really do feel as if I've put in a vigorous exercise session. If it weren't for wanting to help Grayson, I'd go home and take a nap. "This place called The Edison. I'm helping with construction on their hotel rooms. Or the rooms for the staff. I'm not sure exactly. Manual labor, so other than having to watch some videos about how to drywall, it's pretty low tech."

Malachi considers me for a moment. "How did it go watching the videos?"

"Not great, but I got through it." There was that whole panic attack when Grayson suggested making a video. The mere thought of it begins the cascade of anxiety.

"Hotel rooms? The Edison?" Malachi asks. "Is that a wise choice?"

I shrug. "Sure. I mean, it's flexible. Grayson needs the help, and I'm not bad at it. Funny—the work I've done on stage crew and props in the past is how I'm okay with using tools and painting and construction. So my theater background, which is the cause of all of this and the root of all my pain, is actually helping me out."

"And being at The Edison is okay?"

"So far so good. It's making the days go fast, which I don't take for granted. I actually feel kind of ... good."

As I leave and walk up the hill toward the back of The Edison, I'm amazed. I do feel good. It's been so long since I've felt this way.

I have hope.

Chapter 12: Grayson

My head is swimming. Absolutely and totally buried in a muck and fog and I'm not sure I'll ever be able to make heads or tails of anything again.

I want to sleep on the train back from New York, but the activity in my brain is preventing that. Reluctantly, I pull out my notebook and start flipping through the chicken-scratch notes I made over the past three days of auditions.

My goal with being away these past three days was to cast approximately fifty percent of the roles for the summer, leaving about thirty-five percent for local talent. The other fifteen will come from big names that I'm recruiting, like Julianna. I hate casting those because it involves a lot of ass kissing and begging and favors.

Looking through my notes, there's some good potential here. I start matching names to roles and making list after list in the back of the notebook. I still don't know what I'm going to do about the junior production. Henderson was up my ass about it, but none of his suggestions have felt right just yet.

I scroll through texts from my mom again. There's nothing new, but she said Ria has made great progress over the past few days and started priming the walls. I don't know how she's gotten everything done, but I'm thankful for her.

I wish I could text her.

It's odd that she doesn't have a phone. In this day and age, most people can't function without one. I definitely get the impression that there's more to her story, but so far, she's been tight lipped.

In fact, the most she ever talked was the day we did yoga and she accused me of trying to set up Heidi and Joe. What did she reference again?

Oh right. Clueless.

I think I've seen it. Maybe. It's got a cult following. I pull up the trailer on my phone. It looks like a hodgepodge of over the top 90s references. I don't see the appeal. YouTube automatically launches into the next video, which is a Top Ten list about the movie. The host of the list adds the disclaimer that this is about the 1995 movie, not the TV series or musical.

Musical.

A quick search reveals that the movie director released a musical version in 2018. There's also a version of Emma which has all pop songs and is perfect for the junior show.

I text Henderson and a few minutes later, the emails have been sent to buy the rights to the show. The list of songs is great, and I know it'll be fun to do. Songs by Sara Barellis and Katy Perry, just to name a few. The kids will love it.

I pull into the parking lot of The Edison, having driven right to the dorms rather than stopping down at the house first. I have to find Ria and tell her the good news.

She's sitting in the back hall, taking a break. I stop and look around. She's even taped and mudded out here. Incredible.

"Did you sleep at all? How did you get this done?"

Ria looks up. "I don't sleep much anyway. Plus, you weren't here to distract me with the constant singing."

She's joking. At least I hope she's joking.

"Was your trip good?"

"It was. Stressful but good, I think. But that's what I wanted to tell you. I was stuck and you helped me out!" I slide down to sit on the floor next to her.

"How did I do that?"

"Clueless. Well, Emma, to be exact."

Ria shakes her head, obviously not following my train of thought that is perhaps jumping from track to track. "Whatever you say."

"No, seriously, you're a genius. I've still got tons to do, but I needed to tell you that you pulled my fat out of the fire." As much as I'd like to sit next to her for hours and talk, my mind is spinning with everything I've got to do. I stand up, reaching down and pulling her up to standing with me. For the first time in a very long time, the thought of a season at The Edison doesn't seem like a weight around my neck. We might just make it. *We*. "Everything here, it's been so much. I haven't been excited about it; it's been more of a burden, which makes it hard to trudge through."

Ria nods. "I know all about trudging."

I'm holding her hands still. I smile at her response. "I can't thank you enough. I don't know what I'd do without you here. And then ... brilliant!" My excitement starts to well up, as I want to go read the book for *Emma: The Pop Musical* and post for auditions.

With it being the camp, we pretty much take everyone, but I've still got to cast the show. I've got to get the word out about auditions and start making graphics. Adrenaline is rushing through my body. "Seriously, Ria, you are the best!" I lean in and kiss her quickly on the mouth before sprinting out the door and down to the office.

It's hours later before I look up from my computer, bleary-eyed and exhausted. I've made tons of promotional material, emailed my usual camp goers, posted on several theater boards, and even set up social media ads. I look out the window up toward the dorms and am surprised to see the halogen construction lights still blazing.

Ria must have forgotten to turn them off, or she left them on, thinking I'd be back up to help. It's well after midnight, so I won't be doing anything there tonight. But still, I don't want to leave them on. They get hot and the last thing I need is to burn the place down.

Begrudgingly, I make the trek back up the hill to the dorms. A soft voice floats out from one of the back rooms. Dammit. Ria not only left the lights on, but the radio too. Doesn't she realize electricity's not free?

I halt, frozen, when I realize the voice is not only the radio, but Ria too.

Singing.

I'd bet money she's a mezzo soprano.

I stumble back for a minute, listening to her voice, signing along to The Bangles, "Eternal Flame." She's not just singing, but doing the harmonies as well. Ria is a singer.

A damn fine one.

I quietly walk into the room, mesmerized by her voice. With the last chorus of the song, I can no longer restrain myself and join in singing. She looks up, a bit startled, but continues as our voices entwine and twist together, supporting each other. As the last notes drift away, I can't control the large grin from spreading over my face.

We sound perfect together.

"You've been holding out on me! Why didn't you tell me you could sing?"

The shock of my appearance begins to fade from her face. She clears her throat quickly. "Because you sing so much, it's impossible to get a note in edgewise."

She may have a point.

"Well, if I'd have known, I'd have restrained myself."

Ria raises an eyebrow. "Like you just did? The Bangles are an all-girl group. You couldn't even let me have that."

"But the harmonies ..." I protest.

She shrugs, muttering something that sounds suspiciously like "diva" under her breath.

"No, but seriously, what are you still doing here? It's almost one."

She blinks at me, and then looks out the window. Ria turns back to me. "I don't know how that happened. I'm supposed to be asleep."

"The whole world is supposed to be asleep. But here you are ..." I look around. "Painting?"

"Priming. I got going and I only have"—she counts on her fingers—"three rooms left."

"So in three days, you've finished mudding, taping, sanding, washing, and have primed nine dorm rooms, plus hallways?" How did I not notice this when I was up here earlier in the day?

Ria shrugs. "I don't have much else to do."

"But this is insane."

"I prefer to call it not-so-peacefully co-existing with mental illness." And then she starts laughing. "But I'm getting better."

I laugh too, appreciating this sense of humor that's emerging. It's weird, but emerging. At least it puts a smile on her face.

"No, don't. You're perfect the way you are. You're ... amazing. I don't know how I found you ...

or you found me. You did the work of a full crew in three days. I hope you took the time to sleep and eat. You have to take care of yourself too. You can't just take care of The Edison. But now, we might actually make it for rehearsals and opening night. How are you at tiling and plumbing? We've got bathrooms to do after this." Excitement oozes out of every pore in my body. Any fatigue I'd felt evaporated the moment I heard her sing.

This woman.

Could she be any more perfect?

Chapter 13: Gloria

Opening night.

The word hangs in the air, suddenly stealing all the oxygen from me.

My knees feel weak and I sit rather suddenly.

"Did you finally run out of gas? When was the last time you ate? I bet you haven't eaten recently."

Opening night.

Thoughts bombard me like a swarm of angry wasps. I was singing. *We* were singing. Could I have found my voice? My voice. Singing. On stage. This is a theater. Oh God. Just when I find music, it's ripped away again.

My breath is coming in little shallow bursts. I wish I had Malachi's little blue light to focus on. I picture it in front of me, waving back and forth.

"Hey, Ri—are you okay? Your eyes are doing this weird thing."

I blink once, then twice, and then focus on Grayson. "I'm fine."

"You don't look so fine. You're really pale. Seriously, when did you last eat? Maybe we should go to the kitchen and get you something to eat."

In my mind, because I've been picturing The Edison as some hotel or resort, when he says kitchen, I see the kitchen scene from *Dirty Dancing*. "Is it even open with it being off season and all?" I imagine Grayson opening an industrial-sized can of peaches or something equally as gross.

I know this is not what he's talking about, but I hold onto this false version because I don't want to hear the truth.

I can't hear the truth.

"Um, yeah. It's our kitchen."

"Our?" Now I'm totally lost. I don't know why this is so hard. His words, though quite logical, don't seem to make any sense in my brain.

"My mom and me. Our kitchen. In our house. There's usually leftovers or sandwich fixins or something. Let's get you something to eat."

He grabs my hand and starts to pull me toward the front of the building. "I think we're done for the night. Grab your stuff."

Without breaking his grasp, I reach down and pick up my sweatshirt and bag. With his free hand, he disconnects the radio and halogen lights as we go, plunging us into darkness. My grip tightens, afraid to let go.

Afraid to be alone.

Afraid though, of where he's leading me.

Afraid to lose his contact.

The air has a chill to it, but that's not why I'm shaking. We head down the hill toward a small house. Next to the house is an enormous building.

I've never walked out the front door to see this before. "What's that?" I ask, but not wanting to hear what I know his answer will be.

"That's The Edison."

"So The Edison is a hotel?" I ask.

It's not a hotel.

I know it's not a hotel.

Hotels don't have opening nights.

Now all the comments about Grayson being a star are making sense. And the references to *Cabaret*. And the singing. Oh my God, all the singing.

"No, silly. The Edison is a theater."

Because of course it is. There's no other logical explanation. That's the problem when you live in the grips of anxiety for so long. You see everything with blinders on. Blinders you don't even know are there. And because you can't see the world for what it truly is, you set yourself up for failure over and over.

Just because I know this doesn't mean I can change it.

Breathe in one, two, three, four. Out one, two, three, four.

It's only been a few hours—minutes really in the grand scheme—since I opened my mouth and a song came out. Emotion fills my chest, thick and heavy, making it hard to catch my breath. To feel my throat vibrating as the words came out; that endorphin rush. Only to know that everything that caused my loss is right back in the foreground, staring me down. I haven't even fully processed or unpacked that yet. I cannot deal with—

Damn, I'm out of time.

We arrive at the back door of the house, for which I'm relieved because now I don't have to say anything else stupid, though I really want to sit and put my head down between my knees. Instead, I try to ground myself by observing my surroundings. The house has a kitchen straight out of the 1950s, with faded linoleum and painted cabinets and all. I have a feeling this might be next on the slate for renovation. Grayson drops my hand as he makes a beeline for the fridge. "Let's see what Mom left us."

"It's just the two of you?" I'm sure we've talked about this, but I can't remember right now. I glance around the room, trying to stop myself from falling into the abyss again. The kitchen table has wooden legs and an aluminum top. Grayson opens a drawer built right into the table to pull out utensils. I've never seen anything like it before. The linoleum under the chair legs is worn, a testament to endless family time spent around this table.

"I moved back in here when Dad got sick and permanently when he died. It works for us. Mom makes the food on the home front and handles the corporate donors and sponsors on the business end. It works for us that she makes sure I don't starve. And now she's making sure you don't starve either." He chuckles. "At least that's how I rationalize my mom cooking for me at the age of thirty-five. Speaking of which, how old are you?"

"Thirty-two." I almost blurt out that I still live with my parents too. But that would open a whole bunch of baggage I'm not yet ready to unpack. I'm trying desperately to keep it all in and hidden right now, but moments of panic thread through my veins. I need to focus on something—anything—to keep me from fully melting down.

He bends over, reaching into the fridge, and I focus on his firm backside. I'd have to be dead not to appreciate it. But now that I know for a fact he's an actor, I cannot allow myself to find him attractive. Like when he kissed me today—seriously, what was that? Or when he sings and his voice makes my stomach flutter. Or when we harmonized and it was like we were meant to sing together. Or when he smiles and that dimple pops—

"Ria."

Shit.

I didn't even realize he'd turned around and was trying to get my attention.

"You know, I should probably go. It's late and I have to—"

"You're not going anywhere without eating. And letting me drive you home. It's the middle of the night. You didn't drive here did you?"

I shake my head. "The town's so small, it seems wasteful to take my car." And spend money on gas. Not to mention walking is good for my brain.

He gestures for me to sit down at the table, which is in the middle of the kitchen. It's exhausting being wound this tightly. The minute I sit down every single ounce of adrenaline and energy I have seeps from my body and the seventeen hour work day catches up with me in an instant. I feel myself start to doze off while Grayson is puttering about because one minute I'm holding my head up and the next, there's a turkey sandwich in front of me.

I take a bite. Two maybe. That's it. That's all I've got. The emotional rollercoaster of today has been too much. The high of singing. The low of discovering the truth about The Edison. It's sapped everything I have, and everything is shutting down. I'm too tired ...

****

"Holy shit!" I leap up, looking around.

I have no idea where I am.

No clue at all.

Oh fuck.

So at least this time, I feel that my ensuing panic attack is totally justified. Oh my God. I start rocking, sitting at the edge of this bed that I have no recollection of crawling into in a room that I don't know who it belongs to and in a house that I have no idea where it is. I look around. Are there cameras?

I'm lost.

And what if whoever brought me here recorded it. Me. I look down, frantically patting myself, feeling for all my clothes.

They seem to be there, intact.

"Hey, you're up." A cheerful voice calls from the doorway to my left. I haven't been able to look around or focus on anything. It takes everything I have to localize to this voice.

I blink once and then again.

Grayson.

"Where am I?" I ask, though I feel stupid because maybe the fog is lifting, and I could probably figure this out if I could just get my mind to clear.

"You fell asleep at the kitchen table. Mid-bite. I didn't have the heart to wake you."

"Where am I?" I repeat as my heart pounds in my chest and I frantically try to put together what happened.

"The spare bedroom. I hope you don't mind the twin size bed. I have a larger one but it's upstairs and well ..." He shrugs.

"Did you just imply that I was fat?" I don't know why I focus on that. Other than it seems like a better option than the million other scenarios my mind is playing, all of which involve a massive invasion of my personal space.

Grayson smiles, that dimple peeking out. "How did you get that out of what I just said? It was the middle of the night, and you weren't the only one who was tired. It was more of the fact that I was lazy."

"I fell asleep?" I ask again. My head is clearing and the panic is slowly ebbing away. Grayson seems to have that effect on me. Almost like a tonic.

"On the table."

"Did you say mid-bite?" Please don't let it be so.

Grayson laughs, still hovering in the doorway. I try not to notice how his biceps bulge as he hangs on the frame. "Yup. It kind of fell out of your mouth. Pretty gross actually." He wrinkles his nose, but everything else about his face says he's teasing.

I want to relax and poke fun at myself, but something is bothering me. I won't be able to calm until I ask. "You didn't record me or anything, did you?"

My heart is quickening again. No, this cannot be happening again. I cannot have let this happen again.

His brow furrows. "No, why would I do something like that?"

I stand up, pulling the covers up, trying to make the bed as quickly as I can. I can't look at him when I say this. "No reason. I just ... please don't ever record me, okay?"

Grayson steps back as I approach the door. It's like he knows I need physical space. "Sure. Whatever you say. Now listen, since I didn't technically get you dinner last night, let me get you breakfast. Do you want coffee? Do you want to go out? I can cook."

"You mean you can ask your mom to cook?" I'm surprised I'm snarky instead of totally defensive. At least I didn't swing at him.

He smiles and lets me pass. Of course, I don't know where I'm going, so I turn around to face him.

"I'll have you know, I make a killer omelet. I'm known for my brunches," he offers.

"Brunch? What happened to breakfast?" Oh no. Oh no, no, no. This cannot be happening. "What time is it?"

Grayson consults his watch. "Five of nine. Why?"

"Shit. I've got to go. I've got to go now." I start to run down the hall and find the front door. I don't know where my bag is, but it doesn't matter. I throw open the door and try to get my bearings. Even though the house is down a hill from the dorms, it's still up the hill from town. And I'm on the other side now, so I'll have to run up the hill, down the other side, and into town to make my appointment with Malachi.

I'm never going to make it.

I turn to look at Grayson, panicked. "I'm late. I need to go."

He steps toward me, grabbing keys off a hook by the door. "Your chariot awaits." He points toward a nondescript Honda Civic in the driveway. As I slide in, he asks, "Where to, m'lady?"

"Chapel Street." I can't for the life of me remember the number. "It's a white house. Big porch."

As he speeds down the hill, I watch the numbers on the dashboard. Two minutes. "Shit. I'm not going to make it."

"Where?"

It's a fair question, considering he's driving me and all, but still, it's none of his business.

"I have an appointment. I can't be late."

"I'll get you there. Which house?"

We're on Chapel Street already. He must know some shortcut or something.

"That one on the left."

He pulls up and I've got my seatbelt off and the door open before the car fully stops. I don't say anything as I slam the door shut behind me and sprint up the porch steps. Flinging open the door, I race in. Panting, I say, "Malachi, I'm here. I'm not late. I'm here."

And with that, I sag onto a chair, drained from the highs and lows of the morning. I need to crawl into bed for about a week to figure all this out.

"Was that Grayson Keene I saw dropping you off?" Malachi, still sitting comfortably at his desk, parts the sheers on his window slightly and glances out.

"Yeah. I thought I was going to be late, so he drove me."

"Gloria, you only live next door. Why did he drive you?"

It's probably not helpful to lie to your therapist, though I'm tempted. "Um, I slept up at his place."

Malachi's eyebrows shoot up. "Oh, did you now? You wanna talk about it?" A smirk dances across his face.

"I thought therapists were supposed to be impartial and disinterested."

Malachi laughs. "We are supposed to be. But this—this is surprising. I was not expecting you to be at this place quite yet. I want to hear how it all came about."

"Are you a secret gossip?" I lean forward, interested. This is a side of Malachi I haven't seen before.

He laughs. "No, because no one in town will talk to me, and most of my patients don't interact with the townies."

"Are they all agoraphobic like me?"

"I wouldn't call you agoraphobic, truly. You're afraid because of your trigger, not really the outside world. Plus, list for me the things you've done since you've been here."

"Eh, not much."

Malachi ticks off on his fingers. "Coffee shop, park, yoga, job, sleepovers. I don't consider that not much. You've only been here a week."

"It wasn't a sleepover. Not like that. I shouldn't have told you that I spent the night," I mutter.

Malachi laughs. "I see a lot from this desk." He looks at me pointedly. "That's what you were wearing when you left yesterday, and don't take this the wrong way, but you don't look well groomed this morning. You don't smell it either."

My hand flies to my mouth. "Oh my God, I want to die. I was up working on the dorms at The Edison. Grayson was out of town, so I was just motoring through. It was kind of nice. I got into the zone and was really focused. It's been a long time since I could focus for that long."

Malachi nods and smiles slightly, his professional therapist face back in place. I continue.

"Grayson came in midday when I was taking a break. He was all excited about something and he sort of kissed me." I touch my lips at the memory. "I don't think it was romantic or anything. He was just really excited. So then, I didn't know what to do with myself, so I kept working. But here's the interesting thing—"

"Right, because kissing isn't the interesting part," Malachi says dryly.

"Stop." I hold up my hand, laughing. This is a different Malachi today. Or maybe it's a different me. It sort of feels like the old me, just a little. The me that I'd forgotten existed. The me from before. "So when we work, Grayson sings. Like *all the time*."

"I can imagine."

"And his voice is great. It's the kind that a decade ago would have made me weak in the knees." Not only a decade ago, but I'm not ready to open up that can of worms yet. "I used to sing too. Like Grayson. All the time. I haven't sung since that night when ... it ... happened. It's this huge void that I can't fill."

As I'm talking, Malachi picks up his blue light and begins moving it. My eyes following closely, I keep going. "But yesterday, after Grayson came back and kissed me—and it wasn't a big kiss or anything. A quick peck on the lips. Well, anyway, something in me changed. I put the radio on. I opened my mouth and words came out."

I close my eyes for a minute, letting the memory of those notes wash over me.

"Follow the light, please."

Opening my eyes, I continue. "Grayson came in later. Much later. I didn't even realize how late it was. Like after midnight. I was still singing. I've got a lot of lost songs to make up for, you know. And anyway, he heard me and sang with me." I put my hand over my heart which aches with the memory. "Malachi, I've missed singing so much. I've missed this part of myself. And when we sang together, it was like we created something beautiful. Like making an exquisite work of art out of a lump of clay."

I see Malachi nodding from behind the blue light. "Focus, please."

I shift my eyes back.

"And then, Grayson took me to his house and made me a sandwich. Suddenly I was tired. Apparently, I fell asleep at the table, mid-bite. Grayson put me to bed. When I woke up this morning, I totally freaked out. I didn't know where I was. I didn't know what had happened. All I could think was that maybe he recorded me." I stare hard at the blue.

"Do you think he did?"

I shrug. "I don't know. He said he didn't. I mean, I asked. But I don't know how I can believe him. How can I believe anyone? How do I know you're not recording this right now?" My voice is growing tight as the fear starts to emerge.

"Keep your eyes on the light. It's hard, Gloria. That's why you're here. You're trying to reprogram your brain to not freak out. To learn how to trust again."

"Do you think that'll ever happen?" I switch my focus to Malachi as he puts the light down. He's looking out the window.

"I think you are starting that journey."

Chapter 14: Grayson

What do I do now? Do I wait? How long will she be? Is she coming back to The Edison today? Why is she here? What's she doing in there?

Good God, my brain is firing more questions than a three-year-old in a toy store.

She went into the house. It's one of the properties owned by the Andrewses. The nice one. I'm not sure which Andrews sibling lives there. They seem nice enough but keep to themselves a lot. I don't know why. Perhaps the residents of Hicklam have done something to offend them.

Perhaps they're simply shy.

Perhaps they're involved in a naughty cult, like my mom seems to think.

Though somehow, Ria doesn't seem like the type to be in a sex cult. I just can't picture it. She's too closed off and afraid.

Maybe she's a former cult member and the Andrews siblings run a support group for ex-culters. Maybe we'll get some former Scientologists here. If any of the Hollywood group come through, I'll cast them in something at The Edison.

That would be a coup.

I debate about running into Dean's Beans to get coffee, but I don't want to miss Ria coming out. On the other hand, she might be in there for hours because Lord only knows what's going on in there. Whatever it is, she couldn't be late.

Sometimes that girl is more skittish than a cat walking around a bathtub.

I wonder why?

I don't know anything about her. Not really. I'm not even sure what her last name is. It's got to be on that paperwork she filled out for Mom. At least I hope she filled it out. I text Mom to double-check. This is the sort of thing she usually lets fall through the cracks.

Mom texts back that the paperwork is filed and all set.

Good. At least I know Ria will be getting paid for her labor, though I now feel guilty that we're not paying her nearly enough for all she's been doing. She must have put in at least twelve hour days when I was gone, but I'm betting it was even more than that.

I need to be doing more than buying her an occasional coffee and making her a turkey sandwich.

I look up at the white brick house with its two-story porch. Knowing the mill history in town, I'd guess that this was originally a manager or overseer's house while the brick flats next door—where Ria is staying—were the houses for the workers and their families. If they were in the city, they'd be tenement houses, but here in Hicklam, they're in good shape. Low-rise, brick buildings with multiple apartments. I've heard most of them still have the original tin ceilings and everything, though someone a while back mentioned installing dropped ceilings to help with heating.

Even though these buildings are more well-kept than the ones on the lower East Side, they're not fabulous. Maybe Ria would want to stay up at the house. I could ask her.

I text my mom, you know, since she lives there too and all. And considering it's actually her house.

You barely know her. Are you using condoms?

Then she sends an eggplant emoji. Gross.

Okay, things you never want to discuss with your mother. Ever.

No, Mom, it's not like that.

I start to type a long explanation but give up and call her. I don't even say hello when she answers. "I was just thinking it'd help her out. Save her some money."

"But you don't know her. You're being hasty."

A thought about apples and trees runs through my head. "You're right. What's her last name?"

"How am I supposed to know? You're the one sleeping with her. I'd think if you can put your thing inside her, you should know her last name. But don't go by me. I'm the old fart here."

My eye starts to twitch. I want to tell her again that I'm not sleeping with Ria, but once that woman gets something in her head, it's set there. Plus, it's not as if I'd mind it. She's gorgeous on top of being generous. And boy, can she sing.

That's almost enough to give me a hard-on alone.

"Well, I was just thinking that because she's working so hard for us and such long hours, that I don't want her trudging up and down the hill at all hours."

"You know she's part of the cult. Who knows what's going on with those people?"

"All of the Andrews are perfectly nice. They come to most of the shows. Plus, I think Malachi is the only one who lives here year-round. Marvin and Malyia work in the city. They're the building owners and Malachi manages them."

"But what about all the people who come to town to visit Malachi. In and out, day after day. On an hourly basis too. What is going on in there? It can't be good."

"And that's why you don't like Ria?"

"I don't know Ria. I only met her a few days ago to give her paperwork and drive her home. But I don't like that you're already whipped by her. Do I need to remind you what happened with that Julianne girl?"

This is why grown-ass men should not be living with their nosy, old-fart mothers.

Also, it used to annoy me that my mother refused to call her Julianna, instead insisting on Julianne. Now it gives me a perverse pleasure.

"I don't think you can compare Julianna and Ria in any way, shape, or form." Other than their vocal ranges, that is. "Jules is a diva. Ria's about the furthest thing from that."

"So you are interested in her. I thought so." I can totally picture Mom nodding in triumph.

"No, we're friends, I think. I mean, I'd like to be friends. I have a feeling that's what she needs more than anything else right now."

"Whatever you say ..."

I see the front door bang open and Ria head down the steps. "Gotta run, Mom!" I disconnect and fumble to lower the window. Though I am loathe to admit it, Mom's probably right about it being hasty to invite Ria to live with us.

"Hey!" I call. "Need a ride?"

Ria looks up, a bit of a confused expression on her face. "I'm good, thanks."

She continues walking to the sidewalk and makes a left turn. There are no cars parked along this street so I inch forward. "Let me give you a lift. I owe you breakfast at least, since you didn't get to eat your dinner. Please let me drive you home."

Ria stops walking. "Grayson, I'm fine, really. I can take care of myself. Well, I can't, but I'm working on it." She shrugs.

"I bet you can. I'm not trying to swoop in and do things for you. I'm trying to repay you for how you're helping me, and as an advance for all the help I know you're going to give me. Now I insist you get in the car and let me drive you home."

She laughs. "Fine." She crosses around the front of the car and gets in. "Straight ahead."

"Yes, ma'am." I signal and pull the car out. After about three seconds, Ria says, "Okay, we're here."

I look at her. "Seriously?"

She smirks. "You insisted."

"You live next door to the Andrewses."

"It's practical. I have to see Malachi three times a week. And you've walked me to my house before, so you should have known that."

Totally true. In my race to be a white knight, I forgot all about it. Now I look like an idiot. So to cover, I raise my eyebrow, giving her the chance to continue.

Quickly she adds, "He's helping me with the book I'm writing. It's historical fiction centered around an immigrant family in the textile industry."

"Oh, I didn't realize Malachi Andrews was an expert about textiles and mills." I would never in a million years have pictured that.

"I didn't say that. He's helping with ... other things ... that are helping me write the book. I have a standing appointment with him on Monday, Wednesday, and Friday mornings, and he doesn't tolerate people being late."

Interesting.

"Just ask it." Ria's arms are folded across her chest as she leans on the passenger's side door.

"Ask what?"

She sighs. "I'm not in sex cult."

"I didn't think you were!" I protest, a little too loudly, even for my own ears.

She raises her eyebrow in well-deserved disbelief.

"Okay, maybe my mom questioned it. She's nosy and has an overactive imagination."

Ria laughs. "That's totally the vibe I got that day when she drove me home. She asked some weird questions about rituals and tattoos. Speaking of which," she looks out the window, "I am here. I need to shower and change and eat. I'll be back up in a little while. Thanks for the ride."

"Don't you want to get breakfast?"

Ria sighs. "Grayson, I smell. You smell. We're still tired. We spend enough time together. I'll be back up in a hour or so. I promise. You can survive without me."

But I don't want to.

The realization stuns me and I sit up a little straighter. "Sure. Take your time. I have an in with the boss. He won't dock your pay or anything."

"He'd better not." She opens the door. "See you in a bit."

The minute she walks into her building, I want to run after her and kiss her senseless.

This is crazy. I don't know anything about her. I don't know her full name or where she's from or how long she'll be here. And let's face it, it's not like I'm going to have time for anything but The Edison any time soon.

If I can just stay focused and get this job done, I'll be able to get Henderson to take over with Mom and I can get back to auditions in the city. If I can get the renovations completed and we have a successful season, I might actually get back to living my life.

If nothing gets in my way, that is.

That's a lot of ifs.

Chapter 15: Gloria

"Mom, you won't believe it. It's gorgeous! I'll have to get some pictures and send them to you." Two weeks after I finished the dorm rooms, I started work on the main theater bathrooms. It's taken me a month, but man, am I proud of what I've done.

"If you had a phone, you could text them to me." Coming from anyone else, the statement would sound nagging or patronizing. From Mom, it's a gentle prod.

"I don't want a phone. I don't know if having it would cause me anxiety or not. I think it would. What if I'm having a bad day and I do a Google search? I don't want to undo all the work I've done."

"That's a good point. I just wish you were a little easier to reach."

"I've got a home phone."

"Yes, but I can't see pictures that way."

I sigh. "I know. I've been thinking about it, which is better than before."

"You should be better than before. You've been in treatment for two months now. You should be almost done."

"I am. I'm a lot better. Mom, I go to a theater to work every day. That should tell you something." Maybe I leave out the fact that while I'm *technically* in a theater, I haven't been on stage. Not even to walk across it. I've done some dressing room work, as well as working on the bathrooms and the lobby. In a related story, I now know how to lay tile and grout. That's what I want my mom to see.

Grayson's friend, Drew, taught me. No videos this time, though in theory I should be able to watch them.

"But you would have to be home to be able to use a landline. That's where a cell phone comes in handy."

"I'm thinking about it. I really am. I did give you the number for the office at The Edison, in case you need to reach me."

Mom's quiet for a minute. "I thought the point in all of this is for you to get back to normal."

Normal. What is that even?

"I don't know what normal looks like anymore. I can't see myself ever being one to spend hours of time on the internet. It's too unpredictable. Plus I don't need it. My life is full without it. I don't know what I'd give up to do that. There's not much I want to give up."

"Like Grayson?"

Now I'm happy she can't see my eye roll. "Friends, Mom. Not to mention, he's my boss." Of sorts. I'm pretty much his right-hand person at this point. That'll change when Henderson arrives this week. But with the cast and crew busy with rehearsals, I'm basically the foreman. Forewoman. Foreperson.

It's also pretty much a crew of one, so it's not too hard to control myself.

"Do you have a date you'll be returning? What will you do when you get back? Are you going back to school in the fall?"

I forgot how much my well-meaning mother contributed to my stress. "I should be ready to leave in about a month. I'm not sure after that. But I've got to run. Got to get to work. Talk to you soon. Love you, Mom."

I disconnect before she has the chance to ask me any other questions. I'm actually finishing up with Malachi next week, slightly ahead of schedule. Years of cognitive behavioral therapy, mindfulness training, and meditation, combined with my EMDR treatment, seem to be the trick. It's a lot of work, but it's paying off. I can leave as soon as I'm done with Malachi.

He'd like me to hang out for a bit, just to make sure I do okay.

Plus, I don't know what I'd be going back for. I still haven't found anything I want to do. At least not enough to go back to school for it.

I grab my bag and head up the hill to The Edison. It's a different place now that the dorms are open and full of cast and crew. The theater is teeming with activity, opening night only two weeks away. Truth is, over the past four weeks, I've hardly spent any time with Grayson, as he's so busy with the cast.

Probably a good thing, even though I hate it. I crave time with Grayson like a man in the desert craves water.

The prior four weeks had been heaven and hell all at the same time. It's ironic. As I'm doing so much more than I've been able to do for the past several years, I'm only just aware of all the things I can't have in life because of what was done to me.

There's the optimistic part of me that wants nothing more than to charge into the main stage area of The Edison and belt out "Good Morning" from *Singin' in the Rain*. I played Kathy junior year in high school. I still remember the songs and choreography. That kind of muscle memory doesn't leave.

Similar to the memories of what happened following the incident.

The assault, I remind myself.

I was assaulted. First by Aaron and then by Marissa. Though truthfully, I didn't find out about her role in it until months later, when I inquired about pressing charges. Before I had any idea of how bad I would get. Before I chickened out of filing a police report.

Some of that seems like yesterday, while some feels like a lifetime ago. But the treatment with Malachi must be working, as I'm able to think about the incident. My pulse may have quickened a skosh but not enough to even raise my awareness. My breathing is still regular. I'm not huddled in a corner sobbing.

Baby steps.

Actually, these are huge, giant steps.

I've come a long way, baby.

I head right for the ladies' restrooms, ducking under the caution tape spanning the doorway. The water hasn't been turned on in here yet, so I don't want anyone sneaking in and using the toilets yet. *That's* not a mess I want to clean up.

Today I'm finishing the baseboards and trim work. It's all been painted and is waiting for me to pop it back on. I'm an expert with the pneumatic nail gun. Makes me feel like a badass using it.

Filling my life with things that empower me, like fancy tools, has helped with my recovery these past eight weeks. But Hicklam is an artificial bubble, away from the real world. It's not as unpredictable as New York City would be, which had been my original life plan. I know Mom is right, and I have to think about what comes next.

"Oh, you're here. I was worried when I didn't see you this morning, but then I couldn't remember if it was a Malachi day." Grayson pops his head through the doorway, carefully avoiding the tape.

"It wasn't. I was just late because I was talking to my Mom. You know how they can be." I smile up at him from my place on the floor.

"You wouldn't be here if I didn't." He winks at me. "What was your mom on your case about?"

I sigh. "To get a cell phone so she can harass me all day at work."

"Ah, yes. The job of a mother is never done."

"She worries about me, and this would ease her mind. Plus she wants to see all the progress at The Edison. I don't think she believes I can wield this bad boy as well as I do." I wave the nail gun around.

"Easy there, killer. At least take your finger off the trigger. We don't need any flying nails. I'm nervous enough that things aren't going to fall into place."

"What's up now?" I enjoy these moments when it's just the two of us and we talk about nothing and everything. In these fleeting times, I can almost picture a world in which I could open myself up to someone again.

Almost.

He slides into the restroom, using some *Mission: Impossible* type moves and plops down on the floor next to where I'm working. Grayson pauses for a minute as he looks around. "Damn, Ria, this looks fantastic. I can't believe you did all this."

"Drew was a big help. He got me started."

"Yeah, but still. The tile is amazing and the paint looks great. This space looks about three times larger than it used to."

"Getting rid of wood paneling often has that effect, you know." I look around, trying to see what he's seeing. "It does look at lot brighter in here. The new light fixtures are great. Plus they're LED lights, so they'll save you on electricity in the long run. They'll pay for themselves eventually."

"We'll need every drop of that savings we can get." He runs his fingers through his hair, which is in desperate need of a haircut. "I'm still kicking myself for green lighting this whole project."

"Didn't this place need it?"

"Probably. I mean, it needed something, but maybe Mom was right and Dave was ripping us off. He's the one who told us they needed to gut everything down to the studs. Maybe we could have made improvements with less demolition first."

"We're in the home stretch. Once opening day rolls around, I'm sure you'll sell out this place night after night. Things'll be fine." He's alluded to money issues several times. I mean, would I be heading up this project if they weren't in a bad situation?

Grayson quickly places a finger over my lips. "Shh. I don't want any of the cast or crew hearing that we're in financial straits." His gaze suddenly shifts from his finger to my eyes and something changes. Carefully, as if time is moving in slow motion, he pulls his finger down my lips. It takes everything I have not to take his finger in my mouth in the most inappropriate way.

A loud bang from somewhere else in the theater breaks the spell, and Grayson quickly pulls his hand down. "Sorry. I mean, you know the theater type. Actually, you probably don't. There are always the people who are in it for themselves. If they see a way to tank me and The Edison, they may take it."

"I know the type," I say dryly, still trying to compose myself considering the impression of his finger is still lingering on my lips. "You know I won't say anything."

He smiles, standing up. "I know. You're good people, Ria. Honest and open. It's what I like so much about you. Why I'm glad we're friends. 'Cause we are. Friends. And I value and respect your friendship. Okay, well, I should see what that noise was. Gotta run. I'll check in with you later."

He dashes through the door, getting his foot caught in the tape and pulling it down. Sheepishly, he turns and starts fumbling with it.

"Never mind, I'll get it."

I stand up and fix the tape, watching Grayson sprint down the corridor toward the stage area. Apparently I was the only one who felt that moment.

Probably a good thing.

Grayson sure did emphasize how much we're friends. Perhaps he saw the longing in my eyes or something. Could it be that he knows me better than I know myself? I'm trusting him, and we're friends. I'm getting to a point of maybe I would want something more.

Take out that maybe.

He's telling me loud and clear that he doesn't want that. Okay, message received.

Not to mention that he values my honesty and integrity. Ha! I won't even tell him that my name is really Gloria.

Yeah, I need to get a cell phone. That and a plan to get the hell out of here as soon as I'm done with Malachi. I'm already starting to make a mess of things here.

At least I'm consistent with that.

Chapter 16: Grayson

Okay, probably dodged a bullet on that one. As I walk back into the main stage area, I remind myself over and over that kissing Ria is not a good idea.

Not because I don't want to, but because I don't think she's in a place to handle it. I still don't know what happened to her in the past. Whatever it was, it was big. And not good big.

Though I am relieved to hear her talk about her mom. Knowing that she's in contact with her makes me feel a bit more relieved that she's not running for her life from a psycho ex or something.

Not that it would change how I feel about her.

I wouldn't have made it through the renovations without her. The girl can learn anything. *Anything*.

Ten bucks says if I throw her a pair of character shoes, she could walk up on stage and nail the scene.

Thinking back on her voice that one day—the only time I've heard her sing—I'm half-tempted to try it. That is, if I can ever get her in the theater. She steers clear. I'm guessing it's because of the loud, sometimes obnoxious cast of characters. I often forget, especially when doing shows back to back, that people in the outside world don't function like us. That there are people who don't need a double door to fit their egos through.

Myself included.

The Edison, and all its daily grind, is the only thing keeping me humble. Had I continued on my career trajectory, without this weight tied to my ankles, I'd be as cocky and egotistical as the rest of them. I still act like I am, of course. I've got a reputation to uphold, obviously. Instead, I'm tired and scared. Worried that I'll let my mom—and dad—down. Worn out from trying to do it all. But I can't let anyone see that.

No one wants to work for a company in which the management is full of doubt. I think most of my acting skills come from my "fake it 'til you make it" philosophy. They need my swagger and confidence, not the worry that spreads across my face when I look at the bank account.

Which is dismal.

We're running low on money. Dangerously low. Considering we have no income coming in between mid-September and mid-May, that's a long time to make due with what's in the account. And then you add on the cost of this renovation ...

The home equity loan payments alone are enough to give me a small heart attack on a monthly basis. That's before we consider the cost of running the shows and paying the cast and crew and all that good stuff. We have to sell at least seventy-five percent of the seats at every single show to make our payments for the year. That doesn't include frivolities like eating. If we can sell eighty percent, I may not have to sell a kidney to have the start-up funds for next year.

Mom and I severely miscalculated how much this renovation would cost. As Dave started ripping more things out, the expenses went up and up and up. While I hate to admit Mom was right about him overcharging us, we would have overextended our budget long before we finished. Even with going down to paying just one person, it'll be tight.

Normally, between our sponsors and ticket sales, we cover our seasonal costs with enough to live on for the rest of the year. Having to repay the loan on top of that means we need more income.

If I've done my math correctly—and I run these numbers almost daily—as long as we can secure the same level of corporate sponsorship as last year, we should be able to repay the loan by the end of this season. If we can't, we won't be able to make the payments until next year.

I doubt the bank will look kindly on that.

I'd love for Mom to get more in sponsorship to give us some more breathing room, but I can't count those chickens before they hatch.

Ugh. Is that an ulcer I feel starting?

"Grayson, where are you? We're starting," someone calls from within the theater. If nothing else, the rehearsals are at least distracting from all the other things on my mind.

God, I miss the days of living in the city. Waiting tables, going to auditions. Taking any show I could get, no matter how off-Broadway it was. I knew if I kept at it, all the hard work would pay off. I'd make it big and that would be that.

My dreams would come true.

I never minded coming back to The Edison for the summer season. I'd sublet my place to save on rent. Experience. Connections. Work on my craft. It was all worth it.

Until the time when it wasn't coming back for a visit but coming back to stay.

There's part of me that's terrified I'll never get out of this small town. That I'll never get my shot. That'll I never experience that feeling of having made it on the biggest stage. That this is all there is for me.

I shake my head to clear the negative thoughts from swirling around. I should probably do some more yoga. It did help, at least for a little while. I haven't been to a class since rehearsals started, since we usually run into the evening.

I wonder if Ria is available tonight?

"Be there in a minute!" I call into the theater before sprinting back toward the bathrooms. I poke my head in to find Ria where I left her, sitting on the floor with the nail gun.

"Hey!" I call, startling her. She squeezes off a nail and her whole body jerks with the force.

"Shit!"

"Are you okay? I didn't mean to scare you."

"Don't sneak up on me when I'm using power tools. That could have been bad."

"Sorry. I just was thinking maybe I'd do a yoga class tonight. I'm pretty tense about things and that actually seemed to help. You up for it?"

"Let me check my schedule," she says dryly.

Shit. I didn't even think of that. She's here every day. Even weekends. And for long stretches of time, too. I don't notice her comings and goings now that I'm busy with rehearsals, but it seems like she's always here. "I'm sorry. You must be busy writing. I feel like such a shit for taking up all your time."

Her brow wrinkles. "I was kidding. It's fine. I don't have my stuff, so I'll meet you there a little before seven."

"Are you sure that leaves you enough time? I don't know how you possibly get any writing done. You're here all the time."

"I'm doing what I need to do," she replies flatly. "See you later."

The dismissal in her tone is unmistakable.

Maybe it's a good thing I didn't kiss her earlier. I don't need that kind of complication in my life. Not to mention, I don't have the time or energy for any of that right now. Plus, it's not like either one of us will be staying in Hicklam long-term.

Though, come to think of it, I have no idea where Ria is from. She doesn't talk a lot about ... anything. Pulling out my phone, I quickly type 'ria benedetti' as I head into the theater. I want to know more about her. Where she went to school. What she looked like when she was younger. Who she talks to when she's not with me.

"Grayson! Where have you been? The staging for this scene isn't working!" Paul, the stage manager, greets me at the back. "We can't get the bench and light post on and the water feature running in the allotted time. We've got to figure out something else."

I slide my phone into my back pocket and set about doing all the things a proper director is supposed to do. Except the director, Todd Withers, hasn't shown up yet. He asked that I "look after things" for the first week. If his reputation is accurate, he'll show up last minute, change one thing, and take credit for the whole performance.

Whatever. As long as people come and pay to see a Todd Withers's show, I don't care. I'm here anyway.

I'd like to be able to walk away, free and clear, but I carry the baggage of generations with me. Plus, if we lose The Edison, my mom loses her home. Like, her only home. She grew up in that house and has never lived anywhere else. Not to mention, this was her life with my dad. He loved this theater, probably even more than she did.

Sometimes I wonder if she truly understands what's at stake.

Dad was always the grounding force. The level head to her artistic side. She's a painter more than an actor—

Wait.

I slap myself in the head. Mom's a painter. An artist She always used to do the sets for the shows. That's how she and Dad met. She stepped back when my theater career started to get busy and never got back into it, but maybe it's time. Plus it would save on having to pay a set designer.

I glance up to see what's going on onstage. There are people clumped about, and they appear to be discussing different scenes and blocking. Hell, for all I know, they're discussing the latest baseball game, but with this crowd, I highly doubt it. They're fine without me for a minute. I jog out of the side door and to the office.

"Mom, I've just figured out a way to slash the budget a bit."

"Oh, Grayson, that's great. What are you going to do?"

I hate how Mom automatically assumes I'm taking on more responsibility. Truth is, I don't have the bandwidth to carry one more single thing.

"Ask not what your country can do for you. Ask what you can do for your country," I say in my best Kennedy impression. I'm not really sure though. I haven't had to do too many Massachusetts accents in my career.

"Huh?"

"Mom, you're coming out of retirement. You've been promoted to lead set designer."

She blinks up at me, not saying anything.

"Time to break out your paint brushes!" I wave my hands in a little flourish.

Mom leans back in her chair. I sink into the chair on the other side of the desk, waiting for her to respond.

"I don't think so, Grayson. I gave that up years ago. I don't really do that anymore. I'm too out of practice. I wouldn't know what would look good. Why don't we stick with the plan?"

I feel as if she's slapped me across the face, and I jump to my feet. My blood starts to boil. I rake my hands through my hair, wanting to pull and scream all at the same time. "The plan? *The plan*? Since when in God's name has there been a plan? If there had been a plan, you and Dad would have managed this place better, doing small renovations as the budget allowed instead of waiting until the walls were crumbling to fix anything! If there was a plan, you would have hired the necessary support staff instead of dumping it all on me! If there was a plan, we'd have had contractors to—oh wait. We did. You fired them. Without consulting me, but with expecting me to shoulder the burden of their work. So tell me about this plan, Mom? I'd like to be filled in one of these days."

She stares at me, her eyes wide, still saying nothing. Slowly they fill with tears.

Dammit.

I leave without looking back. I can't deal with her right now. The salary for the set designer isn't much—a few grand. But it would be a few grand we could save or use elsewhere, and it may have helped.

I can't figure out why I'm busting my ass to help The Edison survive when Mom doesn't seem to care. I've stepped out of my comfort zone to help. Why can't she step back into hers? It's *her* theater, for Christ's sake. It's almost as if she wants it to fail.

I wish she'd clue me in, if that was her plan. I've only given up everything for it. It'd be nice to know if I sacrificed my whole life for nothing.

Chapter 17: Gloria

Well, I don't think yoga's doing the trick for Grayson.

I've never seen him in this bad of a mood before. Come to think of it, I've never seen him in a bad mood. I can practically feel the tension and stress coming off his body in waves.

As we're in the final savasana pose, I sneak my hand over to touch his. Glancing out of the corner of my eye, I see his eyes closed, yet his pinky finger sneaks in to curl around mine. I focus on my breathing and meditation, willing my calming energy to flow through our hands and into Grayson.

I'm not used to being the one with excess calming energy to spare.

As we gather up our supplies, Grayson tries to shove his mat into the strap, failing once, twice, three times. Gently, I pick them up and slide the strap over the roll and hand it back to him.

"Wanna talk about it?"

He looks around the studio at all the women milling about. The instructor, Cassidy, is hovering and looks as if she's about to swoop in. He hasn't seemed responsive to her advances in the past, so I doubt he'd appreciate another attempt now when he's obviously dealing with a lot. I don't wait for his answer, giving him another option. "Walk me home?" My raised eyebrows let him know that this is not up for negotiation.

He nods and we head for the door.

It's a warm night and dusk is just starting to settle in. The days are getting longer and longer, which I know has helped my mood. We reach my place in just a few minutes. "Why don't you come up?" I look at him expectantly, but then it occurs to me what I might be inadvertently implying. "To talk," I add hastily. "In private where the whole town and crew can't hear."

We walk up the stairs to my flat. I haven't spent much time here lately. The Edison has been much more of a home to me than this place. Though it's furnished and minimally decorated, there's a sterility to it that I'm seeing for the first time. I understand why Malyia wouldn't want to spend a lot on furnishings, with different clientele moving in every three months. And let's face it, people in the depths of depression and anxiety aren't generally known for their stellar housekeeping skills.

"Oh, this is ..." Grayson trails off, clearly at a loss for words.

"Completely furnished before I got here. Not my design aesthetic, but it's clean and there are no cockroaches, so it's fine."

"You're pretty easygoing."

I've been called a lot of things in my life. Easygoing has never been one. Even before. I was a typical theater person. Drama. Drama. Drama.

Attracted to it like a moth to a flame.

"I try." I shrug. "Welcome to my humble abode. At least for the time being."

"So what's the deal? It was furnished? Doesn't one of the Andrewses own this building?"

"Malyia does. Marvin owns some others and Malachi owns the building next door. I think they're looking at a few more places, but you know ... the rental market in Hicklam isn't fantastic."

Grayson looks at me. "I guess it's a good thing for you that Malachi is connected. It's pretty convenient that he's right next door for your research."

I head to the kitchen area rather than engage in this line of conversation. "Do you want something to drink? I have water or ... water."

"Hmm." He scratches his chin in mock deep thought. "I guess I could go for a water."

I pull a bottle out of the fridge and twist open the top before handing it to him. "So, what's eating you?"

Grayson sighs, sinking into a chair at the little dinette set. He lowers his head directly to the table, hand still clutching the water bottle. "I can't win."

"I hear ya, but what about? It sounds like rehearsals are coming along. Plus you know how it is. You have that little span where nothing's working and everyone's terrible and the songs suck and no one knows their lines and then ... poof! It all comes together. Usually one of the last rehearsals. But it always comes together."

Oh shit. I shouldn't have said that. He's going to ask how I know. I suck in a breath, waiting for him to put me on the spot.

"Yeah, I know. It's not that. It's everything with the theater and the financial stress."

Slowly I exhale, thankful he didn't notice my slip. "How did it get so bad? I mean, I don't mean to pry, but if you want to solve the problem, you have to start at the root of it."

Without lifting his head, Grayson answers. "The fine and performing arts are always a fickle business, depending largely on the economy. When the economy's bad, people have less money to spend on these sorts of things. We'd done okay with the recession in 2008. Weathered it without too much damage. People still need their arts to take their minds off of reality. My parents—my dad—was savvy with things like that. I wasn't worried. Everything was fine."

"Until it wasn't ..." I supply when Grayson trails off.

Grayson lifts his head and looks at me, his eyes full. "Until my dad got cancer and outlived everyone's expectations by over a year. Which meant an additional year of expensive medical treatments. But it was my dad. We couldn't not try. In the meantime, he couldn't do much around The Edison so a lot of the slack fell on paid contractors.

We hired out more than ever before, which added up quickly. The upkeep of the building slid until we closed last year, and I knew if we were going to make it, we *had* to bite the bullet and do the construction work."

I nod. I want to pat his arm or rub his shoulders or sit on his lap. Something. *Anything*.

Especially if it involves pressing my body against his.

Whoa. Wait. I cannot go thinking thoughts like that.

"I'm sorry," I say quietly, sitting down on my hands. Literally. I don't trust myself otherwise.

"And my mom seems unwilling to help. I don't know why though. The Edison—it's her legacy. She and my dad met because of it, for Christ's sake. She's a mess and I'm trying to help her, but I'm so mad at her too because it seems everything she's doing is going against what I need her to do."

"Like firing your contractors."

He smiles weakly. "Exactly. I still don't know what I would have done without you. I'm so lucky to have run into you the way I did. That you asked Heidi for a job. That I saw you doing yoga in the park and that Heidi told me you were looking. It's like it was meant to be or something."

"And this job was just what I needed too. You have no idea." What I really want to say is that *you* are what I needed. Grayson is the first non-family member, other than paid mental health professionals, that I've connected with since the incident. I wasn't able to sustain any of my former friendships.

No one wants to deal with someone who's a mess all the time. I'm so lucky my parents were there for me. Somewhere along the way, I read that the difference between bad situations that are tolerable versus bad situations that are toxic is connections to other people.

For nearly ten years, my parents have been a thin thread, keeping me from succumbing to toxicity in every way shape or form. But now, I feel a thread, growing thicker and stronger by the day, between Grayson and I.

Every minute that we spend together, just the two of us, a tiny fiber stretches between us. Those tiny fibers have begun to add up.

"Okay, so what can I do to help? What did you ask your mom to do? Is it something I can help with?"

Grayson shrugs. "I asked her to take over set design and construction. She used to do it. In fact, she went to art school. She was an artist. A painter. She said no. It would save us a few grand."

"Will that few grand make a difference?"

"In the long run, maybe not. On the other hand, it might. I can't afford to be throwing cash out the window. We only have a limited time to make money each year."

I hadn't thought about that. And it hadn't occurred to me how much I've made from them either.

"Stop paying me. I don't want a paycheck anymore."

"Ria, stop. That's the most ridiculous thing I've ever heard. Of course we're paying you. I know you need the money. You want to know what's funny? Weeks ago, I even suggested to Mom that you move into the house with us to help you save money. Now here you are, trying to save me." He looks around the flat. "Writers aren't known for their comfortable lifestyle until they get picked up for Oprah's book club."

I squirm a little, uncomfortable with his admission, but more uncomfortable with the lie that hovers, threatening to snap the thread between us. I should tell him I'm not working on a book. I should tell him why I'm here. He'd understand. "Yeah, so about that—"

"Ria, no more of your nonsense about not getting paid." Grayson stands up. "I've taken entirely too much of your time tonight, and I know you must have hours of work left to do." He looks around the place again. "I'd say come in late in the morning, but we're in a time crunch on finishing those bathrooms. They have to be done by opening day next Thursday."

I stand too, trailing after Grayson as he heads toward my door. "Is the show ready?"

He turns, pulling me into a deep hug. "It will be." He rests his chin on top of my head. I stiffen for a moment and then melt into him. It's been a long time since someone held me when I wasn't shaking in panic.

I'd forgotten that hugs could be for pleasure.

I close my eyes, resting my head on his chest. If only this moment could never end.

He continues, "I don't know that The Edison is going to make it, and I don't know what I'll do if it doesn't. My mom can't take another loss like that. But on the other hand, I don't want to stay here forever. I don't know what to do."

"Yes, you do. You know you have to try." I can't picture him walking away and letting The Edison go under. It's not in his nature.

His chin presses slightly into my head as he nods in agreement. "You're right. What do I do about my mom?"

"I don't know. I can't get a read on her. Probably because she thinks I'm trying to recruit you for my secret sex cult."

Grayson bursts out laughing, releasing me from his grasp. Dammit.

I look at him. "Let me know what you need, and how I can help. I'm all yours."

"You're the best, Ria." He leans in and gives me another one of those non-committal kisses on the lips. It's about the same intensity that you'd kiss someone on the cheek with, but he doesn't try for my cheek. "See you in the morning, and thanks again."

He walks out, closing the door, leaving me standing there, confused.

I didn't come to Hicklam to meet a man, let alone an actor. I've been successful, so far, at avoiding the inside of the theater, but Grayson will expect me to watch at least one of the shows.

I don't know if I can do that.

I could just leave before opening night and avoid the whole conflict. That would be the smart thing to do.

I don't know if I can do that either.

Chapter 18: Grayson

Another opening, another show.

The words from the iconic song dance through my brain. I down another energy drink and go through my last minute checklist. The final week has flown by, getting ready for the opening of *Singing in the Rain.* I'm backstage, setting up props and checking lights. Mom's handling the front of the house, manning the office. She never did step up and do the scenery, but she has been helping by expanding her traditional roles since our throw down.

It's two hours 'til curtain. I expect the cast and crew to start trickling in soon. The noise level drifting from the dorms has steadily been rising over the past few minutes, meaning everyone's awake now, whether they want to be or not.

Convinced that I can't do anything more backstage for the time being, I wander up to the front of the house. Ria finished the men's room yesterday, in the nick of time. Both bathrooms are incredible. She put some design touches in that I hadn't planned, and it really pulls the rooms together. Not that anyone is coming to The Edison for the bathrooms. But considering feedback last season complained about the facilities, I hope at least someone notices all her hard work.

Between the dorms and these bathrooms, I never would have been ready to open tonight. I'd planned on stepping back and only taking an ensemble role for this production, but Henderson convinced me to take the featured role of Production Singer. Not too featured, considering the character doesn't even really have a name. Though I have my one song to sing, so I can't complain.

Henderson knew. He knew more than I did that I needed to be up there, singing. With all the things I've had to do, and all the directions I've been pulled in, being on stage is what makes everything right in my world. As long as I can do that, I can do anything else I need to do.

Adrenaline—or too much caffeine—pumps through my veins as the minutes tick by. Before I know it, it's time to get dressed. I'm not on stage until about midway through the first act, but I can't help myself from standing in the wings, watching and tweaking little things. The house seems somewhat full, though I won't have a good idea until I get out on stage and can really look. They're laughing when they're supposed to laugh and clapping when they're supposed to clap. No one's fallen. No one's flubbed lines in a major way.

All in all, it's going okay for the opening. Sure, there are scenes that need polishing, but we're all professionals here, so we bring our A-game every time.

As I enter the stage, slowly descending the stairs to the opening chords of "Beautiful Girl," my eyes don't attempt to count attendance. Instead, they look for Ria. She's got to be out there, somewhere. I can't seem to locate her, and have to focus on the choreography, which mostly has me swaying back and forth and linking arms with the girls swirling around me, waving their large feathered fans.

I have a quick costume change to get out for my next number as part of the ensemble. I'm wishing I'd sat this reprise out so I could go look for Ria. I'm dying to know if she thought I sounded good.

She knows singing. I know she does. She may not say it, and she may not do it often, but she's a singer. One whose opinion I greatly respect.

It's odd. I don't know much about her. Nothing really, other than that she's writing a book. Though I didn't see a computer or notebooks or books or anything else in her apartment that one might expect someone who's in the midst of a research project to have.

I do know that whatever—and whoever—she is, there's something dark chasing after her. I still can't shake that feeling. And there's something off about her book as well. She never seems to be actually writing. But no matter how much I don't know, there's a feeling of something comfortable.

And I need her. I need her approval and her support and those rare smiles that could light up the entire stage.

God, I wonder if she's ever performed? She's had to have, with a talent like hers. What if she thinks I'm terrible or washed up or a hack? I don't think I could handle it if she thought that. Maybe it'd be a good thing if she didn't see tonight's performance. It's going fine, but certainly not as smooth as it could be going. Or will be going.

So it's fine that she's not here. Maybe I should go out and look for her at intermission. I could text Mom and ask her to look.

"Grayson, come on!"

I don't even know who hisses my name as I'm pushed forward onto the stage for the brief ensemble number I'm in.

Good God. I have got to get a handle on myself.

I refocus on the show and before I know it, I'm back in my character's top hat and tails to take my final bow. One show down, one million to go. That's not true. Only about ninety more to go.

It makes for a long summer.

After the bows, it takes me about an hour to make sure everything is cleaned up and back to where it should be. The stage crew takes care of this, but I can't rest until I'm certain that we're ready for curtain tomorrow. Then I head to the office, where Mom is processing receipts. We sold seventy-six percent of seats tonight. Definitely not terrible for opening night. Lots of people don't want to see the show the first go 'round. Most of the cast won't buy tickets for their families for this performance either.

Perhaps Mom's marketing is working.

I log onto the computer and spend another hour with social media, uploading pictures and tagging them.

"Grayson, honey, you need to stop. It's almost one. You need your rest." Mom's hand rests gently on my shoulder.

"A few more minutes. I only have to—"

"Grayson." Her tone is stern. "Enough for the night. Go to bed."

I blink up at her, unsure of how to respond. There's a large part of me that's really tired and agrees with Mom's game plan. But underneath that, I'm scared that if I don't work through the night, I'll be letting The Edison down. I'll be letting her down. I'll be letting Dad down.

She folds her arms over her chest. I want to know why it's so easy for her to just keep shuffling on, like we're not in dire straits, with everything riding on this season. Does she not understand? Or does she understand and maybe simply doesn't care anymore?

"Mom, do you want us to fail?"

She lets out a huff. "Of course not, Grayson. Don't be ridiculous. How could you say such a thing?"

I want to say because she's been making one poor decision after another and not putting any extra into this. But she's still grieving. She's probably doing the best she can.

"Do you want The Edison to succeed?" I'm asking the same thing, yet somehow it's different.

She looks away, as if she's far off somewhere. "Wants aren't always the priority. What I want, I can't have. But yes, I want The Edison to succeed. Of course I do."

I don't challenge her. If she says she wants The Edison to succeed, then I will stop at nothing to make sure that happens. "Sorry, Mom. Give me a few more minutes. I want to finish up some things. I promise I'll call it a night soon."

"Promise?" She tilts her head to the side, as if she knows better.

She probably does.

I never make it to bed. I never make it up from the desk.

One minute, I'm working on a spreadsheet, and the next, there's a hand gently shaking my shoulder.

"Grayson, wake up."

"Hmm," I mumble, reaching up to hold onto the hand. I must be dreaming because it sounds like Ria. And though I'd very much like her in my bed, I know she wasn't there last night.

But she's here now.

"Grayson, wake up. I brought you coffee and a scone. You slept at your desk."

I blink up at her, bleary eyed. "What are you doing here? You shouldn't be wandering around in the middle of the night."

"Middle of the night? It's nine a.m."

"How did that happen?" I look around the office as if I've never seen it before.

"You tell me. I came up here a little while ago, and there you were, cuttin' z's and laying in a pile of drool. I don't know what happened last night, but I figured it was a rough one, so I ran down to Dean's Beans and got you some sustenance."

My eyes focus on the white cup and brown paper bag. Without saying anything, I reach over and take a sip. Sweet goodness.

Ria perches on the edge of a chair across the room, slowly sipping her own coffee. "How'd it go last night?"

My shoulders drop in defeat, realizing that she really, truly wasn't here. "Fine, I guess. We made the minimum for attendance that we need, so that's good."

She takes another sip. "And the show?"

Her words are a kick to my gut. Of course she wasn't here. But I don't want her to see my pain. I match her sip without breaking her gaze. "Do you plan on coming to see it?"

Her eyes drop. I win.

"Ria, what's the deal?"

I see her swallow, now looking out the window that faces the busy hallway to the backstage area.

Her gaze now fixes on something up above. I look too but can't see what's so interesting.

"I don't know if I can come."

"Why not?"

"I don't want to talk about it."

Part of me wants to slam my hand down on the desk and demand the story. Thankfully, the rest of me knows that would be a terrible thing to do. "You can tell me, you know. We're friends. You can trust that."

"Yeah, I've got to run. I've got to go see Malachi. I just wanted ..." her voice breaks off, the strain evident on her face. "See ya."

She turns and before I know what just went down, is out the door.

I watch the door for way too long, hoping she'll come back in.

Needless to say, she doesn't.

On the other hand, it's been several weeks since she ran out on me like that, so I guess it's good that I've stopped putting my foot in my mouth as much. Or have I? I don't even know what I say or do wrong to upset her.

I wish I did.

Chapter 19: Gloria

"You don't have an appointment."

"I need you," I pant, trying to catch my breath after sprinting here all the way from The Edison.

Malachi folds his hand together and places them on his desk. "What should you be doing in this situation?"

"I know. I'm not panicking."

He raises an eyebrow at me.

"Not yet. And I don't want to. But I have to do a thing, and I'm afraid to try it on my own. Is there any way you can come with me?"

"It depends. I'm going to need more information."

I slowly sit on the chair opposite him. I can do this. I can ask for help. "So, The Edison is open for the season now."

"I'm aware." Malachi nods.

"Last night was opening night. They're doing *Singing in the Rain*. I did that junior year in high school. I was Kathy, the female lead. I know every note in that show."

"So, how did last night go?"

I shrug, looking out the window. "Grayson said it went okay." I'm lying. I didn't actually even get that far with him. "Fine, is what he said. He was more worried about—" I break off, not wanting to break his confidence. "We didn't talk that much about it."

"I take it you didn't go, then."

I shake my head, unable to look Malachi in the eye. "He wants me to. He specifically asked me to go to the show tonight. I want to. I mean, I don't want to, but I want to go for Grayson. I know it's going to be hard, and I worry that it's going to trigger me."

"Why will it trigger you?"

"Seeing them up on stage. I'll want to be there too, and then I'll remember what happened."

"Remember what happened now."

Quietly, I reflect to that night almost a decade ago. What happened when I was on stage wasn't even the worst, but it was the start. That first domino to fall during the darkest point in my life.

"I'm not freaking out."

"If the treatment worked, you shouldn't be. There's a reason why your last session for EMDR will be Monday."

"Am I cured?" I ask hopefully. Malachi's told me all along that I was progressing, but it's been hard to see. Looking back, I can tell, but in the moment, like so many other things with anxiety, my perspective is skewed.

Malachi sighs slightly. He must be tired of the constant insecurity. "Gloria, you were a prime candidate for the Eye Movement Desensitization and Reprocessing therapy, especially to have a good outcome. While your anxiety and depression have increased over the past ten years, you are not someone with an organic mental illness."

"So you're saying I'm processed mentally ill? How do I get the non-GMO kind?" I laugh at my own terrible joke.

Malachi groans. "Prior to the incident, you didn't have depression or anxiety. You don't have an organic, or neurobiological cause. You don't have a chemical imbalance. However, your PTSD created a short-term chemical imbalance that kept repeating."

"I didn't have a chemical imbalance, so I went out and created my own? I've always been the resourceful type." Figures I'd make my life even more complicated.

Malachi nods. "Essentially, yes. Those moments of panic trigger a chemical cascade in your brain and body. The EMDR interrupts that cascade. Since you were relatively healthy to begin with, you have a good chance of doing pretty well."

I think on this for a moment. "If a person already has anxiety or depression, will EMDR work for them too?"

"I don't need to tell you this: Living with a mental illness is just that. Living *with* it. There are no magical cures. It's a load to carry every single day. Some days, the load is manageable. Others, it feels like you have to carry the weight of the world. And the worst part is that because it's your brain, it lies to you. It tells you the world is one way, and you believe it, because *it's your brain*. You know some of these things. You've experienced them. But you are very lucky because before your trauma, you were a healthy individual. Still, there are many people out there, fighting the good fight, walking around with the rocks of depression in their pocket, and we have no idea. It's why compassion and empathy—of which you have in spades—are such valuable tools in the world of building connections."

I think on this for a moment. It's a lot to consider. It makes sense. The last ten years have been such a struggle, lost in my own brain. I've been to therapy, on medication, and doing yoga to help myself. Right after it happened, I couldn't leave the house.

I really am doing much better.

I can do this.

"I want to go to the show. If you're available, I'd appreciate your support, because it's going to be hard for me. But if you're not, I'm still going because Grayson is my friend, and I need to support him."

"I'll be there." Malachi smiles.

"You will? Oh my God, thank you." I sag against the chair in relief. "That means so much."

Malachi laughs again. "We have season tickets. I was going tonight anyway. Marvin and Malyia will be here soon, and we go together."

I cock my head to the side. "All this time, you knew you were going to go anyway? Why'd you make me go through that?"

"A little more clarity and insight never hurts. You're doing better, but you will have to keep working for a very long time. I'm trying to give you the tools to understand and cope."

"If I go, will you sit by me?"

"We have season tickets, so my seat is set. The seats around us are usually full."

"I have an in with the owner. I can probably make something work." I hope my voice sounds light enough where he thinks I'm kidding. I don't want Malachi getting annoyed at me for being too pushy.

"Then consider it done. If you can change my seat, I'll be happy to sit with you."

I look down at my hands. "Will you walk me inside? I'm not sure I can go in."

Malachi squints at me. "You work there. Surely you've been able to go in without difficulty," he baits.

I shake my head. "You know I've never set foot in the actual theater. I worked on the bathrooms and the dorms. I've been backstage a little. You'd better check out the bathrooms and tell me what an awesome job I did. But I was always too afraid to go into the theater itself. Which is bad, because Grayson asked me to help with sets, and I told him I would but then dragged my heels finishing up the men's room so I wouldn't actually have to. I feel badly too, because I know he was trying to save some money, and I didn't help with that."

And now I feel even worse for possibly betraying Grayson's secret.

"Please don't repeat that to anyone," I add hastily. "Can I invoke attorney-client-priest privilege or something?" Shit. Shit. Shit. I can't believe I'm such a screw up.

"As my client, our sessions are confidential. Anything we discuss related to the reason for which I was treating you is covered under the umbrella of confidentiality. Unless you tell me differently, I wouldn't even acknowledge you in public."

I shrug. "You can acknowledge me. People think you run a sex cult. If they think I'm one of the weirdos in your gang, they won't want to talk to me. It's a win-win for me."

Now it's Malachi's turn to shake his head. "I wish people didn't think that about me. It bothers me. Tremendously."

I stand up to leave. "You could, I don't know, hang up a sign. There's no shame in being a mental health professional."

"People don't want to be seen coming and going from a therapist's office. It bothers the clients when they are identified going in."

This is bullshit, yet understandable at the same time. "I wish mental illness didn't have the stigma it does, but here we are." I turn toward the door. "Curtain opens at eight. See you at ten 'til?" I don't want to sit there for any longer than I have to.

****

There is approximately four minutes until the overture starts, and I still can't go in. Malachi is running late. He had a crisis with a patient who is not me. If he doesn't get here, this patient is about to be in crisis as well.

No.

I can do this.

I *have* to do this.

I turn toward the door.

Nope. Not gonna happen.

I turn away and head down the hall to Mrs. Keene's office. Maybe floating around back here will be enough for Grayson.

I am a shitty friend.

In the back hallway, a door opens and suddenly, there he is. Grayson. All six-foot-one of him, in a black tuxedo and tails.

Oh. My. God.

At least this time, when my knees go weak, it's not from panic.

"You made it! You'd better take your seat. We're starting any minute!" Grayson grabs me and pulls me into a quick hug. My mouth is dry and my brain is short circuiting.

If I thought Grayson was attractive in ripped jeans and a T-shirt, I was in no way prepared for formal wear. Yowza.

To see Grayson look like this, his normally unruly hair slicked into a sleek pompadour, I'd get out on stage myself.

My heart thuds practically to a stop. While I'd do a lot to see him like this again, I couldn't ever get out on stage. No matter how much I may have once wanted it. Craved it. *Needed* it.

"You look hot." Oh, God. Did I actually say that? Shit. "You're sweating. The lights aren't going to help. Are you sure the air conditioning is on?" I babble on to cover my for my snafu.

"I'll have Mom check it. Now get to your seat. I'll see you after the show. You're coming to the cabaret, right?"

The lights flash one more time, and I know I can't stall any longer. Practically sprinting down the hall, I make it in as the doors are closing and slide into my seat toward the back of the house.

The theater is packed. Good.

To ease my anxiety that swells a bit each time I look at the stage, I start to count how many people are here. In the end, it's easier to count the open seats. I think the theater can fit around four-hundred people at a time, and there are only eighty-three seats open. That's good. Very good.

And then, Grayson is on the stage, and I couldn't tear my eyes away if you paid me. He should have the lead in every play ever. By the time his number is done and all the girls are posed around him, framing him with their pinky feathery fans, I can barely breathe.

I want to be up there with him.

I know I never could, but for a moment, that longing to be back on the stage peeks through the years of anxiety and fear. I remember the rush. The thrill.

How good it felt.

And how good I was.

And damn, how good Grayson and I would be together. I would do anything to have it back.

If only.

Chapter 20: Grayson

She came and the show was at seventy-nine percent capacity.

It's a great day.

We've just done final bows, and with it being Saturday night, it's time for our post-show cabaret. In the side room, normally reserved for rehearsals, we set up tables and chairs and have a bit of a coffeehouse, catered by Heidi and Dean's Beans, naturally. She makes a killing here, which is why she often forgets to add things to my tab.

Members of the cast and company come out and sing songs from upcoming shows or whatever is speaking to them at the moment. There's very little rehearsal for this. You sing what you are comfortable singing.

It's an up close and cozy atmosphere and our die-hard patrons love it. And an extra five bucks a head for another thirty minutes of entertainment is a win-win for everyone. Not to mention it's a fun way for the cast to decompress after a show.

Josh, the musical director, steps up as emcee, introducing the night and thanking everyone for coming. He decides the order of performance and accompanies on piano, unless we've made other arrangements, as I have for tonight.

Ria's hovering in the doorway, not relaxing at a table with the Andrewses. She was sitting with Malachi for the show. I didn't see her, but Mom made sure to tell me that Ria had requested Malachi's ticket be changed. I don't read anything into it.

Okay, I *try* not to read anything into it.

But Malachi's sitting at a table in the middle of the room with his brother and sister, while Ria fidgets with the hem of her shirt, barely in the room. It's okay. She'll still be able to hear. I'm just glad she's here to hear it.

I'm up.

Josh moves from the keyboard bench to one of two stools set up in the middle of the floor area that serves as our stage. The mics are low to accommodate our sitting. Josh has his guitar. My hands are in my jeans pockets, as is my habit when singing. Countless vocal teachers have tried to break me of this, but if I don't think about it, that's where they go. Right now, I have something else on my mind.

Like how she's going to react.

"For those of you who are new here, I'm Grayson Keene. My family has owned The Edison for several generations. This off-season, we worked very hard at bringing the facilities into the current century, including walls without holes for the cast and toilets that don't rock when you sit on them for the guests. I hope you've all enjoyed that luxury feature tonight." I pause as the crowd laughs a bit.

Seriously though, the bathrooms were not a good situation.

I glance up at Ria, who has taken approximately one step into the room, as I say the next part. "The Edison wouldn't have been ready to open yesterday, had it not been for the hard work and dedication of many. I'm sorry to those who considered themselves my friends who I used solely for their cheap labor."

Josh starts strumming a bit on his guitar.

"But I couldn't have done it without the tireless dedication of one special person. Ria, my friend, this song is for you."

I take the mic with my left hand as I launch into "You've Got a Friend," never breaking eye contact with Ria while I try to tell her, in song, what she means to me. As I sing the first verse and chorus, she's immobile. It's hard to tell, but her eyes may be shining with tears.

Approaching the second verse, Ria begins to move. Without looking away, she weaves through the crowd of tables and chairs and bodies until she's next to me. I remove my hand from my pocket and reach toward her. There's no hesitation as she takes my hand in hers.

Heading into the second chorus, Ria harmonizes with me. The song is meant for that. In fact, Joni Mitchell sang background vocals and harmonies on both the Carole King and the James Taylor recordings of this song. No wonder they sound good.

But that pales in comparison to how Ria and I sound.

As I hit the bridge, I tug her hand and pull her body closer. She needs to be able to sing into the mic for the last chorus. Instead of bending down, as I expect her to, she slides onto my lap. My right arm wraps around her waist as her left arm drapes across the back of my shoulders.

I look into her eyes and suddenly it's only her and me and the music.

The world does not exist.

Frankly, if I wasn't holding a microphone in between our mouths, I'm not sure we'd even be two separate entities.

Her beautiful mahogany brown eyes are wet with tears, though none leak down her cheeks. They threaten to spill and she hastily wipes them away.

It startles me when the crowd erupts into applause, followed by a standing ovation, led by Malachi Andrews. He yells out a "Hell yeah!" and whoops with delight. A sideways glance at Ria shows that she too forgot we were in a room full of people. She stands up awkwardly.

I reach down and take her hand as the audience continues to cheer. Sheepishly, she grins at me. For the first time, there's a light in her face that I've never seen before.

She's stunning, and it takes everything in my power not to grab her and kiss her and carry her to bed right here and now.

Before everyone in the place becomes aware of my growing desire, I tug lightly on her hand, pulling her toward the door. She's perhaps still a bit dazed, but she's laughing and breathless. "Oh, my God. I can't believe I did that!"

We're running now, out of the theater, into the parking lot. "Where are we going?" I ask. I want to head right to my house, but she's pulling me down the driveway toward the road.

"Come on!" She says, louder, pulling harder.

I say nothing as I try to keep up with her, half running, half stumbling in the dark as we head down the road toward town. I wish I hadn't slid my feet into flip-flops before heading into the coffee house. They're quite inappropriate for our midnight jog.

It's only when we turn onto Chapel Street that I even process where we might be heading. I don't know why she's leading me here. Maybe she's really upset and wants to yell at me for putting her on the spot like that. I didn't expect her to sing, let alone on my lap.

Though I'd understand if she said she couldn't help it. It's like our voices were meant to entwine together. I couldn't have stopped it if I'd tried.

She pushes open the outside door, still pulling me as if I was a petulant toddler. We get up the stairs and to her apartment door when she stops. Before I know what's happening, Ria spins around and pushes me into the wall. Her body slams into me as her lips crash onto mine.

I'm stunned for a second—but only a second—and then my mouth reciprocates move for move, tongue stroke for tongue stroke. Her hands are in my hair, pulling and frantic. My hands start at her waist and as they begin to move up, I realize her loose-fitting crop top leaves the perfect route for me to touch her bare skin.

As my hands make contact with her flesh, she gasps into my mouth, which increases my pace to almost frenetic. I pull my hands up the sides of her body, feeling the smooth fabric of her bra, all while my tongue dances in her mouth.

"Grayson," she pants, finally pulling back an inch. It might as well be a mile. I pull her in again.

"What," I breathe, my lips on hers.

She pulls back again. I respect that and lessen my grip on her, giving her the space she needs. "Grayson, I ... let's go inside." She steps back, putting a vast void in between us while she fumbles in her jeans pocket for a key. She drops it once, and I bend down to pick it up. She drops it again, and we both bend down this time. In the process, we smack our heads. I sit back, rubbing my forehead, while she falls back, rubbing the top of her own.

I look at her and laugh. "I don't think that was supposed to happen."

She looks down at the small brass key clutched tightly in her hand. "None of this was supposed to happen."

She leans back into the door, extending her feet out in front of her. It takes me by surprise, as I thought we were in the middle of something. When she doesn't move after a minute, I scoot around so I'm sitting next to her. I think about putting my arm around her shoulder but sense that perhaps space is what she needs in this moment.

I slowly extend my hand and place it on hers.

"You okay?"

"I'm sorry," she whispers.

"I don't know why you feel you should be sorry. You have nothing to be sorry for, unless it's for being clumsy, and even then, I don't think that's something you can really help." Though she's never appeared clumsy before. I wonder what's gotten into her.

Copy that sentiment for the whole evening.

"I ..." She falters again.

"Ria, it's okay. Whatever it is you want to say, you can. I wasn't just trying to seduce you with song tonight. I really meant it. Whatever you need, I'm here for you."

I hear her inhale sharply and then it seems like eons before she exhales. "Grayson, I ... there's something I need to tell you."

I brace myself for whatever it is that she's been hiding for the past two months. Maybe longer. While I want to reassure her again, I say nothing, giving her the space to talk.

"Grayson, I ... I have some trust issues."

Um, ya think? "I think that's natural. Lots of people do. I do."

"Lots of people don't have what I have."

I have no idea what she could be talking about, other than an STD.

"Well, I may need more information than that. Do you want to go inside and talk about it?" I've been waiting for so long to hear what she has to say.

"Sure." She shrugs. I spring to my feet, pulling her up with me. I slide the key out of her hand.

"Allow me," I say, inserting the key into the lock and opening the door to her flat.

We step in and I wait for her to direct me where to go. She heads straight to the kitchen area and grabs two bottles of water, without bothering to turn on the light. I sit on the couch and wait for her, illumination only coming through the windows from the street lamps. She places the bottle down on the coaster on the coffee table directly in front of me.

Then she sits on a stool at the counter and looks down at her water bottle.

Message received.

I'm not going to lie; I'm a little confused by her behavior. Make that a lot confused. Maybe what she has to say will finally explain it.

Ria clears her throat nervously.

"Whatever it is, it's okay," I try to reassure her. She's still looking at the bottle in her hands as if it holds the vast secrets of the world.

"I'm sorry about that," she says finally. Her voice is so quiet I can barely hear her.

I don't know what 'that' she's referring to. I don't want it to be that kiss, because Lord knows, I want to do more of *that*.

"Ria, you can ... tell me." I stumble a bit, wanting to tell her to trust me. I have a feeling that word will set her off so I refrain from using it. "Whatever it is, I'm here for you. I'm not upset about anything, except the fact that you're across the room instead of right here next to me." I pat the couch.

She looks at my hand for a minute before ever so slowly getting up and coming to sit on the couch. We could fit another person in between us, but it's a start. I slide my hand into the void and place it palm up, an invitation for her. After a minute, her hand tentatively inches toward mine, and she rests the edge of her hand on top of mine.

It's better than nothing. However, she's still not saying anything. Maybe it's too hard for her to start. I think back to my first impression that perhaps she was on the run from an abusive ex.

That would certainly lead to trust issues.

I take a bold shot. "Ria, why did you come to Hicklam?" I expect her to remind me about this book she's writing. Once again, there's nothing in her apartment, including a computer, to even suggest that she's working on a book. I've suspected that the book thing was a lie. I just want to know why she's lying to me.

She clears her throat. She's looking straight ahead, focusing on the blank wall. "I came to Hicklam to work with Malachi Andrews."

Okay, here's my chance. I have to take it. "Doing what?"

Her gaze remains trained on the wall. "He's a therapist, specializing in post-traumatic stress disorder."

I let out a breath I didn't know I was holding. The first brick in the wall has come down. "And you have PTSD?"

She nods. "And anxiety and depression."

"I'm sorry," I mumble, not knowing what else to say. "Is it bad?"

Ria finally looks at me. "If you consider having to run out of places because you can't breathe and you're positive everyone is looking at you and you want to die right then and there bad then yes."

Shit.

"Do you really want to die?" I wouldn't have pegged her for suicidal, but I didn't expect this either.

"No, not anymore. In one of those bad moments, I feel like I'm going to or that's the only way out of those horrible feelings. I've never self-harmed."

Phew.

Of course, the next thing my mind goes to is to ask what her PTSD is about. My mind keeps jumping back to abuse, and I'm filled with rage to think that someone may have hurt her in any way.

Obviously she's been hurt.

I decide for a less invasive approach. "So Malachi Andrews is a therapist? That will disappoint my mom so much. She had all these machinations about wild and salacious goings on in that innocuous white house. You know, in hindsight, maybe *she* should be the novelist." That earns me a small smile, and I feel as if I've won the lottery.

"I can see that in your mom's face every time I talk to her. What do I have to do to convince her I'm not in a sex cult?"

I laugh. "Invite her to one of your sessions? But then knowing her, she'll excuse herself to use the facilities and snoop through every room of the house, looking for evidence."

It's Ria's turn to laugh. "I can totally see her doing that. And who knows what Malachi has in his basement. He could have a freaky side. We don't talk about him. We talk about me and my issues. There could be all sorts of shit down there."

I squeeze her hand and shift infinitesimally closer to her on the couch. "Do you want to talk about your issues?"

I expect her to shut down again, but instead she rests her head back on the couch and closes her eyes. "I do and I don't. I wish I didn't have to. I wish I could have just continued mauling you and ripping off your clothes and having my way with you. But I can't."

She's about to tell me something big. But all I can think about is what she just said. She wants me. Like I want her.

I don't care what her issues are. They don't matter. We have to make this work.

Chapter 21: Gloria

He hasn't run for the door, screaming in panic.

Not yet, at least.

I can do this.

I try again. "It's really hard to put myself in a vulnerable place. I feel vulnerable all the time. At least I used to. That's what my PTSD is—was—about."

"What do you mean *was*?"

"Malachi specializes in a specific treatment that has really been helping me. I've tried everything else, and nothing's helped me as much as this has. I can't remember the last time, before coming to Hicklam and working with Malachi, that I was able to leave the house every day."

It's pretty hard to leave the house when you're convinced everyone has seen you naked, during a very vulnerable and supposedly private moment. Which, for a while at Anniston College, was the truth.

But I don't want to think about that right now. I want to be here, present, with Grayson. Grayson who looked ravishing in a tuxedo, but downright delicious in his ripped jeans, white T, and leather flip flops. My heart—and somewhere else—flutters just thinking about him on that stool, hands in his pockets.

And then he started singing to me.

I realize it's been a beat since I've said anything. This must be killing Grayson. He's a talker, often filling the void of silence with endless prattle. You know, the opposite of me.

"I'm really doing better. A lot better. But I still think this is going to be hard, so I'm going to apologize in advance."

"Ria," he says softly, "can I ask you something?"

I want to say no, but I owe him answers. The truth. I nod.

"Did someone ... hurt you? Like physically?" His hand is squeezing mine tighter and tighter, and I bet he doesn't even realize it. His other hand is balled up tightly as well.

"Not like what you think."

I feel his body sag into the couch as his hand goes limp in mine. Suddenly, it feels as if he's too far away. I have to get close to him again. I shimmy over and then throw my leg over his, pulling myself onto his lap. It's the second time tonight I've sat on his lap.

It's a place I really like to be.

And from the feel of it, it's definitely mutual.

His hands grip my waist. I wish—*again*—that I wasn't wearing this stupid crop top. It makes it too easy for him to slide his hands up. I mean, I like that, but then I start to panic.

A little.

There's also part of me that loves the feel of his hands on my bare skin. I'd love for that part of my brain to be able to take over right about now. I lean in and kiss him lightly, much like he did to me that day sitting out in the back hall.

"Grayson, I'm in a weird place right now."

He kisses me a little more intensely and pulls my hips down into him. "I'd say you're in just the right place."

I smile against his lips. "Not physically, silly. Mentally. I want this. I *really* want this. You have no idea. But I'm not sure what I can do or when. I'm all sorts of messed up."

He pulls back slightly.

I tug him closer to me and kiss him again. Then I explain, "I'm okay with this for now, but I might not always be. But it's not you. It's me. I want you to consider yourself warned."

"I'm warned. Is there anything you don't want me to do?"

Now I lean back and look into those gorgeous green eyes that I noticed the first day in the coffee shop. I lift a finger and slowly trace it over his cheek where his dimple is. His eyes close as I touch him. "I'm not ready to have sex with you. I ... I can't put myself out there like that again yet."

His eyes fly open. "You said no one hurt you, but is your trauma ..." he pauses, searching for words, "... is it related to sex?"

I nod, the tears appearing instantaneously. "I don't want to get into it now, but yes. And so it's not something I've been able to do since ..."

"How long ago?"

"Ten years."

Grayson's hands fall. "Oh God, Ria, you were practically a kid."

"Twenty-two. Old enough, but too naive for my own good." I wish he would put his hands on me again. I feel secure when they are there. Grounded. Home.

It's only been a few hours, and I'm already craving his touch.

Is this how it is for addicts? Is this why people with mental health issues become dependent on drugs so quickly? The way I feel when he's touching me ...

No pharmaceutical has ever made me feel that good.

"I don't know how all this is going to work. I ... I want this to happen, Grayson. I do. So much. But I also know I'm not ready yet."

He nods, his gaze intent on my face. "You tell me what works and doesn't work. I don't want to make you upset. I ..." Now his gaze drops. "I know I have in the past. I've said things that made you run away. I don't know why though."

I owe him more of an explanation. But I'm afraid if I tell him everything, he'll never look at me the way he is now. "I think I'm better. Even words used to trigger me. The treatment has worked a bit, at least for now. Have you noticed that I haven't freaked out all month? I thought I was going to today, simply walking into the theater, but I didn't."

The confusion is evident on his face as he looks up. Dammit, I've said too much.

"The theater is part of the problem?"

I nod. "Yes, being on stage and performing is part of my trauma."

He shifts underneath me, so I roll off of him. Grayson immediately gets up and starts pacing. I can see him moving through the shadows of my dark apartment. As soon as I click the lamp on, however, I wish we were still in darkness. Grayson looks like a man in anguish.

Probably because he is.

I stand up and move toward him, taking his hand.

He looks at me. "Have I made this worse for you? Why didn't you tell me you couldn't be at The Edison? You should have said something."

Unsure of what else to do, I sit down on the floor, pulling Grayson to come down too. "Lay down," I instruct. I wait until he's settled, and then I lay down too, my head next to his, with my feet pointing in the opposite direction. This way, I won't be too tempted by his body. "I won't lie. When Heidi told me you needed help getting the rooms ready, I thought it was a hotel—an ugly one admittedly—but a hotel that needed cleaning. I was up for it because I wouldn't have to talk to people. But then, I realized it was construction. But with it just being the two of us, for the most part, I figured I could handle it. After all, I'm here trying to get better. I didn't even realize that The Edison was a theater until I was too far in to walk away."

"I remember that. I thought you were so tired you were delusional or something."

"But it was still okay because it's not like I had to get on stage or anything. I don't know if you noticed, but I never actually go *in* the theater. Tonight was my first time."

"So you're a theater virgin?" He's coy and seductive. If only he knew what really happened.

"For The Edison, yes. If you hadn't specifically asked me to go see the show, I probably would have avoided it. I made Malachi change his ticket so he could sit with me in case I freaked out."

"Did you?"

Our noses are about an inch apart. I smile tightly. "No. I thought about it, and the panic wasn't even close. Tonight was huge for me."

"But then the cabaret ..."

"I wasn't sure I could even come in for that."

"I've heard of stage fright before, but this is extreme."

"It's not stage fright. Not like I'm scared to get up and perform, even though that's how it might seem. I used to perform. A lot. I was a musical theater major in college." I haven't said that aloud outside of a mental health professional's office in years. "The stage was my life."

It's freeing to be able to talk a little about this without totally losing it. I wish I could go into what came over me tonight that gave me the strength and courage to sing with him, even though there were people there. People who could have been recording me. In that moment, it didn't matter. I felt the pull to him, the gravity of his words, and then my body took over as it used to seconds before a performance. I didn't think. I just felt. And sang.

But I can barely process this myself, let alone articulate it. I stop talking and let memories of that feeling wash over me again.

"Now everything is making sense. You don't get a voice like yours with harmonizing ability from singing along in the car. You're a mezzo, right?" Of course Grayson can tell.

"Yup."

"Did you finish college? What happened?"

"I dropped out at the end of my senior year." Practically failed out is more like it. "Everything happened toward the end of spring semester. I bombed my finals and withdrew. I didn't have enough credits to graduate. I couldn't go back. But unfortunately being on stage—quite literally—is all tied in with my traumatic event. The one thing cost me my whole career. I haven't known what to do, other than be a freak, since."

"Are you coming back to the stage?" I'd have to be stupid not to hear the hope in Grayson's voice. "Say the word and any role is yours. I don't care who I've already cast. You want to be Roxie Hart? Done. I'll fire Julianna."

Cold washes over me. I try to focus on what he's said. "Who's Julianna?"

"Julianna Rickey. She'll be coming in in a few weeks to start rehearsals for *Chicago*. It's our big show of the summer. She's a typical stage diva, so terrible to work with. Not to mention, she's bringing her stupid big-shot boyfriend to be the director and oh, did I mention, we used to date?"

His delivery relaxes me. "That's a lot of information all at once. I take it you are not one of her biggest fans."

"In terms of talent, she's great, of course. In terms of personality, the lyrics from *You're a Mean One, Mr. Grinch* run through my head. Any day, I'd take the seasick crocodile."

"How long were you too together?" It's easier for me to focus on this than the role that she'll be playing. I don't want to think about *that* at all. Though, truth be told, I don't really want to think about Grayson with someone else either.

"Three years. We were in the company in *Company* and the rest is pretty much musical theater cliché. Boy and girl meet. Boy and girl have wild, passionate sex, fueled by spending all waking time together. Boy and girl pretend not to get jealous when the other gets a better role. Girl cannot handle when the boy gets a national tour. Girl dumps boy when he loses the tour because his father is dying. Pretty typical stuff really."

"Totally typical and not specific at all. I hate her already. I admit that I haven't been keeping up with the theater world. Avoiding it actually. Why'd you even cast her?"

"She's doing it as a favor to me, as long as she can bring her douche bag boyfriend. She's got a big following. The last two years, her career has really taken off, and it practically guarantees sell outs for the full three weeks. I can't afford not to. The Edison doesn't have time for my wounded ego. I have to do this for Mom. I can't bring back Dad, but I can save the life they built together."

And this may be why I'm falling in love with Grayson.

For a "typical" theater guy, he's anything but.

He pulls his knees up to his chest. "While I'd love to stay and have this nose-to-nose chat with you, my old back is protesting. I should be going." He rolls up to a sitting position and stands up. As soon as I get my feet in front of me, he reaches down and pulls me up, into a hug. He kisses me slow and soft, and I cling to him because my legs have suddenly forgotten how to support me.

I could kiss this man forever.

"Stay," I whisper. My voice surprises me. "Please stay and hold me tonight."

"Can I keep kissing you?"

"You'd better." I pull his hand toward the bedroom.

"Well, it's a tough job, but someone's got to do it." He grins.

Indeed.

Chapter 22: Grayson

It's stupid, but I'm totally in love with this girl.

Woman.

Ria Benedetti is all woman.

I just have to take my time and earn her trust. I can do that.

I wake up and Ria's sitting up in bed, her large Cincinnati Bengals T-shirt tenting around her slight figure, but at the same time revealing she's not wearing a bra.

I hope I'm man enough to be cool about all this without jumping her or making her otherwise uncomfortable.

Then I notice that the circles under her eyes are larger than I've ever seen. "Did you sleep at all?"

She shakes her head. "It's fine."

"It's not fine. Were you okay? Is it because I stayed? You should have woken me up."

"Nah, you were snoring so nicely. Plus, you have to look fresh and pretty for today. You have two performances."

I lean in and give her a quick kiss on the cheek. "It's asking a lot, I know, but you can t ... tell me." I stutter over the word 'trust' again. She's not ready to be sold a line. I mean it, but she may not be in a place to hear it yet.

"I thought I'd be okay with you spending the night but maybe I started to worry a little bit."

Ah shit. She's not comfortable around me. Doesn't trust me. I hate this worried look on her face. "Worry about what? Snoring? Drooling? Farting in your sleep?"

That earns me a smile. Good.

"I'm nervous being in a vulnerable position. I've been living in my amphibian brain for too long."

"Huh?"

"You know, the amphibian brain—the primitive part that's responsible for staying alive. The part that has the fight or flight reflex. When you are in moments of anxiety and states of panic, that's the part of the brain that takes over. It's the amygdala. It overrides all rational thought. My amygdala has been in charge for too long."

I vaguely remember reading something online one time about how humans are the only mammals that sleep on their backs with their stomachs exposed. Most mammals keep their soft abdomens tucked away so that predators can't get to the fleshy organs for a quick kill.

Who knew this was all related?

"And is your work with Malachi supposed to make that better?"

She lifts her shoulders a little, letting them drop back down quickly. "It is, until I tried to fall asleep. But I'm doing much better. Really, I am. Some things are going to take time."

"I've got all the time in the world. Speaking of which, what time is it?" I look around for my cell phone. I'm almost certain I put it on the nightstand before I went to sleep. It's not there. Maybe I left it in my jeans pocket. I reach around and feel my backside, but it's not there either. I look at the night stand again. I distinctly remember putting it there, as I wrestled with myself about whether to keep the pants on or off before I crawled into Ria's bed.

Dropping to my knees, I begin searching the floor and under the bed. The damn thing has to be around here somewhere.

"What are you doing?" Ria peers over the edge of the bed.

"I can't find my phone. I know I put it here last night." I tap the edge of the night stand. "But it's gone. Maybe this place is haunted."

Ria's face turns a deep blush. "I have it."

I kneel up as she retreats to her side of the bed. "What do you mean you have it?"

Her hand sneaks under her pillow, and she slides it out. "I swear I'm not a closet klepto or anything. I promise. But it's why I couldn't sleep."

"You're afraid of the phone?" Then I remember her horror when I asked if she had a phone and her talking about how her mom wanted her to get one. "Oh, right. It's part of the thing."

Ria nods. "I think, maybe, if we want to try this again someday, if you didn't have your phone, maybe I could sleep." She looks down. "I mean, if you want to. It's a lot, I know. And since there's a distinct possibility of this going nowhere, I understand if you don't want to do weird."

I lean in and give her a quick kiss on the tip of her nose. "I wish you would tell me why, but I respect that you're not there yet." I look at the phone, which is off. I power it up and the time very much indicates that I need to leave. "You tell me when and I'll leave the phone home. Or at least give it to you to lock up. Whatever you need." I stand up and head into the bathroom.

By the time I'm finished, Ria is standing by the door, practically ready to shoo me out. She's staring at her feet.

"Don't be embarrassed; you're not the one doing the walk of shame. And since we ran here, it literally is a walk," I joke.

"Let me drive you. It's the least I can do. You were very nice to me last night."

"Ria." I capture her chin in my hand, forcing her to look at me. "I'm sorry that your past has been not nice to you. But I plan on doing everything in my power to show you that some people are worth it. That some people won't betray your trust. And if you need me to stand on my head wearing a tutu while painted purple, I'll do that. You let me know. But for right now, you get some sleep. You look exhausted."

A watery smile spreads on her lips while her eyes spill over. "Grayson, I wish I could be the person you deserve."

"You be you, and I'll work to deserve that."

I lean in and kiss her one more time before heading out the door and down the stairs. I jog across the street to visit Heidi and grab a latte.

"Grayson, honey. Oh my God. I'd say the show was great, which you already know, but the coffeehouse cabaret. I died. *Died*! You and Ria are like, the best thing ever. You should put out a record or something. Is she going to be in one of your shows? Please tell me that you're a thing."

"We're a thing."

I probably shouldn't say that without talking to Ria first, but I know deep down, it's true. I can't imagine going a day without seeing her or talking to her or touching her. There's no going back now.

"Did you know she could sing like that?"

I nod, "Yes, but I didn't expect her to join in. I was trying to dedicate that to her. But it sounded okay? I mean, obviously, we didn't rehearse."

In my head it sounded perfect. Of course, in my head, I dance like Gene Kelly. The latter is not always true.

Heidi puts her hand over her heart. "God, Grayson, if Joe didn't have my heart, I'd have fallen in love with you two right then and there. If there's ever two people who belong together, it's you and Plain Coffee."

I smile, thinking back to the time when I knew nothing about Ria except she didn't like my bad jokes and did yoga. What a difference two months makes.

"So what's the deal? Is she moving here permanently? Is she moving in with you? She's still renting from Malyia Andrews, right?"

Heidi's train of thought barrels through my daydreams with the crushing reality of small town living. I don't need Ria's private business to get out, nor do I want to scare her away with talk of commitment way above what she's ready for.

"You know, Heidi, I'm not sure Ria's where I am yet. You know, I'm an acquired taste."

"Yeah, for anyone with a pulse."

I grin. "I mean, my lifestyle, The Edison ... it's not for everyone." Immediately Julianna springs to mind. I had to beg her to do the show here. She's already made demands about her accommodations. She's going to hate being here in Hicklam. "I don't know what Ria's long term plans are. We haven't officially even been out on a date, so let's not order flowers for the wedding quite yet."

As I walk back up the hill toward home, I can't help but think about the differences between Ria and Julianna. I wonder what Ria was like before her ... trauma ... as she calls it. Was she the typical stage diva? Was she like Julianna? Is that why I'm attracted to her?

I shake my head, as if I was having this conversation out loud.

While I got more sleep than Ria last night—or was it this morning—I could use a three-hour nap. Unfortunately, between office work, social media, and the two upcoming shows, I barely have time to run through the shower and shave before heading into The Edison for a jam-packed day.

Despite how much I have to do, all I can do is think about Ria. What it felt like to hold her in my arms and taste her on my lips.

"Grayson!" Mom yells, shaking my shoulder. "What are you doing? The curtain goes up in three minutes. You can't still be in the office. You aren't in costume and—oh God, you don't even have your makeup done yet. What are you doing?"

Shit.

I'm off my game. Off my routine. I didn't even do my vocal warm up before hitting the stage. I missed a note, causing a side-eye from one of my cast mates.

I never miss notes.

I stay focused enough to get through my quick costume change before intermission. As Act One draws to a close, the last thing I expect is Mom, waiting for me backstage.

"Grayson, a word in my office." She's using her business tone. I feel like I'm eight years-old again and about to get reprimanded for not doing my homework.

"Where were you this morning?"

"Mom, I'm thirty-five years old. I don't have to justify myself to you. I can come and go as I please."

"Not when you neglect your duties here."

"Duties? I made it on stage in time. It was fine."

"You were pitchy and uneven and not focused. And you missed the interview with Ted McGuin for WXYZ this morning."

Shit.

"I'm sorry, Mom. I forgot. Something came up."

"Something or someone?" She raises her eyebrow in that way she does.

"It's not like that, Mom. This is ..."

"I saw the two of you last night. It is different. Different that is all-consuming. And that's something you don't have time for right now."

I want to rage against my mother for pointing this out, but she's right. After I complained to her that I had too much on my plate and dumped some responsibility on her, I don't have time for a relationship, let alone one that is going to require as much mental energy as Ria is going to need from me.

Dammit all.

"Don't go sitting there, like I killed your kitten or something. You have to finish this show and do another today."

I stand up to leave, dejected. She's right. As much as it kills me, my mother has a very valid point. But Mom's not done yet. She moves in for the jugular. "And in case you were wondering, we are only at seventy-two percent this afternoon. Perhaps if people had heard you on the radio, they would have run over for the show."

"Mom, stop. I don't need the guilt. I don't need the pressure. I don't need any of it."

"I've already lost your father. I'm afraid if we don't have all of your focus, we'll lose The Edison too. Then I'll have lost everything."

She's not the only one who has lost so much. "Mom, I've been here working my ass off all year, but especially the past eight weeks since you fired Dave and his crew. I didn't see you out there, picking up the slack. But I was, and Ria was right along side of me. I get that this might not be the right time to start a relationship, but you know what? Maybe it is. Maybe Ria's what I need so I don't forget myself. What I want in this world. Because I've been working so hard, burning the candle at both ends and for what? You can't even cover a fifteen minute radio spot? You and Ted have known each other since you were kids. You couldn't sell the theater, which has been in *your family* for sixty years, to the audience? Then why the hell are we even trying?"

I storm out, slamming her office door harder than necessary.

As I spin around to head toward backstage, I crash into someone. I grasp the arms in front of me to keep us both from toppling over.

"Grayson, are you okay?" Ria pants, as if the wind's been knocked out of her. Probably because it was.

"No. I have to get back." My hands drop to my side, but quickly, she grabs me, pulling me so I have no choice but to look at her.

"Is this because of me? Of last night?"

I don't want to upset her so I don't say anything. Unfortunately, she takes that as a confirmation. Shit.

"Do you want me to leave right now?"

I shake my head.

"Then, we'll figure it out. You tell me when and where and how. That's what I came to tell you. I fell asleep after you left and when I woke up, all I could think of was how lonely I was without you there. So whatever I need to do, I will. Let me help you."

I can't meet her eyes.

"You've already done so much. I can't take anymore from you. Besides, what if it's not that easy?"

She laughs. "Grayson, life isn't easy. If it was, we wouldn't appreciate the things we have. You've got stuff; I've got stuff. And it's going to take me a while to get through my stuff. But I don't care how long it takes me to get there, someday I plan on appreciating the hell out of you."

I finally meet her gaze and grin slightly. "It's going to be tough, and maybe I'm not what you need."

What I want to say is that maybe I can't be what she needs, even though I want to be. There's not enough of me to go around.

Chapter 23: Gloria

Well, that could have been worse.

It also could have been a lot better.

It's not like my timing is great. In fact, it almost couldn't be worse. Grayson has so much on his plate right now. Maybe I shouldn't ask him to take on one more thing.

Instead, I head to the back row of the theater for Act Two. Today's show is easier to watch than yesterday's. That's progress, right? For tonight's show, I might even move up a row or two, if there are seats available.

I only went in today because Beth at the booth assured me that there were empty seats. As much as I'd like to support The Edison, I can't afford to spend forty bucks a day on tickets. Seventy on Saturdays and Sundays if you count the matinee and evening show.

Hell, I can't even afford to be here. As of Monday, I'll need to find a new place to live. Housing is covered while I'm in treatment, but Monday is my last appointment with Malachi. He's sending me off to face the big-bad world all on my own.

If everything goes according to plan, I won't be alone. Grayson will be there, by my side.

It's more than I ever thought would happen here.

I wonder if, as a staff member at The Edison, I could stay in the dorms? I'll ask Mrs. Keene in between shows. Now that the bathroom work is done, I'm finishing up some last-minute touch-ups on the lobby and rehearsal room. I should be done with that work by Tuesday at the latest.

So maybe, staying at The Edison won't work either.

After the applause and obligatory ovation following the conclusion of Act Two, I make my way to the office to talk to Mrs. Keene. Loud voices force me to pull up short.

"I've arranged for Ted to come in and talk to you now. Take that makeup off your face. It's terrible."

"Mom, it's a radio interview. No one will see that my contours aren't perfect."

"I still can't believe you missed it this morning. You were the one who set it up. Didn't you have it on your calendar for today? Didn't your alarm go off?"

Guilt fills me. When I took—no, stole—Grayson's phone, I turned it off. I was fearful that he'd reach under my pillow and sneak it out and record me while I slept. I thought if he had to fumble with turning it on, I'd probably hear it. And now, he missed something because of my paranoia.

Great.

"Just smile at Ted and turn your charm on, Ma. You remember what charm is, right? Like when you're nice to people."

Ouch.

"Grayson, do not speak to me like that. I raised you better, young man."

There's a long silence, in which I decide it's time for me to move on. I can't keep listening at the door. Things are bad in there, and they don't need someone prying.

I know what it's like to have your privacy invaded.

Dropping my head, I turn around and head out the door. The May Saturday has turned muggy and there's a thunderstorm threatening. I hope it holds off until I get back to my place.

I look around my little flat as the thunder crashes outside the pane of glass. I don't have tons of stuff to pack up. Clothes and toiletries mostly. A few books. It takes all of ten minutes. I can be out the door as soon as my appointment with Malachi is done on Monday morning.

The rest of the day is spent cleaning the apartment, making things shine as much as possible. Sitting on the bathroom floor, I think about my first day here, when I scoured the apartment for hidden cameras.

I haven't looked for a hidden camera in at least a month. Conveniently, I dismiss my behavior the night Grayson stayed over. Maybe it was irrational, but I saw it as survival.

I don't feel like there are eyes on me all the time. While I was at The Edison today, everyone was on their phone at intermission, and it didn't even freak me out.

For the most part.

Maybe that's enough growth. Maybe I don't need to shoot for the stars and try to have a relationship too. Maybe I'd be safer being by myself. Especially because being with Grayson will always mean being around the theater. He's the exact wrong person for me. Maybe I should listen to the Universe this time.

But I don't want to. I want to trust that no matter how hard this might be, or that how inconvenient the timing is, that this—whatever—is growing between Grayson and myself is worth the work.

Just like I was worth the work.

Of course, trust in anyone, including myself, is a leap for me. Though as I think about it, each day that I've been here, I've been trusting Grayson a little more. Opening up in ways I thought to be closed off forever. I have to trust myself finally.

The rain that has been pouring steadily for hours finally seems to be giving out. I need to tell him that I can give him space or support, as long as he can do the same for me. It's how partnerships work. It doesn't always break down fifty-fifty, but as long as there's a give and take, it can work.

I put my sneakers back on and run up the hill. The evening show is letting out. I wonder if there will be another coffeehouse cabaret tonight. It would make sense to have it on both Fridays and Saturday evenings, as long as the people show up for it.

I sit down on a bench by the side door to wait for the cast to finish up.

"Oh, Ria. You're still here." Mrs. Keene's voice is flat.

"Um, I left but came back. I was hoping to talk to Grayson."

She sighs as she sits down on the bench next to me. "I don't know what to do about that boy."

Um, maybe realize that he's a grown man?

I sit in silence, waiting for her to continue.

"You know, I don't know anything about you. Where you're from. Why you're here. What you want in life."

"Well, Mrs. Keene, I came to Hicklam to work with Malachi Andrews. He's renowned in his field. An expert in EMDR therapy, with which he's been treating me for the past two months." I should tell her with EMDR is, but I don't. Let her figure it out. "I know you thought otherwise, but I'm sorry to inform you that there is no sex cult. Only therapy."

She smiles a little and shrugs. "But a sex cult is better gossip. Why is it all so secretive?" While I appreciate her attempt to lighten the mood, her joke falls flat. Mostly because I don't like the way she treats Grayson.

Or me.

"There's a significant stigma surrounding mental illness. Not everyone is so open about it. I suffer from Post-Traumatic Stress Disorder, which led to bouts of depression and anxiety. Malachi has helped with the PTSD, so the other stuff isn't a huge issue right now. But I'm lucky. I only lost ten years of my life to this. Some people lose their entire future."

"I'm afraid we're going to lose our future."

"The Edison." My response is not a question but a statement.

"I can't lose it. It's all I've ever known. It's all I have left."

"Then why aren't you doing more to help? Why do you keep getting in his way?"

She looks at her hands. "Everyday, I tell myself I'll do more. That if I sleep well enough, I'll have the energy. All I have to do is get up and do. But somehow ..."

She doesn't need to finish the sentence. I recognize the signs of depression.

"Maybe you need some help."

Mrs. Keene looks up sharply. "And who exactly will help me?"

While I want to suggest Malachi, I start with a more palatable answer. "You have Grayson."

She looks down at her hands. "For now. But I know he doesn't want to be here. And if The Edison goes, so does he. I don't know if that will upset him all that much, to be honest. It doesn't matter to him."

Depression or not, I've heard enough of this bullshit. She has to see. I jump to my feet. "How can you say that it doesn't matter? Have you seen how hard he's been working? I don't think he sleeps at all, practically working around the clock. And now that the shows have started, he has to be in rehearsals on top of everything else. I don't know how he can keep going. And I don't know how he made it this far."

She continues to stare at the ground. "But he doesn't want it. He doesn't want to be here. He wants something else. A life we took from him. I don't know why he's still here."

Can this woman really be so blind and obtuse? "Um, because he loves you and his family legacy, maybe? Because he wants to take care of you. To protect you from further loss. I know he wishes for something else. Something more. But I've also seen him work tirelessly to get this place ready for opening night. I've seen him rehearse and teach and joke with the cast. He is a person who feels utterly comfortable, right here. But he can't do it alone. He needs help. Instead, you're working against him at every turn."

She looks up, anger blazing in her eyes. "You have no right to say that to me. You're not part of this. Part of us. The Edison is all I have left."

"That's not true, and take it from a person who knows what it's like to lose almost everything. When I was at my lowest of low and the darkest of dark, my parents and my brother were there for me. They didn't know what to do, and they didn't know how to help, but they showed up each and every day for me. Just like Grayson's done for you. This place, it's a place. But Grayson is your son, and he should mean more than a few buildings."

I storm away, unsure of where this passion and vigor has come from. I know I should be more compassionate. More empathetic. Hell, I should be sympathetic. But in this moment, I'm angry with her.

And then I wonder if this is how my parents feel dealing with me. Damn it. I should go back to her.

I'm not ready for that yet. However, for the first time in a very long time, I feel as if the clouds have parted and revealed a bright shining light on my world. There's a clarity here that hasn't been present since before.

I feel inspired.

I feel good.

I feel hope.

And after my conversation with Grayson's mom, there's one person with whom I need to speak. I jog quickly down the hill to my flat.

"Hi, Mom," I say breathlessly, grabbing the phone as soon as I walk in the door.

"Gloria, are you okay? What's wrong?"

"Nothing. I had to run home to get to my phone. And yes, I know, a cell phone would change that. I'm going tomorrow to get one."

She laughs. "I'll believe it when I see it. Or hear it. What's going on then? You sound different."

I plop down on my couch. "It worked, Mom. It really worked. This therapy. I feel ... good."

"It's more than that."

My poor mother has been through so much with me. All those countless nights, holding me as I cried and trembled. All those times I thought I could leave the house when I had to turn back without getting out of the car. All those movies we watched so I wouldn't go over the cliff. I've put her through so much. A wave of guilt washed over me, threatening to pull me under.

"Gloria, what is it? I don't like this silence."

I close my eyes, willing myself to rise up through the waves. "I've met someone, Mom. I think I'm in love." The admission startles even me. I didn't think it was that, but of course it is.

"Grayson." She knows me. She doesn't even need to be here to see it.

"Is it that obvious?" I laugh.

"Let's put it this way: I started keeping a tally of all the times you mentioned his name every time we talked. I ran out of paper."

"Better this than of all the times I had panic attacks."

Now it's Mom's turn to laugh. I wish she were here in front of me, mug of green tea in hand, to have this conversation. "It's nice to hear this in your voice. I wish I was there with you."

"I was thinking the same thing."

"But you should be home soon enough. Or are you coming home?"

Her question has merit. I don't want to leave, but I don't have a lot of options either. "I don't know yet." I fill her in on my housing dilemma. "At least I didn't have to deplete the last of my savings to pay for this. The job helped a bit with the costs. Not to mention I only needed eight weeks of therapy, rather than twelve. I have a little left."

"What would you do if you came home? Are you considering going back to school?"

"I haven't thought about it." What I mean is I haven't wanted to think about it. As part of the legal settlement, Anniston College will allow me to return and finish my degree whenever I am ready. The settlement is what I've been living on for the past decade.

It's hard to hold a job when you freak out over the stupidest thing or have a problem being on surveillance camera. That removes about ninety-nine percent of work opportunities.

"No one there will know you. I'm sure even the staff has totally changed over."

"I can't afford to go anywhere else, but I don't think I can go back there. Plus, I don't know what I want to study. It's not like I'm going back to musical theater."

And then, there it is. The pang of longing. I think back to last night. God, was it only twenty-four hours ago?

"I sang, Mom. With Grayson. In front of people. I did it."

In a thick voice, she chokes out, "Oh Gloria, honey. That's so ..."

My tears are now flowing as well. "I know. And when we sing together, it's like magic, Mom. I feel like a whole person."

Mom's quiet for a minute, which means she's carefully choosing her words. "Gloria, honey, I'm sure Grayson is wonderful. Please don't be hasty though. Think things through. Don't mistake performance chemistry for the real thing. Sometimes the magic of music can play tricks with your mind."

It's as if she's dumped a bucket of ice cold water over me. "Gee, thanks, Mom. Just what I needed to hear. I'm glad you're happy again, Gloria, but remember all your past mistakes that totally fucked up your life? You're doing it again."

"You know that's not what I'm saying. I'm simply asking you to take your time. We've spent the last ten years picking up the pieces. Can you afford to shatter again?"

As I disconnect, I want to hate her for saying it. But what I hate is that she's right. What if I can't take this risk?

Chapter 24: Grayson

"Grayson, can I talk to you?"

"I'm busy, Mom. Working. Like you want me to. Having nothing but The Edison in my life. Doesn't that make you happy?"

My mother enters the office, sitting tentatively in the chair across from me. "I'm sorry."

I glance up, raising my eyebrow. "About what?"

"Don't make this more difficult."

Sitting back, I fold my arms across my chest. "I would have to know what *this* we're talking about in order not to make it more difficult."

"I'm sorry I haven't been more help with the business. I ... it's been a struggle. *I've* been struggling more than I wanted to admit. I could have done more."

"You could have and should have. Also, you should not be making major business decisions that shift a large responsibility onto me without consulting me first. Either I'm your partner, or I'm not. You can't expect me to work like a partner, while treating me like a child."

"That's a valid point."

"Is that it? I have to prepare our social media for the week, as well as finalize travel arrangements for the next cast. Have you sent out the email reminders to the camp participants about outstanding balances? I don't want to buy scripts and scores until we have a financial commitment from the lion's share."

She nods and says, "Let's go through what needs to be done. Together."

We talk business for a few minutes, coming up with detailed and thorough task lists that for the first time in months seem to shift a bit more onto Mom's plate. It doesn't ease my workload, but it makes it feel a skosh less overwhelming.

"Okay, what gives?" I ask, settling back in my chair. It's about one in the morning, and the fatigue of the day is overtaking me. I'm not sure I have the energy to stand up, let alone walk all the way to my house and my bed.

"Ria was here."

My head whips around, looking for her. I've been forcing myself to concentrate on the mountain of work in front of me, rather than the fact that she didn't come today. "What do you mean she was here? Today? Tonight?"

"She was at the matinee, and then came back at the end of the evening show, before the cabaret. I spoke with her."

"And?"

"I'm not sure."

Now I'm on my feet, my fatigue forgotten. "Not sure about what?"

"Her. There's something about her that I don't—"

"Mom, for the love of God, she's not in a sex cult. Get over it."

Mom waves her hands, trying to placate me. "Sit down, Grayson. I know. She told me about her therapy. She also told me that you're trying to save The Edison. For me."

I cock my head, looking at my mother like she's lost her mind. Which, maybe, she finally has. "Obviously."

She shrugs. "I wasn't sure if you wanted it to succeed or not."

"Why wouldn't I want it to succeed?"

"Because then you'd be free to pursue your career, free and clear. Without any baggage holding you down. That I'm holding you down."

I can't even look at her. Is that really what she thinks? That I could walk away, losing the only home I've ever known without looking back? That I wouldn't care what happens to her, as long as I'm on the stage? I've heard enough.

"Well, Mom, thanks for the great faith in me. I'm glad it took someone I've known for two months to convince you that I'm not a total piece of shit, as if my actions over the past thirty-five years have left doubt in your mind."

Tears fill her eyes. "Yes, and I feel stupid for that. Since your father got sick and well ... I haven't had the clearest of heads. I haven't been coping nearly as well as I thought I had. I've barely been coping at all. But she did make me see it."

"I told you, she's a good person. I don't know why you didn't trust that. Oh, right. It's because you have no faith in me."

I walk out from behind the desk, pushing past my mother. Every time we take one step forward, we take three steps back.

"I don't want to see you hurt. What do you even know about her?"

I whirl around. "I know she cares about me. She's fragile but strong. She's a hard worker and won't stab me in the back. She's ..."

"Look her up, Grayson. Before you get more involved. Do a Google search. That's all I ask."

"Whatever," I mutter, storming out. My first instinct is to go to Ria's, but it's the middle of the night. Someone pounding on her door might scare her. I wish I could text her.

Seriously, why doesn't she have a phone?

I remember her saying that there is a phone in her apartment, but to get the number, I'd have to go back to the office and go through the personnel records. And with Mom still in there, I vote for option B.

I slide into my car and ease it quietly down the driveway before turning the headlights on. If there's a light on in Ria's place, I'll knock. If not, I'll go home and try to get some sleep.

The presence of a warm glow from her apartment window causes the energy to surge through my system. I didn't know what I was going to feel if her apartment was dark, as it should be at this late hour.

I take the stairs two at a time, forcing myself to rein it in before banging on her door. Instead, I take a deep breath and knock lightly. "Ria? It's Grayson."

It feels like an eternity before she pulls the door open. Her hair is piled in a messy knot on the top of her head, and she's in that oversized Bengals T-shirt again.

And nothing else.

My mouth is suddenly dry as all my blood runs south.

"Are you oka—"

I don't wait for her to finish as I step toward her, cupping her face in my hands as my lips crash down on hers. I have never needed someone the way I need her in this very moment. She stumbles back a few steps but doesn't pull away.

I think I would die if she pulled away.

Her arms wrap tightly around my neck as I slide my hands down her back to her waist. After a minute, I go farther until I'm cupping her fantastic ass. She moans slightly into my mouth and that's all it takes to bring me to my breaking point. I lift her up, her legs wrapping instinctively around my waist as I carry her toward the bedroom.

I break our tangle of lips for a moment to look into her eyes that seem lit up from within. There's no sign of fear. Nothing telling me to stop. Still, it's not enough. I need to make sure she's alright with this. "You okay?" my voice pants out.

Her face is serious. "For now. I'll let you know."

I lay her down on the bed, pulling off my T-shirt and kneeling over her. As my hands begin to glide up her body, she puts her own hands down on top of mine, halting my exploration.

"Where's your phone?"

"In the car."

"Really?"

I nod. "You can frisk me, if you want. In fact, I encourage it. Perhaps a strip search?" I arch my eyebrow. That grants me a small smile.

"I believe you."

Her faith in me, previously so fragile, causes my chest to constrict.

I inch my hands toward the hem of her shirt but again am stopped.

"Don't take the shirt off."

I nod in agreement, saying nothing before moving my lips to that delicate skin at the base of her neck. Ria's hands are on mine again, pulling them up her body, underneath her shirt, and toward her breasts.

Her nipples harden under my fingers and I want to wrap my lips around them. "Can I pull up your shirt a little? I want to taste you. I promise I won't take it off."

She nods.

I shimmy down on the bed, lifting the fabric delicately so that I can suckle her tight brown peaks. Her hands are fisted in the bedding as she arches her back, pushing her breast further into my mouth. The pressure against my zipper is painful. But I can wait. I need to make sure she's taken care of first.

I look up and see her eyes closed, her mouth open, a moan escaping. My mouth begins to trail down her body. One hand remains massaging her breast, while the other gently skims beneath the elastic of her underwear. Her body is warm and relaxed, but that's not enough.

"I'm going to—"

"For the love of God, Grayson, if you don't go down on me right now, I'll scream. I appreciate your concern, and I'll let you know but—"

She breaks off with a strangled cry as I pull her panties to the side and my mouth finds her. She's wet and hot and tastes like heaven. Her hands weave tightly into my hair as my tongue explores her most intimate area. My fingers tease at her opening before sliding into her.

I could stay between her legs forever.

She begins quaking beneath my ministrations, spasms rocking her entire body as she calls my name. Her body slowly goes limp so I kiss a trail up to her breasts. I return to teasing them a bit before flipping her shirt down. My grin spreads from ear to ear.

Her lids are heavy as she looks up at me. "Thank you," she drawls, one corner of her mouth lifting in satisfaction.

"It was my pleasure," I say, shifting my body on top of hers, holding my weight through my arms.

"No, it was distinctly my pleasure, of that I'm sure. Now it's your turn. Take those pants off and do you have something?"

I push myself to standing at the foot of her bed, reaching into my back pocket for my wallet. Clichéd, I know, but practical.

As I'm extracting the condom, Ria has scooted toward the end of the bed and is fumbling with the button on my jeans. She opens them, making short work of the zipper before freeing my cock, which has sprung through the opening in my boxers, like it has a mind of its own.

Frankly, at this point, it does.

She sucks in a small breath before dragging my boxer shorts down my legs. I stand there, letting her do as she pleases. Turnabout is fair play, after all. Her hands run up and down my hips, caressing my buttocks before trailing around to the front. She leans forward, as if she's about to take me in her mouth, but then pulls back.

Without looking at me, she reaches over and takes the condom out of my hand. She rips open the foil packet and unrolls it down my length. Oh God, her touch is light and smooth and almost enough to make me lose it right now.

As she gets to the base of my shaft, she cups my sack. I groan and bite my lip. I'm not sure how much longer I can hold out.

Yet another reason to be grateful for condoms. In addition to protecting both of us, it will spare me from the embarrassment of finishing too quickly.

Though that is still a distinct possibility.

Ria must sense my need as my body trembles under her touch. Her hands walk up my body, pulling me down toward her. She slides back on the bed, still sitting but with her legs spread and bent, giving me a beautiful view of her in all her glory. She nods as I lean in, kissing her deeply.

She lays back and I pull myself over her. "You ready?"

Now she's biting her lip, but it doesn't seem out of fear. More apprehension. Her pupils are wide in the dim light. She lifts her pelvis, grinding it against me. It's what I need. I slide into her gently. Her hips curl in toward me, welcoming me into her flesh. I push in further and she groans. Her kissing becomes more frenetic, matching the speed of my thrusts.

As her nails dig into my ass, I feel her clench and quiver around me. It's too much, and I can't hold out any longer. I groan as I climax, her body gripping me tight.

All my energy leaves with that last thrust. Collapsing down on her, I gasp for breath.

"You okay?" Her voice sounds as breathless as I feel.

"Yeah, I'm great," I pant. "And you?"

"Your heart is racing. Please don't have a heart attack on me. I don't want to have to explain that to your mother."

I laugh, shifting my weight up and pulling out of her. I quickly head to the bathroom to clean up. When I return, she's watching me intently, as I walk around her apartment naked as a jaybird.

I hop into bed next to her and pull her to my chest, and kiss the top of her head. Instead of waxing poetic about feelings that I don't even understand anyways, I sigh contentedly and drowsily whisper, "Thank you," before drifting off to sleep.

Chapter 25: Gloria

I did it.

We did it.

And man, was it fabulous.

I don't remember sex being that good, even if I did have to leave my shirt on. The thought of being totally exposed was too much for me. But at least I got through everything else. Got through. Like it was a chore to be endured.

If that's what chores are like, call me Cinderella from now on.

I even fell asleep with him. I'd like to think it's because I'm at a whole new level of trust, which I am, but I think it has more to do with barely sleeping last night and then being thoroughly satisfied.

In a good way.

The best way.

But now, in the morning light, with a few hours of restorative sleep, my mind is doing that fantastic thing where it starts to race and overthink and, well, freak out.

I don't know why. I am mostly positive—though I can never be totally sure—that Grayson didn't record us. Me. He said he left his phone in the car. He hasn't been in my place to put in hidden cameras or anything.

Unless he has. Maybe he—NO.

No. No. *No.*

I will not let myself fall down this dark rabbit hole again.

I work through my strategies for staying in the present. Grayson has never given me one iota of reason not to trust him. Instead, he has shown patience and respect and empathy. I really need to talk to Malachi about how to work through this. Good thing I have one more session.

One more session.

That's it. And then I'm leaving.

I look up at Grayson, who's just come out of the shower, with a towel slung low around his waist. Water runs in little rivulets down his dark hair, curly with moisture.

"Ria, what is it? You look like you've seen a ghost."

I want to shrug it off and say it's nothing. Deny it. But if I expect the truth from Grayson, I have to give it to him myself. "I'm leaving. Monday."

He falters. "Monday? That's tomorrow. Why? Don't go." He checks himself quickly. "I can't tell you what to do, but I don't want you to leave."

I look down at my hands, tightly wound in my lap. "Tomorrow's my last session with Malachi. I only get the apartment while I'm under treatment. I don't have anywhere else to go. I have to go home and figure out what I'm going to do next."

Grayson perches on the edge of the bed and tentatively reaches out for my hand. I can't meet him, so he puts his hand on top of mine. "If you don't know what you're going to do, why do you have to leave?"

I look around, unsure about how he can't see the obvious answer. "Um, I don't have a place to live. And I can't afford rent right now. It was included with the cost of the treatment, which is why people come here to see Malachi. It's part of why he's the best—he makes everything possible so you can focus on recovery. But even with what I made working for you, my savings are almost totally depleted. I haven't been able to hold a steady job and I've been living on the settlement money or my parents' subsidies. I mean, I live with them. I couldn't keep my own place after it all happened."

Normally, I'm ashamed to admit this. Seeing as how Grayson lives with his mom, he can't look down on me for that.

"Settlement? Were you in an accident?" His brow creases as if he's trying to figure out a difficult calculus problem. He's trying to put the pieces of my shattered past together.

"There was an incident at college. *The incident*. It involved a serious security breach on the college's point, so they gave me a settlement. They also will allow me to return and finish my degree, but I'm not sure I can—or want—to go back there."

"And you said you were a musical theater major? I take it you wouldn't go back to that. What else would you study? What do you want to do?"

I finally raise my gaze to meet his. I can tell him. I *should* tell him. But if I tell him why I can't go back to my major, will it change the way I look in his eyes? Will he immediately search out the video and see me humiliated? I'm not ready for that. I don't want him to *ever* see. "That's the problem. I don't know. I kept thinking I'd wake up one day and this would be behind me and I'd get back to living. Except ten years have rolled by. I'm alive, but not living. At least not until now."

"Surely you haven't been sitting in a dark room all this time. What have you done? Anything you liked?"

How do I tell him that being around people is hard? That working with computers and technology is virtually impossible. That the only thing I ever wanted in life was to be on the stage, and I miss it like I'd miss oxygen.

That, maybe, he'd understand.

"All I ever wanted to do was perform. Once I couldn't do that anymore ..." I take a steadying breath. "I've taught some yoga classes at the Senior Center, but it was too much. Done some house cleaning. Dog walking. Cat sitting. Odd jobs, here and there. It's been tough because I do better when I'm scheduled and busy but then sometimes the schedule gets overwhelming for me. Sort of a double-edge sword, if you know what I mean."

"Running The Edison is not what I'd planned on doing. I mean, I thought I'd come back, maybe do a show here and there. But I thought my primary job would be on Broadway. It's been ... an adjustment having to give that up. I know it's not the same in any way, shape, or form. Just sometimes life takes us in unexpected directions."

"Yes, like off a cliff, running through the woods, swimming through an alligator-infested swamp. You know, but it's all good exercise, right?" My words betray my deep-down bitterness that I had to go through this because other people were cruel.

Grayson pulls me to him. "No, what I'm saying is that if I wasn't here, fighting tooth and nail for the old girl—if my dad hadn't died, if my mom hadn't lost her ever-lovin' mind and fired the crew—if none of that had happened, I never would have met you. So, while I didn't appreciate it at the time, maybe I'll trust in fate this once."

"Fate is a hard one for me to get on board with. It's hard to believe I was meant to suffer the way I have." I look hard into Grayson's face. He's kind and good, and I do believe he cares about me. I think. "But yes, I'm glad we met."

Very glad.

"So you can't rent this place?" Grayson's up and pacing. I sort of wish he'd get dressed because his practically naked body is distracting for me.

"I don't think so. I'm sure Malachi has his next client coming in, and they'll need the space. And can you put your pants on? It's hard to think with you like that."

Grayson smiles and does a sexy little dance, letting the towel drop to the floor. While it's meant to be provocative and funny, I'm too uncomfortable to enjoy it. The large windows are right there and it's broad daylight and anyone might see. I drop my head, letting my hair fall around my face, as if it might protect me from prying eyes.

"Okay ..." he says slowly. My reaction is enough to make him stop and get dressed. Now I feel guilty for making him feel bad.

Ah, the endless cycle continues.

"Grayson, I'm sorry." Yup, that's the next step. Apologizing for being broken. "It's not that I don't think you're sexy or appreciate your body. Believe me, I do. It's just the windows and what if someone sees you?"

He pulls his jeans on. "Are you ashamed of me? To be seen with me?"

"No, of course not."

"Then why do you care if someone sees me here?" He pulls his T-shirt down over his head.

"Not sees you here. Sees you." I wave toward his crotch. "All of you."

He plops down on the edge of the bed and pushes toward me with his hand. "Heck, when you've been in theater as long as I have, probably everyone in town has seen most of me. I mean, I was in *Hair*."

Hair was notorious in the theater community, with the majority of the cast going completely nude toward the end of Act I. In keeping with the spirit of freedom, cast members could opt out and sing from the wings. In college, we'd discussed doing the show and many of us had long, mostly drunken and pot-filled discussions about what we would do.

I'd said I would do it. I probably would have too, if given the choice.

The choice.

That's what it all comes down to. I didn't have a choice.

"I'd always thought I'd be fine with doing that scene. We'd talked about doing it my senior year in college." Aaron was all over it, excited for the chance to direct the show.

"Yeah, I wasn't as comfortable as I thought I would be. It was a little creepy, thinking about all the people who have seen ..." he looks down at his lap. I half-expect him to call it 'Mr. Happy' or something as equally ridiculous. "At least I was in the back row, so that's how I've rationalized it and kept a little of my dignity."

While I had my dignity stripped.

"Okay, let's move on from *Hair*," Grayson says. "If you have to move out but don't want to leave Hicklam yet, the answer is simple. Move in with me."

I sort of wish I was driving right now because I'd slam the breaks. "Hold up," I raise my hands, as if under arrest. "Um, no."

I don't know what to do but this conversation has me about to crawl out of my skin. I get up from the bed, pulling a robe on over my long T-shirt and shorts. If I could put a snow suit on to cover up, I would. But it's May and I don't have one anyway because I'm not four anymore.

Perhaps I should invest in one.

"Ria, no, that came out wrong." Grayson likewise jumps to his feet, his hands in the air as if trying to calm me down. "I meant move into the house. Or the dorm. Up to the property. Not *in* with me. I mean, you're welcome to and all, but I know we're not there yet. I just mean to ..." he trails off.

I look at him for a moment. I'm screwing this up, and it hasn't even started.

"Grayson, I'm going to freak out. A lot. Over stupid shit. Over nothing. I don't mean to. I don't want to. I'm sorry. I can't say I'm sorry enough. I can tell you to not take it personally, which you won't be able to do, but it's not personal. Ask my mom. I'm all sorts of messed up, and I'm trying to be better. I shouldn't have slept with you because I'm probably not ready."

I take a deep breath, trying to muster up the courage to continue.

"When will you be ready?" His eyes are wide. Sincere.

I shrug. "I have no idea."

Grayson walks up to me, clasping both my hands in his. "Then I'll wait. Tell me what you need and I can do my best. And if my best isn't good enough, I'll do better."

Tears start flowing down my cheeks. I can't wipe them away because he's holding onto my hands tightly. "You can't do better than your best. If it's your best, then that's all you can do."

He leans in and kisses me softly on the nose. "You know what I mean. Let's figure this out. Together. But you have to stay here in order to do that."

I think about what his mom said last night and how overworked he's been. "The last thing you need is another distraction."

"What I need is you right by my side, jumping in and helping out. There's nothing you can't do. Drywall, paint, tile. I sort of need a right-hand man. Er, woman. I need you. Stay."

Dammit, he has me.

Chapter 26: Grayson

"Closing night for *Singing in the Rain*. You ready to move on?" Ria asks. She's sitting on the floor in the living room, notebooks and sheet music spread out around her. It's the perfect picture. Since she had to give up her flat, I convinced both Mom and her that the best solution would be for Ria to stay with us. While she could have picked the dorms, she said she felt safer staying in the house that had less traffic.

In the guest room, naturally.

That was Mom, but Ria didn't disagree.

Anyway since Ria is now in charge of running our camp, it's great that she's so close. Not to mention I can be here for her as much as she's been here for me.

"Yup. Rehearsals have been in full gear for *Rent*. We open on Thursday." I'm playing Benny, the scuzzy preppy disloyal building owner.

"It's sounded great, from what I've heard." Ria barely looks up from her work. In order to get her to agree to stay in Hicklam, she insisted on doing as much as she can at The Edison to lighten my load. She's working on set design and staging for our camp production. Campers will be here in five weeks, but between *Rent* and *Chicago* for three weeks after that, the time will fly by.

"I do love this show. I remember going to see it when I was a freshman in high school. We drove up to Albany to see the touring show."

She looks up. "High school? Weren't you a bit young for it at fourteen? Drugs, AIDS, drag queens, menage à trois? That's heavy for a kid."

"I was a theater kid. We grow up fast."

She looks back down. "I guess that's true. When you're a kid in the shows, you're around so many adults all the time that they seem to forget you're there and innocent. And then the shows are often too adult for the cast. I mean, who thinks *Sweet Charity* is a good idea for a bunch of teen girls?"

I slide down on the floor next to her. "Any time you want to sing "Big Spender" to me, I'm game." I lean in and give her neck a kiss. She bats me away.

"I'm working here. My boss is a huge pain. He's so demanding."

I lean in again, this time gently pushing her down to the floor. "Tell me about these demands. What does he ask of you that's so taxing?" My hand wanders up her shirt, teasing her nipple through her bra. Her back arches, pressing her breast into my hand.

"Oh, you know the typical. *Let me go down on you. Let me please you. You didn't have enough orgasms. Let's try for another*. Really," she pauses to moan as my hand wanders south. "Quite. Tedious." Her words are coming in short gasps.

I lean in and suck gently at the base of her ear. This particular spot drives her wild. Her hands start pulling at the hem of my shirt and then stop. Her entire body goes limp under mine. Quickly, I get up. Ria remains laying on her back on the floor. Her knees are bent up as she presses the heels of her hands into her eyes. I see her diaphragm rise and fall, slowly and deliberately.

She's trying to get back into control.

I have no idea what I did to make her feel out of control in the first place, but it was pretty obvious that she stopped being a willing participant.

Without uncovering her eyes, she says quietly, "I'll be fine in a few minutes. I'll talk to you later, okay?"

I may be totally ignorant when it comes to what I've done, but at least I'm smart enough to know when I'm being dismissed. Still, shaking my head, I review what just happened. Something quite similar—with the exception of that particular conversation—happened last night. She was fine then.

So what was different now?

I replay the conversation in my head. We were talking about the different shows, growing up in the theater. *Sweet Charity*. Her boss being demanding.

None of it seems like it would be triggering, but I guess that's the thing with triggers. I've tried to read up on PTSD in my spare time, just so I'm a little better informed. What would be most helpful is if Ria would tell me what her incident and triggers are, so I can not be insensitive.

The conversation has me wondering about what she was like on stage. She's quiet and subdued, but I've seen those lively streaks in her. I can only imagine what she was like before something stole her joie de vivre.

Maybe there are some videos online of her on stage. Quickly, as I'm walking up to the theater, I pull out my phone and Google, "Ria Benedetti."

Nothing comes up.

Literally nothing.

Google is asking me if I meant Ray Benedetti or Myra Benedetti. It's like she doesn't exist.

She avoids computers and social media like the plague, but how can a person in her early thirties *not* have any sort of internet footprint? I've got to be spelling her name wrong or something. Maybe there are two n's in her last name or—

"Grayson, there you are. I have been waiting forever for you to get here. It's just like you to keep me waiting. Some things never change."

The voice is like nails on a chalkboard. Maybe not even that pleasant.

Shit.

"Um, that's funny, Julianna, because you aren't due to come in until tomorrow. Rehearsals for *Chicago* don't start until Tuesday."

"Yes, but you close tonight. Don't we want to get started?"

"I've been over this with you. We strike the sets on the Monday after close. It gives the company time to decompress and get into the mind frame for the next show. We have a lot of last minute things to do before *Rent* opens on Thursday. Most of us aren't even thinking about starting rehearsals for the show after just yet."

It's not like I haven't explained this to Julianna before. We'd talked extensively about how things ran at The Edison during the years we were together. And I went over it with her and her agent numerous times while brokering the deal for her to work here this summer.

The deal which included her bringing her boyfriend as the director. It's fine. One less thing for Henderson and I to have to figure out.

"Yes, well, I wanted to talk to you about something. You see, A.J. will be here on Sunday. I told you he'd be starting a bit late. Well, he's really weighing other commitments and this is a strain for him to have to come here and direct." She makes it sound as if he's curing cancer or erasing childhood poverty.

"Henderson and I will handle the directing, if you need us too. If it's too much for A.J." I stumble over his name. I'm not jealous. Not at all. Julianna dumping me was the best thing that ever happened to me, until I met Ria, that is. She's toxic and demanding. Actually demanding; not in the kidding around way Ria said I was.

"No, it's not that. A.J. is one of the most brilliantly talented humans I've ever met. He's so ..." She clasps her hands to her heart and stares off. It's such a fake stage pose that I have all I can do not to roll my eyes.

"I'm sure he'll do great things here, when he finally shows up."

"Yes, well, that's the thing. He's got a special fondness for this show. Some special attachment to it or something. Anyway, he says there's one more thing he wants guaranteed before he comes up here."

Oh shit. Here it comes. The unreasonable demand.

I sigh. "Lay it on me." In my mind, I'm remembering the numbers that Julianna's draw will bring in. The cash flow from sold-out performances. Our pre-sales are already over eighty-percent. Whatever I need to do to make her happy, I have to do.

For the sake of The Edison.

I'll give them my room. My house. Catered meals. Whatever it is.

"So A.J. can be quite possessive of me. And with me playing Roxie Hart and all ... well, he thinks he should play Billy Flynn."

My role. Billy Flynn.

"Okay ..." I drawl, unsure of why that makes a difference. "I'm supposed to play Billy."

She laughs, that overdone stage laugh. Jesus, is she ever *not* performing? "Yes, that's what A.J.

had a problem with. All that time we'll have to spend rehearsing, with me in such close proximity."

Naturally, she's referring to the number, "We Both Reached for the Gun," which is done with Billy Flynn as puppet master and Roxie Hart sitting on his lap as his marionette. Interesting. That's too much for him but he doesn't care that she has a simulated sex scene with someone else.

"Will he be playing your lover, Fred Casely, too?" Obviously, Julianna is much *too special* for any riff raff to be in close proximity.

She casually lifts a shoulder and lets it drop. "He doesn't care about that role. Only about you."

"Why me?" Seriously, why? Does he think I want Julianna back? No way in hell. Let's face it, I'm basically using her for her draw. And to be honest, there's no basically about it. I'm using her.

"He thinks it might be too much temptation."

"For who?" I bark in laughter. I sit down in the first row and fold my arms over my chest. I can't believe I lasted for almost three years with her. How did I not realize how insufferable she was then?

"Obviously, for you." She rolls her eyes, still performing.

"Okay, I've heard enough," I say, coming to my feet. "If he wants Billy, he can have Billy. It's fine. Ensemble is fine for me." Hell, I can sit this one out. I have a feeling catering to Julianna and her demands will be a full-time job in and of itself.

"Oh, no, that won't do. A.J. wants you to play Amos."

I'm sure he does. The foolish chump of a husband. If it were any more obvious about what A.J. was trying to do, he'd challenge me to a duel. I turn around, ready to tell her off, when I catch a glimpse of my mom standing at the back of the theater.

"Braedyn is cast as Amos already. I wouldn't want to take his role. It's not cool." It's also against everything we stand for here at The Edison. That kind of shit may happen elsewhere, but not here. Our subject matter may not always be family friendly, but this is a family theater.

"A.J. says you play Amos. And what A.J. wants, I want. You understand?"

I sigh, resigned. I want to fight, but there would only be one loser here and it won't be Julianna. "Yes, your majesty. I understand. Ensemble sounded good. It'd give me more time to spend with my girlfriend. Frankly, even Amos will free me up. This makes my day." I smile sweetly at her. "Good luck getting settled. I'll see you at rehearsal on Tuesday."

And with that, I turn and walk back out of the theater. Inside, I'm seething, but Julianna's not the only one with good acting skills here.

A.J. my ass. She wants to make me jealous. I don't know what I'm going to tell Braedyn without sounding like the biggest dick in the world. I'll find a way to make it up to him. Another role. A bigger part.

I've got to get in touch with him before the word spreads through the cast and crew like wildfire. And if I know Julilanna, which I do, she'll light that match as soon as she can.

I head up to the office to pull up Braedyn's cell number so I can text him to come down early. Call isn't for ten more minutes, so I have a narrow window before this could potentially implode.

Once in the office, I pull up his number and shoot him a quick text. The main phone rings, so I answer, as I have been doing since I was about seven, "Thank you for calling The Edison Theater, Hicklam's hippest happening place. Show times today are at two and seven. How may I help you?"

"Yes, may I speak with Gloria please?" A woman asks.

"Um, I'm sorry. There's no Gloria here."

"Isn't this The Edison?"

"Yes, ma'am."

"My daughter works there."

"I'm sorry, you must be mistaken. There's no Gloria here." I say again.

"She has to be," the woman insists. "I talked to her yesterday. She gave me this number if I couldn't reach her other one."

"I don't know what to tell you. I know everyone in the cast and crew here. We don't have anyone in this production whose name is Gloria."

"But she said she worked there. Oh God. I knew I never should have let her go. All that way by herself. She just wants so much to get better. If she's not there, has she been lying to me all this time? Where has she been? God, if that stubborn girl would just get a damn cell phone so I could track her like every other normal overprotective parent then—"

Wait.

"Um, ma'am. Excuse me. What does Gloria look like?" I don't need her to tell me. "Is she about five-three with dark brown hair and the most exquisite mahogany eyes and perfectly tanned skin and she does way more yoga than any human should and has the most perfect mezzo-soprano voice ever?"

"Is this Grayson?"

I smile. "Is this Mrs. Benedetti? I'm sorry, I didn't mean to scare you. Ria's here. Not, here, here. She's at the house and this is the office phone. But I can run up and have her give you a call." I look at my cell. Braedyn is on his way down. Shit.

"Why did you say she didn't work there? You scared the piss out of me."

"I'm sorry. The Gloria threw me. I know her as Ria. I didn't know it was short for anything."

Makes sense and I feel like the colossal idiot.

It also makes sense as to why the Google search came up empty.

"Can you please have her check in with me today? I just need to make sure she's okay."

I have no idea what Ria—Gloria—has been telling her mom about us, so I'll toe the line. "I'll make sure to pass on the message. I saw her a little while ago and she was fine." Of course, that's a lie, but I'm not going into details.

Braedyn comes bounding in as I'm disconnecting. I ask him to sit down while I tell him of the latest development. I have a feeling, and not for the first time, that Julianna may be more trouble than she's worth.

If only I had any other viable solution to save The Edison.

Chapter 27: Gloria

I probably have some explaining to do.

I owe you an explanation.

It's not you, it's me, because of course it's me.

Possible scenarios for what to say to Grayson have been running on repeat through my mind all afternoon. And evening.

Lucky for me, he's been tied up with his two final performances, so I haven't had to commit to an awkward turn of phrase just yet. I sort of thought he'd stop back over in between shows. Maybe he thought I needed space.

I didn't know people as thoughtful and considerate as Grayson existed.

You're comfortable getting on stage totally naked. I can barely let you see my breasts.

I'm afraid someone is always watching me.

You see, I can't get frisky in public places because of that time my boyfriend recorded us having sex, and I didn't know about it.

I was recorded having sex without my consent, and it was purposely put out on the internet.

I steal over to the theater, perfectly timed to watch Grayson perform his number. God, that man is sexy in a tuxedo.

Not to mention out of one.

If I were running this place, I'd only cast him in roles which required him to wear tuxes and suits.

I'll get my fill of him like that when *Chicago* opens in two weeks. *Rent* will have him in parkas and sweaters and the terrible fashions of the early 90s. I'll try not to let that kill my libido for him.

I don't think I have to worry.

The only thing putting a damper on the sexy time is me. That, and the fact that Grayson is busier than a one-legged man in an ass-kicking contest. I'm trying to do as much as I can. I'm even going to work with the campers. I can rehearse with them and teach them. It might be a nice compromise, still getting some of the feel of being on stage without having to go up there.

Malachi was supportive.

Even though I'm discharged from his official EMDR program, he's keeping me on as a client for some counseling until I go back home.

If I go back home.

For the first time in a decade, I can maybe picture myself having a life. Not living with my parents. Leaving the house daily. Having a job.

Of course, it would be infinitely better if my job didn't involve one of my biggest triggers, but we can't have everything, now can we. And the totally fun thing about my PTSD-fueled anxiety is that I can be triggered by the stupidest thing anyway. At least if I know what I'm facing, I am better prepared to deal with it.

And at least now I can walk into a theater without hyperventilating.

Though the worry beads around my left wrist are still getting a workout.

I head over to the house to wait for Grayson to come home. It'll be a while. It's customary to have a drink—or several—upon close of a show. It wouldn't surprise me if Grayson doesn't come stumbling in until the wee hours of the morning. I'd like to wait up for him and tell him why I acted that way. He has to know. I can't keep this from him anymore.

As I sit in my room and wait, I start to worry that Grayson won't come to me tonight. That I've scared him off and he won't knock on my door. God, he's been so understanding. More than understanding. Superhuman, really, in his compassion and realization of my needs.

Like giving me my own room when we could be sharing one.

He said his mother was old school, but he knew I wasn't ready.

Or maybe he's just a decent human being, and I'm not used to that.

It's almost like he knew I needed to comb every inch of the space, looking for hidden cameras and recording devices before I'd be able to undress, even though there's no way he could know that. And even then, it took me a few days to get comfortable.

I've been here for about a week and today is the first time I was able to walk from the closet to the bed—a whopping six steps—in the nude.

I don't think this will be a shock to Grayson. He gets it. He knows I can't be intimate with him in his room, even though the bed in there is a double, as opposed to the twin I'm sleeping in.

Maybe tonight I'll surprise him.

I've got enough time to look around his room for cameras. I have to check. It's the only way I'll be able to relax in there.

Ignoring the guilt that's nibbling within, I ease open Grayson's door. His room is an odd blend of ten-year-old boy and grown man. There's a shelf that holds trophies and awards. A spelling bee. A talent show. National Honor Society.

Grayson really is perfect. My attention goes to another wall. It's lined with framed eight by tens. Instead of school pictures showing his growth, they're all Grayson's head shots. I'd say he was about seven in the first one, if the missing teeth are any indication.

Slowly and carefully, I run my fingers around the rim of each frame. Nine in all. Then I pick up every trophy and award, turning them over before replacing them and moving onto the next.

The computer will be problematic. It's a laptop, so at least it can be closed. But still, I don't even want it in the room. I disconnect the charger and pick up the device. Even holding it in my hands is making my skin crawl, like this inanimate object is personally responsible for all my pain and suffering over the years.

I'll put this in the downstairs office and then it won't be—

"What do you think you're doing with that?"

Oh shit. Mrs. Keene's voice startles me, causing me to bobble the computer in my hands.

I look from the computer in my hands to her and back again. What am I supposed to say?

Well, you see, Mrs. Keene, I'm planning on seducing your son in here tonight because his bed is bigger and we can get more creative, but I can't have him recording it and emailing it to everyone he knows.

"Um, I was going to email my mom."

Lame but safer. Much safer, if the glare in her eyes are any indication.

"Grayson isn't here right now." Her tone is cold and clipped. I guess I don't blame her.

"I know. I was going to shoot a quick email and bring it back before he got home. What time do you expect him tonight?"

"Why don't you leave him a note and he can come find you? He knows how to do that." It's impossible to miss the disdain and disapproval dripping from her voice.

My grip tightens on the computer. "Mrs. Keene, why don't you like me?" I have to know.

Her mouth sets in a firm line as she looks me up and down. And up and down again. I clutch the computer in front of me, willing it to be a lead shield from which to prevent her eyes from seeing me.

I know this feeling.

I hate this feeling.

The prickles start at the base of my skull as my skin tightens, feeling as if there are tiny bugs crawling all over me. My throat is tight and my heart quickens. The blood is rushing to my ears, pounding like a drum.

"My son is the most important thing in the world to me."

I need to respond in a rational way. However, my grasp on rational is quickly slipping away as panic is threatening to bust through the door.

"Grayson is important to me too. He is the most wonderful person I've ever met. Kind and compassionate. Patient. Giving to a fault. You must be so proud of him and the job he's doing here." I don't know where that speech came from, but I mean every single word.

She looks taken aback for a moment. "Why, yes. Yes he is. And he deserves someone equally as wonderful."

Ouch.

"I know he does. And I also know there's probably nothing I can say to change your opinion of me. Your mind is made up that I'm not good enough. You think you know me and my story. The truth is, maybe I'm not ready yet for Grayson. I probably shouldn't be in a relationship right now, as I'm just trying to figure out how to live again. But I also know that I deserve to be happy and what a special gift he is. Right now, the most foolish thing I could ever do is to walk away. So instead, I'm going to do *whatever* I need to do to support Grayson and be the partner he deserves. Now if you'll excuse me, I want to email my mother."

I push past her, my breath coming in short spurts. Definitely not supplying enough oxygen to my brain. And I'm still clutching the demon device as if my life depends on it.

"Gloria, wait!" Mrs. Keene calls after me, but I'm not stopping. I don't need to hear what she has to say. Her use of that name says it all.

I used to love my name. I was named after my grandmother, and she was the coolest of cool. I loved that we had that bond and that of all her grandchildren, I was the only one with her name. There are no less than three songs with my name. Oh the thrill I'd get when Laura Branningan would start calling, "Gloria."

Then, that other song—the song that haunts my nightmares—begins racing through my head. *G-L-O-R—*

STOP.

In the hallway at the bottom of the stairs, I drop to my knees, laptop falling to the ground beside me. Pressing my hands into my eyes, I rock back and forth. Back and forth. Back and forth, willing the images in my head to go away.

The grainy video.

If the song hadn't specifically identified me, I'd always thought that *maybe* I'd have been able to remain anonymous. Thanks to Marissa, setting that lovely soundtrack, everyone knew.

Everyone saw.

And now, here it is, back again.

If Mrs. Keene knows, it's only a matter of time before she tells Grayson. I thought I was ready to tell him, but I can't. I can't bear it if he knows. I don't want him to ever see. Ever.

"Ria? What are you doing? Are you okay?" Suddenly he's there, as if I conjured him up in my mind. Pulling me to him. Scooping me up in his arms, pressed tightly to his chest. He holds me there until the trembling stops. Then, with strength I didn't know he possessed, Grayson stands up from the ground, holding me as if I weigh nothing.

And how many times have I wished that I could weigh nothing and evaporate into nothingness? I thought I'd left that feeling behind me, but now it's back. The thought of Grayson ever watching the video is bringing it all back.

"Shh, Ria. It's okay. You'll be okay. I promise. I got you," he murmurs into my ear.

I shake my head in disagreement. Nothing will ever be okay again. Ever.

"Can you tell me what happened?" Grayson asks quietly.

I want to remain silent. Then I remember that silence nearly killed me when it first happened. "Your mother."

Grayson settles me down on my bed before taking a step back. "Ria, tell me. What happened?"

I slam my fists down onto the bed. "She ruined it all!"

He tilts his head, confusion spreading across his face. "How so?"

"*She knows*," I hiss. "She knows all about me. She knows I'm not good enough for you. She's going to tell you, and I can't deny it. You'll never look at me the same way again. She's ruined everything. All my progress. All my growth. All my healing."

I curl up into a little ball, my knees pulled tight into my chest.

"Ria, don't hide it. You have to talk to me," Grayson says, squatting down in front of me. I don't look up at him. I can't. "Ria," he pleads. "Please?"

I can't.

Ever again.

Chapter 28: Grayson

There are so many things I want to ask.

That I want to know.

But she won't even look at me.

When I found her at the bottom of the stairs, curled up like a wounded animal and rocking, I expected to move her and see some gushing abdominal wound.

She's been ripped open, alright. Just not physically.

I'm not an expert like Malachi, but I do know this isn't Mom's fault. The result of Mom's instigation? Possibly. But this is due to her *incident*.

God, I wish she would confide in me. It's not like she has a secret past as a porn star or something. Whatever happened, I'm sure wasn't her fault.

I can't imagine what happened between Ria and Mom to send Ria running like this. Mom has never been aggressive. But she hasn't been herself since Dad died, either. She's not the mom I knew. More like an angry husk of a person. Maybe she did say something mean to Ria. I'll make her apologize in the morning.

I knock lightly on Ria's door, but she doesn't answer. I try the handle, but it's locked. She's never locked the door. I dash to the kitchen and scrawl a note.

I'm here for whatever you need. Please let me help you.

I slide it under her door and retreat to my room. Sleep comes in fits and starts and provides no rest or relief. I'm worried about Ria, locked in her room. Alone.

At least feeling that she's alone.

I stumble down to the kitchen to find coffee and my mother, in that order. After pouring a large mug, I say, "What happened with Ria?"

My mother doesn't say anything, still scrolling through her phone.

"Ma, what happened with Ria? She's very upset."

Finally my mother looks up, her reading glasses perched on the end of her nose. "What do you know about her exactly?"

"Lots." I don't know where she's going with this. I sit down at the table, opposite her. "Enough."

"Do you know why she's in town? Really why?"

I nod. I don't want to betray her confidence, but I also need my mother to back off. "She came to work with Malachi Andrews. He's a therapist. Apparently quite good, if it brought her here all the way from Ohio."

"I found her in your room last night. She had your computer. She says she was taking it to email her mother."

That's odd. I didn't think she liked computers or technology. She doesn't even own a phone. Then I remember that her mother was looking for her. "Oh shit, her mom was trying to get a hold of her. She called The Edison number. I forgot to tell her!" I jump up from the chair, determined to get the message to Ria.

"Yes, well ..." my mother says slowly, "she said she was borrowing your computer to email her mother. But I don't believe her. She's lying about a lot of things. I don't know how much you should trust her. You've always been too trusting in your relationships. Remember Julianne?"

I stop, not wanting to turn around and look at the woman who gave birth to me, because I'm afraid of what I might say. I close my eyes and count slowly to ten. "Mom, give it a rest. Ria's a good person. I'm not sure how I'd be making it without her, and I won't have you upsetting her for no reason."

"Oh, there's a reason."

I shake my head and walk out before I can no longer resist the temptation to not engage her. If I didn't know better, I'd almost say Mom is ... jealous. That's how she's acting, at least. How doesn't she see that Ria makes me happy? Not to mention the tremendous help she is with the incredible workload.

If nothing else, Mom should appreciate that, which is exactly what I tell her.

She doesn't have time to respond as Henderson comes storming through the back door. "I just talked to Braedyn. Are you kidding me?"

I shrug. "I don't know what else I'm supposed to do. That was Julianna's demand. I'm fine stepping down as Billy Flynn. I don't need it. In fact, I'd be fine being ensemble. But she insisted."

"It's a dick move." He folds his arms over his chest. "You and I are the producers here. We get the say."

"You know as well as I do that being the producer is really key for 'he who puts up the money.' And as the person who needs to make the money on this, we need Julianna to sell out those shows. So whatever we have to do to make her happy, we have to do. I feel terrible about Braedyn. It's not how we run things at The Edison. We don't stab each other in the back, but yet I did it."

Henderson nods. "She doesn't bring out the best in you, certainly. I can't believe you were with her for that long. How did you stand her?"

I glance over at my mother, who's back on her phone, as if our previous conversation didn't happen. "See, Mom? It could be a lot worse. I could still be with Julianna."

She doesn't even look up. Whatever. She's checked out again.

When we get through this season—if we get through this season—the two of us are going to have to have a long, hard discussion about how this place needs to run. And how much support that will require.

We've got to budget to make sure we can hire people when we need to. Though, now that the lion's share of the renovations are done, in theory next winter should be much smoother. And though I'm loathe to admit it, we ended up saving a money by firing the contractors.

On the other hand, if we had kept the contractors, the renovations would have been completed long before opening night, and I would have been able to focus more on growing the business.

Maybe I wouldn't feel so tired and defeated.

My only high point since March is Ria, and I'm not sure where we even stand.

Not to mention that simply knowing Julianna is on the same property is dragging me down.

Dammit, I'm on the verge of a massive pity party.

Henderson and I head over to the theater. "How can I make this up to Braedyn? Everything's been cast, for the most part," I ask, desperate for something—anything—to absolve me from my sins.

"Give him one of your roles," My co-producer says, as if it's the most obvious solution. Mostly because it is.

"Yeah, man. I ... I'm so stressed I didn't even think of it. It's done. I'll even ask him which one he wants."

I pull Braedyn into the office, apologizing profusely again for taking his role away. He's still pissed, but acquiesces quickly when I offer him his choice of my roles for the rest of the summer.

I really don't care which one he takes.

I'm all out of fucks to give.

After Braedyn leaves, now in the role of Seymore Krelborn in *Little Shop of Horrors*, I head outside for a minute. I need to get in to tear apart the set and start assembling the one for *Rent*. We've got a song run through this evening. Dress rehearsals commence tomorrow. We only have two days to polish it before opening on Thursday. Not to mention we'll start doing the music for *Chicago* tomorrow morning.

It's a lot.

And I'm tired. Not just tired, exhausted.

But on the other hand, I can't imagine living any other way.

Though it'd be nice to just show up and do the plays without having to worry about the business aspect. As much as I'd like to think I'm handling this well, I'm not. Last season, it was all about getting through without Dad.

This year, I'm realizing this isn't sustainable in its current form.

Maybe Mom sees it too, and that's why she's acting so weird. We're going to have to talk, and she's not going to like what I have to say.

I can have my career or I can have The Edison. I can't do both.

And she's certainly proven that she can't run this place. If I don't do it, there's no way it can continue on.

"Hey—" A voice startles me out of my pity party. I hadn't heard Ria approach.

I look up at her, unable to say anything. My realization is making my head spin and my heart heavy. My family's legacy or me.

Gingerly, she sits down next to me. "I had a bad night last night."

"I noticed." I should be supportive. I should tell her it's no big deal. But that takes more energy than I currently have to spare.

"It could have been worse, and I'm doing okay today. They used to last days and weeks and months, even. The treatment I did has really helped."

"That's good," I say flatly.

"Grayson, what's wrong?" Delicately, she touches my shoulder. I shrug her hand off. Her arm falls to her side like it's made of lead.

I look at her. "I'm glad you're feeling better. Truly, I am. But I have nothing to give you right now. I'm out. I don't know how I'm going to get through today let alone this week let alone this summer. I can't be everything to everyone. I've spent it all, and I've got nothing left."

Ria stands up. I expect her to walk away, but she doesn't. Instead she pushes my shoulders back, preventing me from leaning my elbows on my legs. She moves one leg over me and sits down on my lap. Then, she takes my face in her hands. I have no choice but to look at her.

"Did you talk to your mom?"

I don't want to go down this road. No matter what I do, I'm going to let someone down. I'm going to hurt someone I care about. Ria deserves a white knight. Mom needs me to be Dad. They hate each other so no matter who I side with, someone will be hurt. Not to mention I can't run the theater and be true to myself.

To thine own self be true.

Shakespeare's immortal words run through my head. Well, not just through my head. I apparently say them out loud too.

"Listen, Grayson, it's not how I wanted you to find out. Hell, I never wanted you to find out." Her back is ramrod straight, and she's trembling again.

Huh?

"You have to let me explain before you say anything."

As I look into her eyes, I remember something. "Your name is Gloria."

All color drains from her usually golden skin. Her eyes are large as saucers. Slowly, barely perceptibly, her chin dips then rises back up.

"I don't like to be called that anymore," she whispers, her voice tight and strained. "My family, Malachi. That's about it."

"Yes, I know. Your mom called the office looking for you yesterday. I told her there was no one who worked here named Gloria. I almost hung up on her before I realized she was talking about you."

"My mom? Called? You talked to her?"

"Yeah, sorry I didn't get the message to you. By last night ... well, with everything with Julianna and Braedyn and then you ... I forgot. Your mom called. You're supposed to call her back." I add again, "I'm sorry."

Nervously, she clears her throat. "Um, did you talk to *your* mom?"

If she wasn't right in front of me—on top of me—I'd probably curl up again. "Not about you. We fought about theater stuff. Again. She's acting weird. Really closed off, but intervening enough to stand in my way at every turn. I don't know why she's being so difficult. I think she's more messed up from losing my dad than I realized. Maybe it's because she realizes she's going to lose The Edison too ... and it's pushing her over the edge."

I slide my hands onto Ria's thighs, around to her hips and waist. Her muscles are tight enough to bounce a quarter off of. Tension wafts off her in waves.

"Grayson, there's something I have to tell you."

Chapter 29: Gloria

It's now or never. I have to tell him.

I don't want to tell him, but I can't have his mom telling him. Or worse, him googling my full name.

Ria Benedetti brings up a lot of empty results. There are no links, no articles, no pictures, and certainly no video. Gloria on the other hand ...

I look around, realizing that we're in a relatively public spot, just outside the side stage door. It would be easy for someone to walk by. On the other hand, if I don't do it now, I'm going to lose my nerve. I take a deep breath and start.

"You know how it is, doing shows. It's easy to get caught up and there's a lot of ... well, hanky panky that can happen within the cast. At least in college, though I knew it to be true in high school as well."

He nods, a small smile twitching the corner of his lips. "I am familiar with such hanky panky."

"So I was a musical theater major, which meant I did a lot of ... well, musical theater. The summer before my senior year, I did *Into the Woods*. The director was this big shot on campus. He was working on his MFA and even was a TA for a class, and we were all so enamored with him. We all knew he was going to make it big someday. I was convinced he didn't even know I was alive. I was Rapunzel, so I wasn't even in most of the show.

Then, the day after wrap, when we were striking the set, I ended up without a ride home. It was pouring, so I didn't relish the thought of walking in the rain."

I remember that day like it was yesterday. Even though it was August, the dampness in the air made me want to curl up under a thick blanket and drink hot chocolate.

"I kept putting off leaving, hoping the rain would clear or even let up for a minute. But there it was, coming down in sheets. So then, the director, Aaron, came up behind me as I was standing in the doorway and asked if I wanted a ride. Of course, I was all over it. One because it meant not getting soaked. Two because it was Aaron. In the car on the way back, that old Extreme song, 'More Than Words' came on, and he sang it to me."

"He sounds like a douche bag," Grayson interjects.

He has no idea.

"He brought me back to my apartment. My roommate was out. By the time we got inside, we were soaked because he insisted on being chivalrous and walking me to my door, so I invited him up for a towel."

Seriously, it was like something out of a bad rom-com movie. We were barely in my door before the clothing came off, and not because it was wet either.

"So, long story short, we were together. It was great. Aaron was so talented, both as a director and an actor. I don't know why he gave up performing, other than he liked the power rush that came with being in charge. But he was dashing and charming and charismatic."

Thinking back, he was probably also a narcissist. Actually, I've had several therapists confirm he was a narcissist.

"And as for our relationship, he liked ... things." I drop my gaze to the ground as I say this. I want to move away from Grayson, to not be touching him when I say this. Instead, I force myself to stay where I am, with his hands firmly holding onto me.

No matter how much my skin is starting to crawl.

"Let's just say, vanilla sex wasn't his preferred flavor. I didn't actually love a lot of what we did. I mean, it was fine. Pleasurable, even, but not my cup of tea. I never felt really comfortable with it."

"Did you tell him that?" Grayson's voice is strained and low. His face is tight with worry.

"Um, I tried in a joking way. I never came right out and said no. But suffice it to say, it wasn't ever me who initiated with the bondage or the toys." I suck in a deep breath and hold it for seven before exhaling. Now comes the bad part.

"One night, I woke up to Aaron restraining my arms and legs in bed. While I was irritated that he woke me up, and again, I didn't need or particularly want all the *stuff*, it was fine. He only did it that once, so I didn't think much of it."

"You were okay with it?"

I shrug. I wasn't but I didn't say anything. I could have said no. I *should* have said no. I didn't.

"Around the same time that spring, we were doing *Chicago*. I was Roxie. This girl Marissa was Velma. She hated that I was with Aaron. She often said he wasn't critical of me because of our relationship and often alluded to the fact that the only reason I got the part was because I was sleeping with him. In reality, she was a better dancer than me, so that's why the casting shook out the way it did. But she never bought that."

"Is this going to be a life-imitating-art of Velma's husband and sister?" Grayson asks, referencing the plot of the musical.

I shake my head, taking another deep breath before I start. "Apparently, the night Aaron woke me up, he'd turned on the camera so he could record us. Me. The way I was in bed, with nowhere to go, the camera was trained on me. And to the outside observer, it was pretty demeaning. He had some fetishes and dom tendencies, so there was a fair amount of degradation."

I feel the heat rising to my cheeks, but still I muster the courage to look at Grayson. It's taken me a long time and many hours working hard in therapy, including my time with Malachi, to come to terms with the fact that unwillingly going along with Aaron was not the same as consent. It was another one of his power games. I was a victim. But at the time I was young and stupid and star struck. It was hard for me to believe that someone like him wanted to be with someone like me. Of course he did. I was easy to manipulate.

No more.

Grayson, not unexpectedly, is at a loss for words. "I ... I'm sorry. I ... can't ... how awful! It explains a lot. Everything, really." He pauses for a minute. "Is that why you leave your shirt on or have the covers pulled up to your chin?"

I nod. "Yes. No matter how many times I check, it's hard for me to be sure that there's not a camera recording me."

Understanding dawns on Grayson's face. "That's why you took my phone."

Another nod. "I was afraid that once I fell asleep, you'd record me. I know it's not totally rational, but that's why I came here."

His hands travel up my back and pull me into a tight hug. "Thank you for telling me. You didn't have to, but it helps me understand what you're going through so much better. Now I understand why fooling around on the living room floor didn't work for you."

I put my hands on his shoulders and push myself back a little. Staring into his intense green eyes, I say, "No, Grayson, that's not it. I mean, that's not all. There's more to the story."

His hands drop. I close my eyes as I say this last part. "Aaron, in addition to his bedroom proclivities, was a cheater. He was also apparently sleeping with Marissa. That started somewhere around tech week, when I was sick as a dog, as is what happens typically during this last week before the show." I'd often find myself so run down I'd fall ill before every performance.

"So even though she was sleeping with him, it wasn't enough because everyone thought of him and me as a couple. He'd shown her the video. It was on his computer. So the night before closing, Marissa logged into Aaron's computer. As an MFA student, he also worked as a TA in some classes and was considered faculty because he was directing the show. This gave him access to student databases. Like, every student on campus."

I swallow hard. As soon as I say this, it will be out there for him to see. He'll go and look it up and he'll see it. "So Marissa emailed the video to every student at Anniston College, along with every faculty member. At intermission, Marissa went through the lobby, telling people to check their email. When I was onstage that night, almost every person in that audience had seen me naked. Had seen me tied up and debased. And a video like that, sent to over five thousand people, can't be contained."

Believe me, my parents tried. Their lawyers tried. The college's lawyers tried. But if you Google 'Gloria Benedetti,' the video still comes up. As does stories about my lawsuit against the college. And because I was identified in the video, some awesome people out there set the video to Van Morrison's "Gloria," thus ruining the song for me forever.

"It went viral. It's out there still, ten years later. And everywhere I go, I feel like people have seen me naked. Probably because they have."

Grayson lifts me up off his lap and stands up. He begins pacing in front of the bench. I pull my knees to my chest, watching him rake his hands through his hair.

"Gray—"

He doesn't say anything, which might be worse than him freaking out.

I put my forehead down on my knees. Tears fall softly. I told him and survived. I didn't even panic. I'm sure I've lost him though.

I used to think no one would want damaged goods, especially someone who lets themselves be used. But this is who I am and I am worthy of love and respect. One incident of not respecting yourself should not last a lifetime.

Grayson needs to see this too.

Grayson paces for a few minutes. Then finally he squats down in front of me, pulling me into his arms. "I will never, ever let anything like that happen to you. Do you hear me? I will do everything in my power to protect you. And so help me God, if I ever run into either of those pieces of shit, I will pound them into the ground."

I look up. His eyes are red-rimmed and glassy. "Please don't watch the video," I say, even though I know asking him not to will most likely encourage him to.

He takes my hands. "I promise I won't."

We look at each other for a long moment before he stands up, pulling me up off the bench and into his arms. "Ria, I'm so sorry this happened to you."

I nod, unable to speak through the tears.

Tears, not panic.

I push back from Grayson, realizing the enormity of this moment. "Grayson, I'm crying."

"Yes, and I'm sorry."

"No, I'm crying. I'm not panicking. I'm not hyperventilating. Sure, I don't feel awesome, but I'm not in fight, flight, or fright mode. My amphibian brain is no longer in control!"

I want to jump up and down with excitement.

Even after reliving the worst time in my life, I'm still standing.

I'm back, better than before.

Stronger.

Strong enough for anything.

Chapter 30: Grayson

Ria feels better. I can see it in her face. There's a lightness—a glow—that wasn't there previously. Or maybe it was and that Aaron douche bag and Marissa stole it from her.

How could people be so cruel?

I don't understand it, but I know it to be true. It's not like I was all hunky-dory with Julianna taking someone else to bed. *My bed* to be exact.

And she wasn't even apologetic for it. She didn't make excuses or lie. She looked me straight in the eye and said, "Grayson, I'm bored of you. You don't have the potential I thought you did."

She always viewed my ties and loyalty to The Edison as a negative, rather than a positive. I won't lie—there have been times when I've felt the same way. I certainly felt it when the first round of chemo meant that my parents could no longer afford to help me with my rent.

But that's how families work, helping each other out during times of need. If I didn't have the emotional ties and family tradition keeping me here, there's the financial. This is what I can do to support them after they've done so much for me.

Julianna never understood that.

I bet Ria does.

She snuggles into my shoulder, sitting here on the bench outside the stage door. It's like there's been an entire shift in the world. Hard to believe it happened in such a mundane place.

"Grayson, you're quiet."

"I was thinking about things," I answer, unable to articulate the jumps my mind has been making from one thought to another. "You said your parents and brother were supportive?"

I feel her head nod against my shoulder. "Yes. They were what kept me alive. My poor mother. She had to take a leave of absence from her job to take care of me. My brother took up MMA to work out his aggression. Also, like you, I think he planned on some ass-kicking should the occasion arise. My dad didn't know where to look, but he was there you know? He basically pretended like things were normal. It helped, believe it or not."

"That's great. I mean, they sound great. You know what one thing I like about you is?"

"The fact that I'm practically a porn star?" She laughs.

I wince, thinking about my previous deal breaker. *It's not like she has a secret past as a porn star or something.*

She must see my expression. "Too soon for that joke?"

I nod, closing my eyes and trying to regain my train of thought. "I like that you understand family and how it works. That you don't question me for giving up my tour to come here. That you don't tell me I work too hard and that it's not my problem."

All the things I tell myself.

"How would you feel if The Edison went under while you were on tour? Or because you were two hours away and too busy to help?"

"Terrible. I don't know that I could live with that." I think about it. "Not to mention, I got to spend a lot of time with my dad toward the end that I wouldn't have had the opportunity for otherwise."

"Not only have you done and continued to do the right thing, there's one more thing you haven't considered." Her voice is soft, and I have to strain to hear it. Either that, or the grounds of The Edison are becoming more noisy.

"What's that?"

"If you weren't here ... if The Edison wasn't here, we would never have met. You wouldn't have made that terrible joke in Dean's Beans that day. Even your mom firing the contractors has been a blessing. And trust me, finding blessings hasn't always been easy for me. Yet now, because you're in my life, they seem abundant."

My arm around her shoulders tightens as I pull her into me. Her lips, soft and yielding, welcome me. With her, I am home.

"I see some things never change. Another cast, another hook up. You're so predictable,

Grayson." Julianna's voice is nails down a chalkboard.

I sigh, resting my forehead on Ria's for a moment before turning to face Julianna. "Is there something I can help you with? I don't suppose you're here to help with the sets."

Julianna scoffs. I'm aware of Ria tucked into my side, her thigh pressed into mine. "Oh, Julianna, this is Ria. Ria, Julianna. She's the one I told you about."

Truthfully, I haven't told Ria that much. Because Julianna doesn't matter to me. I thought she would. I thought it would hurt to see her again. That being around her would be like having a wound fresh and open.

Frankly, I don't give a shit about her, other than what she can do for The Edison.

God, that's freeing.

But Julianna, being Julianna, strikes an exaggerated pose. "Yes, I'm here as a *favor* to Grayson." Her voice is thick with an accent of old money. Seriously, she never stops performing. "I'm Roxie Hart."

Ria stands up. I notice that even though Julianna has several inches on her, Ria's impeccable posture gives her a commanding air. "Yes, I've heard. Roxie's never been a favorite of mine. She leaves a bad taste in my mouth."

That's an understatement.

"But it's the quintessential part. You'd have to be *mad* not to want to be Roxie." Her accent is killing me. Who does she think she is?

"Actually, I find her rather tedious. I much prefer characters who grow and change. At the end of the day, Roxie is still the same terrible person she always was, stopping at nothing to get what she wants."

"It's an admirable quality, the way she perseveres."

Ria shrugs. "If you want to call it that." She turns to me. "Grayson, I'd better get back to work. Thanks."

She squeezes my shoulder before heading over to the office. She doesn't give Julianna a second glance.

If I was questioning it before, there's no doubt in my mind. I love this woman.

"Can you believe her? I want her out of the cast." Julianna's hands are on her hips.

"She's not in the cast, so no worries. She doesn't do shows." *Anymore. Because some back-stabbing wannabe starlet like you ruined her life*.

Okay, maybe that's not fair to Julianna but on the other hand, her actions in the past twenty-four hours have shown that she's not necessarily filled to the brim with morals and ethics.

"Listen, we're doing music from one to three, then we'll be switching over to running through *Rent*. We're starting with 'All That Jazz' and 'Cell Block Tango.' Obviously we'll run through solos at some point during rehearsal, but you're on your own to work on those."

"Well, then I guess you don't need me today," she scoffs.

"That was sort of the plan. You weren't supposed to be in town until tomorrow. I wasn't going to waste time on your songs if you weren't here. See you later."

I head inside the theater, guilt creeping up because I've been missing for so long. The cast and crew has the *Singing in the Rain* set totally dismantled and scaffolding that will set the framework for the East Village is rising steadily.

"Looks great, everyone! Thank you! We'll be working on our *Chicago* songs from one to three and then switching back to *Rent*."

Josh calls the names of the two songs that we'll be rehearsing. I nod in agreement. Our pit band is small but talented. They're learning a whole new score and songs, all while perfecting the one for this upcoming week. It's hectic and frenetic, but they do it seemingly flawlessly.

Let's face it, the whole operation runs well. If Dad's medical costs hadn't whomped us, we'd be fine. The renovations wouldn't have strapped us for cash. I wouldn't have had to bring Julianna Rickey in to save us.

But I wouldn't have needed Ria either.

I guess Dad's medical care, while it couldn't save his life, may have saved mine.

I'd like to think he's looking down on us, smiling at the way the cards played out.

Chapter 31: Gloria

Every day, the songs from *Chicago* occupy larger chunks of rehearsal, which means I have to listen to them more and more as I'm working in the costume rooms. It would be easier on me if I could work somewhere else right now, but I can't. Camp starts in just a few weeks, so I'm trying to see what we have in inventory that I can make work. With the cost of camp being so high, I don't want parents to have to provide any more costuming than absolutely necessary.

I also don't want to have to make Grayson buy anything new either.

Also, the busier I stay, the less I have to think about the fact that when The Edison closes on Labor Day, I have to go home. There won't be anywhere for me to work. And if the season is successful, Grayson will be heading back to the city, leaving me without a reason to stay here.

If The Edison fails, Grayson will be heading back to the city as well. Either way, he's done with Hicklam. And any way you slice it, I have to figure out what I want to do with my life. Living in New

York City, not that Grayson's asked me to go with him, isn't an option. The city is too big and there are too many people. I'm doing well, but Hicklam is small. It's not the real world. Hell, the nearest Wal-Mart or Target is thirty minutes away.

I can exist here, in this bubble.

And it's not like he's asked me to stay with him.

I still have over a month to figure that out. I won't worry about it now. I'll stay grounded in the present.

The present that has the songs from my trauma playing on repeat. Literally.

With matinees of *Rent* on Saturday and Sunday, there isn't time for rehearsals for *Chicago*, so I had a reprieve for two days. Oddly, during that time, I sort of missed the music that had at one point been the soundtrack to my personal nightmare. It's not bothering me as much today.

I've become desensitized, which means my therapy worked.

"Ria, can you please deliver this to Grayson?" Mrs. Keene startles me as she hands me a drink. I didn't even hear her come in. "He left it on the desk, and I have a meeting starting."

I stare at the water bottle in her hand. He's been singing. I could hear his voice occasionally, as well as when he yells directions to the cast. The big-shot director that Julianna insisted be hired as part of her conditions was scheduled to come in last Friday but he pushed it off to Monday. Here it is

Tuesday morning, a mere ten days away from opening night, and he's still not here. That guy is also playing Billy Flynn. Without a Billy to practice with, Grayson's been singing both parts, in addition to directing. He's got to be parched. I guess I can head into the rehearsal room to help Grayson out. Hearing the songs live won't kill me.

I hope.

Taking the bottle from Mrs. Keene, I don't say anything. We have an uneasy truce, mostly because we don't speak to each other unless absolutely necessary.

Slowly, I stand up from the floor where I've camped out, sorting sizes and colors of various garments. The truth is, my back is pretty sore, so getting up and walking around isn't the worst thing in the world for me. If only I didn't have to head in *there*.

But Grayson needs this, so I buck up and square my shoulders as I go in the room. It's not like I don't know what I'm going to hear or see.

Indeed, the choreography is much the same as when I did it in college. Aaron was a big Fosse fan, so he stuck to the original staging and choreography, which is what they seem to be doing here as well. I mean, Fosse is classic but sometimes it's nice to freshen things up a bit.

However, this is typical Fosse, right down to the shoulder rolls, pelvic pulses, and finger flicks. I could probably still do most of the routines in my sleep. In fact, that was something, at the height of my anxiety, that I did to calm myself down—run through dance routines. The monotony of the steps would help me fall asleep.

They're running through "Me and My Baby," which is one of the lesser known numbers, mostly because it was omitted from the movie version. It was one of my favorites.

And I hate to admit it, but Julianna is good, even if she's not going all out. She's marking steps, but I can see her potential. Her gaze darts to the doorway, where I'm standing, and she stops, mid-song. The orchestra awkwardly stops, random instruments clanging offbeat as the musicians try to figure out what's going on.

Grayson stands up. "What's up, Jules?"

I hate that he has a nickname for her. At least this time, the pit in my stomach is jealousy rather than anxiety. Even so, I don't like it.

"I'm not feeling that well. I think I need a rest. You know how the pollen up in this Godforsaken place is killing me. I'm taking a break."

She looks over at me.

"Jules, we're in the middle of the number. Can't you make it through?"

She plops down dramatically. I think she does everything dramatically. At least everything I've seen so far.

Grayson looks at me and shrugs. I walk cautiously into the room and hand him his water bottle. He smiles and takes a long, hard pull. He nods to a chair, and I take the hint. I sit down tentatively, holding on tight to the front edge of the chair. "Okay guys, pick it up from where the ensemble comes in."

Josh counts it off and they start playing. The ensemble sings their part. The two dancers strut back and forth across the stage, an empty spot where Roxie should be. The last third of the song doesn't call for Roxie's vocals anyway, not until the last line. As the cast is singing, I find myself getting sucked in. My feet twitch and tap with movement, walking through the steps. I can't tear my eyes away.

The song ends and everyone turns to look at me. There's a look of disbelief on several faces. Julianna jumps up. "What exactly do you think you're doing?"

It's only then that I realize I'm singing the last line, holding the note out. It's a B that slides down to G, sustained for twenty-two counts.

I told you my body remembered.

I take a deep breath, refilling my lungs with the air they've just dispelled. Julianna's got her hands on her hips, demanding answers.

"Grayson, what is this?" She waves at me. Like I'm a thing, not a person. "Did you get someone to come in to be my understudy? I told you I didn't want an understudy. I don't need one."

Grayson sighs, raking his hand through his hair. "And you know that that's tempting fate. What if you get the flu? What if you break an ankle? What if you have diarrhea? The best way to endure health and wellness is to have an understudy ready." He glances over at me. "But, no, Ria is not your understudy. She's simply tremendously perceptive and pitches in where we need help. And since you left the cast hanging by not singing, it was best to finish the song as intended. Ria obviously saw that."

"But she *sings*?"

I see the cast sharing knowing glances. They all know I sing. They also know I'm painfully shy and introverted. Well, that's what they think, and I'm content to let them continue on with that assumption.

It's easier than the truth that I don't have the mental strength to do the only thing I've ever loved.

"I'm more of a backstage kind of person." I shrug.

Julianna looks me up and down and then turns away.

I can't believe the man I'm sleeping with slept with her as well. Yuck.

On the other hand, I slept with Aaron while he was sleeping with Marissa, so who am I to talk about yuck?

Josh calls out, "Okay, we should move on. What's next?" He consults his music. "Gray, you want to do it?"

He heaves himself up. "We don't have to. We can go on to the next one."

"There are no more ensemble numbers that don't need either Billy or Roxie so ..." Josh trails off, giving Julianna a sideways glance. I frown. Where is

Billy? The guy Julianna insisted play him, displacing Grayson from his role.

Grayson sighs and takes his place center of the floor. He begins to sing "Mr. Cellophane," lamenting the woes of being the invisible man. He's so soulful and sad, that I can't control the tears from falling down my face. I'm sure Braedyn is talented, but my God, Grayson ...

He's meant to be a star.

He's wasting his talent here. He could be the next Jeremy Jordan or Lin-Manuel Miranda. Or Michael Crawford even.

He should be on Broadway. No more time in a podunk town. No more time spent painting and dry walling with me. He should be on stage, night after night, show after show. If I thought he was charismatic and charming that day in Dean's Beans ... well on stage, he practically glows.

I knew it when I saw him in *Singing in the Rain*. Or at least I thought I did. Compared to this, that performance was nothing.

This song is his soul.

And it's telling me that he feels unseen. Unappreciated. Invisible.

I think of how thoughtful and patient he's been with me. How understanding. So understanding. More than even my dad was ever capable of.

While I could have pictured Grayson in the role of Billy Flynn, the charming, slick lawyer, the role of Amos Hart is much more suited to the true Grayson.

He should win awards for this performance. I mean, hell, they still have over a full week of rehearsals before they open. He's only going to get better.

And then an idea hits me.

Not a fully formed idea, but enough of one. I quickly stand up and hurry out, trying not to disturb the rehearsal.

I've got to find Mrs. Keene.

Chapter 32: Grayson

The good news is that ticket sales for *Rent* went well. Very well.

Ticket sales averaged around seventy-six percent, which means I'm not behind yet. I don't want to tempt fate by saying I'm ahead, even by a percentage. I should actually thank Julianna for switching my role in *Chicago*. By playing Amos, in theory I'm required to be at a lot less rehearsals. Of course, it would help if the director and star of the show showed up so I didn't have to do his job, as well as my own. Once he gets here, I can work on the business end of things, including the social media campaign to sell out these shows. Saturday night of *Chicago* opening weekend is already at ninety-two percent.

They look to be our highest numbers since before Dad died. Actually, since before he got sick. If this season makes the numbers and we can pay back the equity loan, we are in a decent position for next year. Without that loan hanging overhead, if every season had these numbers, I'd be able to hire management staff.

If only.

My alarm goes off and I roll over to find my bed empty. Ria was here when I fell asleep. I'm sure of it. She's been able to come in here at least, but every morning she's gone. I understand.

I don't like it, but I understand it.

On the other hand, I slept in a bit, which I desperately needed. If it hadn't been for my alarm clanging, I'd probably sleep until noon. I'm sure she was up at the break of dawn. As long as there isn't a torrential downpour, she religiously gathers up her mat and heads down to the park. Hell, if she can do yoga on a fifty-degree day, you know she'll be out there on a balmy seventy-degree morning.

She's taking on a lot of stress, being here. Being with me. I see how she's constantly pushing herself outside her comfort zone. She hasn't come into any more rehearsals, but I was surprised to see her in there in the first place. And when she sang ... amazing.

Julianna is talented, no doubt. But she's also getting lazy. She's definitely phoning it in, which makes me apprehensive about how this will all come together. She literally sits down in a chair, flitting her hands through the dance steps, rather than practice with the cast. It's not hard to see the irritation on the face of the ensemble members, as well as the other characters, who are trying to act without the two main leads.

Yes, our star and director, A.J. something, had to take an extra week to "reset his energy" before coming to us. Julianna went back to the city on Friday to be with him. They're coming back today. We need to get the *Rent* set torn down so we can get up on stage as soon as possible tomorrow morning. It's going to be a long week.

Yippee.

I can hardly wait.

Basically, rehearsals have been a gigantic clusterfuck. This needs to be our best show ever. We're four days from opening, and we've never run the full show with the leads. I know Julianna knows the show back and forth, though she rarely does it full out. But what I don't know is how much this A.J. guy is going to want to change the staging and choreography. In some brief text messages, he told me to "keep it pure to the original." Of course, then he wanted the black costuming which hails to the 90s revival rather than the 70s Fosse original.

It's not hard to see this guy is a douche bag.

I hope he can sing and act and dance as much as Julianna says he can. It would be like Julianna to leave us in the lurch with some schmuck who can't carry a tune. He's well known and respected as a director. His YouTube profile seems legit, but you know you can't trust everything you see on the internet.

A feeling of dread hits my stomach like bad seafood. I am such an idiot. I can't believe the fate of my family's legacy in the hands of Julianna Rickey. From what I've seen, she's fine in the role of Roxie

Hart. Talented even. But still, I can't shake the notion that somehow, this is all going to blow up.

And there's that nagging feeling that I should have cast an understudy again.

I head to the kitchen to get some coffee, only to find my mother and Ria bent head to head at the table. They both startle when I walk in, obviously up to something.

"What's up?"

"Nothing," Ria says quickly.

Last I knew, Mom was suspicious of Ria. Now the two look like Pinky and the Brain trying to plan to take over the world. It doesn't take a rocket scientist to figure out they're up to something.

"No, seriously, what are you two plotting?"

"What makes you think we're up to anything?" Mom asks, trying to make her eyes wide and innocent. For the record, I did not get my acting chops from her.

I pour myself a cup of coffee and sit down, stirring the cream and sugar in. "Because you have your heads together, you're whispering, and you both looked like the cat that ate the canary the minute I walked into the room."

Ria stands up. "Honestly, Grayson. Don't be so oversensitive. We were talking. That's it. Sheesh. Now I've got to run and go see Malachi."

I cock my head. "Malachi? I thought you were done with your sessions."

"This is a counseling session, to check in and see how everything is working for me. Like a tune up for your car, but for my brain."

I grab her as she walks by, pulling her onto my lap. "And how is everything working for you?"

She laughs as she starts to put her arm around my shoulder. I'm sure if Mom wasn't sitting right there, she'd kiss me. As it is, this much contact is a lot more than she's used to doing in front of someone else. Her arm hovers there tentatively before dropping down to her side.

In order to lighten what has the potential to become a heavy mood, I swing her legs to the front, shifting her onto my right leg, and then slide my right hand up the back of her shirt. I begin singing the chorus to "We Both Reached for the Gun," which is always staged in this position. Ria laughs and flops into the movements expected of a very guilty Roxie Hart as her lawyer, Billy Flynn, spins a tale of disbelief for the media.

It's fun, playing around with Ria like this. As we finish, Mom starts clapping. "You two would be great together on stage."

I steal a glance at Ria, whose face is flushed. I know we would. I wonder if there's any way I could convince her to try it.

Ria shakes her head. "I'm afraid those days are long behind me. There's too much history ... too much out there. Too much at stake for me to ever put myself in that position again."

Mom stands up, clearing her coffee mug to the sink. "That's understandable. And a shame, because I can see how talented you are. But understandable nonetheless."

After Mom leaves, I pull Ria in close to me. "You really won't ever consider going back out there? It's such a waste for you to be in the office or behind the scenes."

Ria pulls away, standing up. "That's like saying that because an Olympic athlete can never compete again, they don't have anything else to offer. I'm not on the stage because I can't be."

I put my hands up, "Whoa. Ria. I didn't mean to upset you."

She puts her hands on her hips. "I saw a speech online this one time. It was by an athlete. A ski jumper named Kaitlin Reynolds. She had been training for the Olympics and about a year before women's ski jumping was finally allowed into the Olympics, she was injured and could never ski again. I remember in the speech she said, 'Sometimes, no matter how hard you work, life doesn't go as planned. Not achieving that one goal you've decided is important doesn't mean you're a failure.' I wrote that quote down. Actually, I wrote it over and over, like a mantra to myself. Because at the end of the day, on top of the anxiety and panic and fear that everyone around me had seen me naked, there was the disappointment in myself. That I'd never become what I was convinced I should be."

"But it's not your fault."

"Isn't it? What's stopping me from walking right back on that stage and belting it out? It's not like I don't know what to do. I obviously do. The only thing preventing me from getting up there is me. But I also know that if I do get up there, it will break me beyond repair."

My heart breaks a little, listening to her anguish.

"I want the stage more than you know." She looks at me. "Or perhaps you do know. But you get it every day. I can never have it. Like taking a kid to the candy store and not letting them eat. That's how I feel here."

And then her hands fly to her mouth, eyes wide with shock. "Oh my God, Grayson. I didn't mean that. I love being here. I lo—"

I stand up, pulling her tightly into me. "I love you too."

I do. With all my heart. There's not an ounce of doubt in my mind that I am head over heels for Gloria Benedetti.

Chapter 33: Gloria

"But what are you going to do when the season ends?"

I hate that my Mom is always the voice of reason, and I hate that she always asks this question. I also hate that my mind keeps going back to Grayson saying he loves me. He can't mean that. It's too soon.

He doesn't really know me. He hasn't seen the video. If he had, he wouldn't be able to love me.

I try to pull myself back to the conversation at hand, as opposed to the one that occurred an hour ago in Grayson's kitchen. Has it only been an hour? Time loses all meaning when your mind is reeling from a declaration of love. "That's too far ahead for me to think. I've got camp starting in two weeks. That's going to take a lot of time and effort. I'm focusing on that." Not to mention I'm on the edge of my seat with what I'm working on for Grayson. I'm nervous about this plan of mine to help make The Edison a hit.

"I know, and I'm glad to see you able to focus."

Her words reference the years where I could barely remember what I was doing when I walked from one room to the next.

"I'm back." But even as I say it, I know it's not true. That me—that Gloria—died that day, still standing on the stage, realizing something was amiss. This me—Ria—is slower. More cautious. So much more cautious. Ready to be hurt. Afraid to be loved. Afraid to love.

Except, I'm taking that chance. At least I'm trying to.

Grayson's made it possible for me to do that. He showed me that I can have faith in someone. That I can be vulnerable and not have that vulnerability exposed. I can't fully let go. I'm not sure I'll ever be able to do that again. But there are times—fleeting moments—with Grayson when I feel it might just be possible.

After hanging up with my mom, I spend another hour or so in the costume closet. I've got a clear vision of how I want this show to look. I cannot wait for the campers to get here. Grayson insists I'll have some real talent to work with. And it doesn't even matter if I don't. I hope to create an experience that helps these kids fall in love with theater. That they find camaraderie and confidence. That it makes them proud of themselves and of each other.

All the things I found in it before Aaron and Marissa ripped it away from me.

I'm excited to give that to them.

Not to mention, being in the costume closet is keeping my mind occupied. Today is the day that *Backstage Magazine* is sending someone to cover rehearsal. That's what Mrs. Keene told me in the kitchen this morning before Grayson came in. It works perfectly because Julianna Rickey and her big-shot director will be here and in full effect. *Backstage Magazine* doesn't normally cover off-Broadway this far off of Broadway, but Mrs. Keene pulled some strings. The reporter is going to do a feature on The Edison and Grayson. Hopefully it will be enough to keep the audiences flocking in droves to little old Hicklam.

And hopefully someone recognizes how talented Grayson is.

I head over to the theater to watch some of the rehearsal. I don't know who the reporter is or when they will be in. I think they're coming on the noon train, which will have them arriving in a few hours. While I'll be happy when they move onto the next show, I'm tolerating the music from this one more than I thought I would. Since my treatment with Malachi, I can handle things in small bits, desensitizing me to the things that once totally triggered me.

I don't even freak out when Grayson calls to me. "Hey Ree—can you do me a huge favor?" Then he smiles that hundred-watt smile. The one he knows I can't resist.

"Anything for you." I smile back, my knees a little mushy. A flutter of excitement runs through me, knowing what I've arranged for him.

"We've been running "We Both Reached for the Gun," and it's just not the same without a Roxie. Can you do it with us? I'm filling in for Billy." He pauses and exhales. "Again."

"Where are Julianna and her big shot director?" I sort of forget that we're in a room full of people when I say this, but from the laughter and snickers, I'd say they are Team Gray all the way. I look around, but don't see her here.

"I guess they missed the early train. Supposedly they will be here soon."

Panic begins to swell. I look around again. I don't see an unfamiliar face here, so at least the reporter isn't in yet. I look at my watch. It's already noon. "Don't you guys open this week? Like in a few days? Shouldn't they be here rehearsing?" The murmurs and grumbles going through the cast indicate that I'm not the only one who's had these thoughts. Perhaps the only one stupid enough to say them out loud, yes. But this is definitely not a novel thought.

Then I realize Grayson's asked me a question. One he expects an answer to. In front of all these people.

Shit.

How could he put me on the spot like this?

I glance around and see the weariness in the eyes of the cast. Between their grueling schedule of running one show at night and rehearsing another all day, they're already wiped out and it's early in the season. And no matter how hard they work, they can only do so much without the two lead roles here.

I need to consider doing this for them. Let me think. We're in the rehearsal space. The same one used for the after-show cabaret, so it's not like I'd be up on stage. The crew is busy taking the *Rent* set down, so it's the last rehearsal in this make-shift space. Maybe I could do this. I'm filled with equal parts dread and fear, with a hefty dose of yearning swirling about. Want. Need. The desire to reclaim this part of me that was so big.

That I've missed so much.

Grayson walks up to me where I'm standing, frozen and paralyzed with indecision. "Ree? It's no big deal. Don't over think. And breathe."

His words snap me out of my immobility. No big deal? *No big deal?* I thought he got it. I thought he understood. Just as I am about to launch into him, he says, "It's no big deal if you don't want to run it. It's a long shot, but I thought I'd ask."

Air whooshes out of my lungs.

He does get it.

Buoyed by that knowledge and a surge of love filling my chest, I square my shoulders and declare, "Let's give it a rip." I smile tightly, trying to quell the nervousness building in my stomach. I don't really have to do anything, other than sit on Grayson's lap and flop a bit. With the exception of one spoken line, I don't even sing in the song.

This is for the cast who have been working their asses off and need the lead characters to play off of. They're professionals enough to adjust to the nuances and changes that Julianna and her BSD (as I've now come to think of him—I know he goes by some initials, but I can't remember which ones) will bring. So if this helps them, I can try.

I can do this for Grayson.

I know he'll protect me if things start to go south.

I begin ransacking the corners of my brain, trying to remember what I'm supposed to do and come up blank. It was always this way for me right before a dance or performance. I was famous for saying, "how does this one start?" I could never think about it. If I knew it (which I usually did), the minute the music started, my body knew what to do. I take a deep breath as the music starts, willing the same thing to happen.

Even though we'd just played around with this in the kitchen a few hours ago, now it's different. I need more tension in my arms. Is my head in the right position? This is all about broken lines and the fluctuation between tension and flaccidity.

Aaron's words begin to float through my head. *Tighten your cheeks. Widen your eyes. Extend your fingers. Tilt your chin left. Up a little. Not too much. Broken lines.*

His directions fill my mind and my chest tightens. *He's not here. He's not here.* I chant in time with the music. *Not here not here not here.* I force myself to focus on the nuances of the movement. Of the song. Of Grayson's calming hand on my back.

Calming that is until we get to the chorus, and I bounce on Grayson's leg like a box of rubber balls dropped off a roof. It's physically demanding, not to mention exhausting. I get a little dizzy going from that to the upright position so quickly as Grayson stands me up for the bridge. I wobble a little, catching my balance only before I topple over. Definitely not the still statue I should be portraying.

As Grayson pulls me back to his lap, he winks, breaking me out of my too serious thoughts. I'm not performing this on stage. I don't have to be perfect. We're only here to help out. I could be having fun with this.

Fun. A novel concept.

And so I do have fun, shimmying and clapping, standing up for the chugs and Charleston toward the end. Grayson pulls me down into the final pose and the music crashes to the end.

I did it.

Sure, I'm breathing heavy, but this time it's from exertion rather than panic. I may not be able to do this in front of people, but I got through this.

Aaron has no longer won.

Slowly, I'm reclaiming my life.

I can't wait to tell Malachi.

Grayson pulls me into a tight hug, swinging my feet off the ground as he spins in a circle. "That was fantastic, babe. I can't believe you just did it all like that. You haven't even been watching our rehearsals, have you?"

He puts me down and I look at my feet. They should be in character shoes, not these sneakers. "Muscle memory."

Henderson pushes in. "Did you say muscle memory? When did you play Roxie?"

Ugh, I don't want to get into this. I certainly don't want to give him any details that he could use to look me up.

Why hello, paranoia. Good to see you're back, old friend. Wouldn't want you to have missed this good time.

"A while ago. I guess I just remember it."

Grayson steps back, one of the dancers talking to him. "Okay sure. I'm sure it's no problem." Eyes dart toward me.

I don't know what the no problem is, but I'm not sure I like the sound of it. Especially not with the way he's looking at me. "Ree, can you do 'Me and My Baby?' We all know you know it, and the dancers and ensemble want to run it."

I look at the eager eyes, all trained on me. My heart is still pounding, and I can't tell if it's exhilaration or panic. They're sort of similar in how they make my body feel.

I'm probably wrong, but I'll go with exhilaration, if only to stay on the positive side of things for once. "I don't know if I remember the dance. Or if it's even how you are choreographing it. What if I mess it up more?"

"You saw it the other day. Do you remember enough to walk through it at least?"

One of the dancers steps forward. "It's okay if you don't really know it. I just need to make sure I have the timing. It's different when someone is singing. We won't pick you up, if you don't want."

I think about that, running the song in my head. They need to look their best when the reporter shows up, and that's going to be hard if they are missing the main characters. "A straight arm lift, right?"

He nods and the other dancer in the routine steps forward. "Put your arms out."

I comply and they lift me up. My armpits hurt when they put me down, unused to the pressure of being lifted from there. I have a feeling my whole body is going to be hurting. While it's all familiar, I'm sorely out of practice. Quite literally.

Grayson looks at me. "You okay?"

I nod. I think I am, at least. Remember, I'm not on not a stage. People aren't watching.

"You ready?"

I give him a small smile. "About as ready as I'll ever be." I turn my attention toward the orchestra. "Hit it, maestro."

The actors start their dialogue which leads in. And then it's my turn to start singing. My voice is a little shaky at first. But as the tempo picks up, I find my footing. I remember enough of the staging to move downstage and upstage, left and right with the two male dancers. I flub some words, unsure of the verse. One of the dancers feeds me the line and I pick back up. It's almost time for the ensemble to take over singing while we have our dance break. It's familiar when they move into line with me, and I am almost solid on the lift.

Almost.

I teeter a little on the landing, making me miss a step.

Singing is one thing. Dancing is another. Putting them together is like trying to thread a needle while running a relay race. My head is absolutely swimming and while I remember moving stage right while doing a series of kicks, I can't think of what comes after that.

I can practically hear Aaron yelling "Good God, Gloria, you have got to work on your cardio. You look like you are going to pass out." He was always on me about that. My burning chest chides me, tormenting me with his voice inside my head.

I feel like I'm going to pass out. I swallow the air, moving from one side of the stage to the other in a series of runs and jumps, faltering and falling behind. I have to catch my breath for those endnotes. Everyone's heard me sing them already. I can't flop now.

I suck in a deep breath, ready to belt when I hear Aaron say, "With an inhale like that, you're never going to sustain. Jesus Gloria, I thought I taught you better."

But this time, the voice isn't in my head. It's coming from the doorway where he is standing. With Julianna.

Now I don't have to wonder if it's exhilaration or panic.

I know for certain.

Chapter 34: Grayson

I always thought I understood what a deer in headlights looked like. Hell, you live in this part of the country, and by my age, you've seen a lot of deer in headlights.

Ria brings new meaning to this.

All color has drained from her face and the sharp breath she inhaled to sing her final notes is trapped. Her body is rigid and taut. Her pupils take up her entire iris, blocking out all of that gorgeous mahogany, leaving large black endless voids.

"Hey, don't freak out. It's okay. No one expected you to get up and do a perfect performance. It's fine."

She stands there, frozen. Though as I step closer, I realize she's not standing still. She's shaking. I need to do something. I—

"Christ, Grayson. I told you I didn't want anyone being my understudy. Especially not *her*. She's terrible. Where did you even find her?"

I turn to see Julianna and A.J. in the doorway. I'd heard someone call out while the number was running, but I was so focused on Ria that I didn't pay attention. And she still needs my focus.

There's a very good possibility she's going to pass out.

I have to get her out of here. Turning back to her, I scoop her up in my arms and make a dash for the door. At least Julianna and A.J. have the decency to step aside as I brush past. I bring Ria into the office and close the door behind me.

If I ever wondered what terror looked like, now I know. It's not the overdone stage representation I'm used to. Her eyes take up most of her face. There's a blankness to them that's quite unsettling, even as they dart back and forth, unseeing. Her cheeks are drawn and her mouth is frozen open. Despite the fact that I'm holding her close, I know she's so far away right now.

I sit down, still holding her, and pull her into me as close as I can. My arms tighten around her as I begin to rock back and forth like you would with a baby. Softly, I murmur into her hair, "It's alright. I've got you. You're okay. You're safe." Over and over I say this, hoping she hears me.

A minute goes by. Then five. Then ten.

There's no change. She's still the same. I wonder if this is what they used to describe as catatonic? I don't know what to do. I'm not helping her. Am I harming her? A wave of guilt and dread washes over me, nearly causing me to lose my grip on her.

I did this to her.

I made her get up there when she wasn't comfortable. Wasn't ready. I exposed her, like I promised I wouldn't.

I thought she was better. I didn't know she was this fragile. This easily broken. I thought ...

It doesn't matter what I thought. This isn't about me. This is about Ria and I need to fix this. I have to help her. Hugging her tight with one arm, I use my other to fish my phone out of my pocket. Quickly, I Google the number for Malachi Andrews. Thankfully, he answers.

"Hello?"

"Hey Malachi. It's Grayson Keene, up at The Edison." I cut right to the chase before I have to waste any time on pleasantries. "I need you to come up here immediately. Ria needs you. It's bad."

"On my way," he says succinctly before disconnecting.

I drop the phone and tell her, "Malachi's on his way. He'll make you feel better. He'll be here soon."

I'm not even lying when I tell her this. Thankfully Hicklam's such a small place that I can assure her help will be here soon. I continue rocking and murmuring reassurances, totally certain that I'm not doing the right thing.

What is the right thing when you've hurt someone you care about?

Malachi comes running in. As I glance up, I can see multiple members of the cast hovering outside the office. I mouth, "Go away" and hope they understand. I appreciate their caring. I'm sure Ria will too.

Malachi looks at her and then at me. "What happened?"

God, I feel like such a shit. "I asked her to step in and do a number. The actress was late getting back and the cast needed to run the songs. We did one together and she was fine. I asked her for another." I look at Ria who is still staring off into nowhere. "She was a little hesitant, so I sort of begged her. She was fine. A little trouble with some of the words and dance steps, but considering it's been ten years, you know, she was great. And then ... she wasn't."

God, what she could have been if only she hadn't been destroyed? How could people be so selfish?

"He's here."

Her voice is so faint, I can barely hear it.

"What?" Malachi asks.

Still unblinking, she responds, "He's here. At first, I thought I was hearing him in my head. His directions. His critique. But it's not in my head. It's real."

Malachi looks at me. "Who's here?"

I shrug, thinking that maybe she's hallucinating or something. "*Him*," she hisses. "*He's here.*"

I look at Malachi, not sure what she's talking about. Malachi narrows his eyes. "Him? Who's him? Who's here?" Malachi also looks around the office, as if expecting someone else to be in here with us. When he sees that no one else has mysteriously snuck he, he turns his gaze toward me.

"Who was at the rehearsal?"

I shake my head, not able to make sense of her words. "The cast and pit band. All people she's met before. She'd been in rehearsal for a while too." My mind feverishly rewinds, trying to go through what had happened. "The actress who Ria was filling in for came in, with our director. They were late getting up here from the City, which is why we needed Ria to fill in."

Jesus, Gloria, I thought I taught you better than that.

A.J.'s words, dripping with condescension float through my brain. I knew he was a prick before I even met him, not that I've even officially met him. It's going to be a long month with them if he's criticizing the minute he walks in the door.

But something's not right.

Jesus, Gloria.

Gloria.

He called her Gloria.

My blood runs cold as my skin tightens. It can't be. I'm sure my facial expression mirrors hers. "That's *him*?"

A.J.

Aaron.

She nods, almost imperceptibly.

Rage rises within me and if I weren't holding tightly onto Ria, I'd be charging after that piece of shit. I'm not sure who is shaking now. I have a feeling it's me.

Malachi needs no further explanation. "Ria, I need you to do something."

What the fuck, man? How can he ask anything of her in this state?

"Ria, stay with me. I need you to tell me one thing you taste." He looks at me and mouths, "rub her scalp" while motioning me for me to do so. Okay.

"Blood. I bit my cheek." Her voice is barely recognizable.

"Tell me two things you smell," Malachi continues.

"Grayson and the lawn was just cut."

"Three things you can hear."

"I hear Grayson's heart, and it's too fast. I hear your voice. I hear ..." She pauses, straining. "I hear the lawn mower."

I hadn't heard most of those things, until she pointed them out.

Malachi keeps going. "Four things you can touch."

"Grayson's shirt." Her hands start to move, no longer clutched into fists by her heart. "His pants. His hair." She reaches up and runs her finger through my hair. Then she extends her finger and runs it along my mouth. "His mouth."

"And lastly, five things you can see."

Ria looks around the room. "You, Grayson. The desk. Papers." Her gaze turns back to me. "Your eyes."

I find myself staring into her own eyes. They are deep and endless pools of sadness and pain.

"Better?" Malachi asks.

"Yes," I respond. As Ria's been itemizing all her senses, I've been mentally cataloging mine as well. And I do feel more calm.

Malachi laughs a little and the edges of Ria's mouth pull into the smallest of smiles.

"Right. You didn't mean me," I say sheepishly. "What now?" I look from Malachi to Ria and back again. No one says anything for a moment. Then two. "Um, Malachi, can I talk to you for a minute in the hall?"

He stands up, so I work to gently position Ria down on the loveseat where I'd been holding her. This loveseat was in our den when I was little. I used to use it for the basis of my blanket fort. What I wouldn't give to build one and bring Ria inside and never come out again. She looks more relaxed, but isn't back to her old self.

Her old self.

I don't think I've ever seen it. Maybe passing glimpses here and there. After ten years, I wonder if she can ever get back to it again.

I think I need to set up an appointment with Malachi, even so I can better understand what's going on with Ria, as well as what to do or not to do. It's certainly going to be a lot more complicated than I ever realized. I have to know what I should look out for.

Like casting her assailant in my show.

"What do we do now? I have to get her out of here. I can't have her in this building."

Malachi nods. "I agree. I take it she's staying here with you?"

Now it's my turn to nod. "At the house. She has a room there. Will she feel safe there?"

Malachi purses his lips together, thinking for a minute before he speaks. "I think that depends on what you're going to do."

"Right. Right. Of course," my head is bobbing up and down as fast as my mind is racing. *What I'm going to do*. "I'll get the bastard out of here right now."

Malachi pulls out his phone and taps furiously. "I'm texting Malyia to see if the flat Ria had rented is still available. I think it is, but I want to double-check. She might feel more secure there."

"Yeah, of course," I'm still nodding. "Whatever she needs."

Malachi looks at me sternly. "Grayson, you have to fire him. Right now. Get him out of town. If you value Ria at all, make him gone."

Malachi turns back into the office.

Obviously he's going. I can't have him here. There's no doubt about it.

Chapter 35: Gloria

"Mom." My voice is hoarse, whispered, as if I've been yelling or screaming. I haven't. I haven't even been crying. It seems my vocal cords are as paralyzed as the rest of me.

"What's wrong, baby?"

"Can you come out here? Right now? I need you."

"I'm on my way. I'll be there as soon as I can."

She disconnects, not even bothering to ask why or what happened. I look at the clock. It's about two in the afternoon. Depending on how long it takes her to leave, she'll be here before dawn at the latest. She'll drive all night to get to me.

I should call her back and tell her to be safe; that I'm fine.

I'm not fine. I'm the furthest from fine there is.

Malachi brought me back to my flat. He helped me search for hidden cameras, wordlessly picking up item after item and showing them to me, so I would know I was safe. He pulled the curtains closed over the drawn blinds, making the place small and dark.

He suggested I call my mom.

Now here I sit, in the dark and silence, hugging my knees and rocking back and forth. What are the odds of this happening?

Let's face it, none of this would have happened if I'd stayed far, far away from the theater world, like I knew I should have. Why did I let myself get sucked back in again?

Grayson.

God, Grayson.

I can't really say what happened after I realized ... you know. Time escaped me. I don't think I lost consciousness, but there's a distinct void from that chunk of the day. I do know how he protected me. How he called Malachi. And I saw the look in his eyes. He's going to kill Aaron.

I need to leave so this doesn't ruin him. The Edison.

The reporter from *Backstage Magazine*.

It all comes flooding back to me. Someone is coming here to do a story on how wonderful this place is. And they're going to walk into the most epic shit show ever.

Fuck.

I have to stop Grayson before he blows up and ruins everything.

Not even bothering to put shoes on, I run out my door and up the hill. Small stones cut into my feet, but I barely feel them. I don't feel my body at all. It's like my head isn't connected to the rest of me.

I'm too late.

I hear the melee before I reach the door. My arms feel like Jell-O as I try to pull the outside doors to the theater open. They might as well be made of lead. I finally manage to pull it open wide enough to squeeze through and run to the rehearsal room.

It's as I feared. Grayson and Aaron roll around on the floor trading blows. The majority of the cast stands around, gawking and shocked. Frantically, my gaze searches for someone who can help. Where is Henderson?

I don't see him so I rush forward, and try to grab Grayson's arm. He moves too quickly, and I pitch forward, tumbling into the fray. Before I know it, I'm flat on my back, staring up into the eyes of Aaron Michaels. A sinister grin spreads over his face as his arms form a cage around me. "I guess I shouldn't be surprised, Gloria. You always did like it a little rough."

This time, instead of fear and panic filling me, anger surges through my veins. My leg rises, swiftly and sharply bringing my knee into contact with his groin. Aaron's eyes widen in shock as his face contracts. His body slumps over as he cradles his genitals, a low moan emanating from his lips.

I look over and see Grayson on his hands and knees, panting, Blood trickles from the corner of his mouth and from his right eyebrow. His nose is fine. No black eye. I glance down at his hand, which doesn't appear bruised or broken either.

Leave it to two actors to fight without actually inflicting damage.

As Aaron is still rolling around, moaning, I stand. And then I do what I've needed to do for a decade. I step closer and kick him in the nuts again. "You are scum. You are below the most worthless, scummiest scum of the earth." I pull back my leg to kick him for a third time when I'm pulled back.

"That's enough, Ria." I look to see Henderson holding me back. He picked a fine time to intervene.

Then I hear the shrieking. "We are going to sue you. All of you. You are going down. Someone call the police. You are all witnesses to this assault."

Dear God, does Julianna Rickey *ever* stop performing?

As the adrenaline continues to course through my veins, I downshift from a physical attack to a verbal. And I direct it at Julianna. "Go ahead. Call the police. But before you do, will you answer me one question?"

She holds her phone in one hand, raising an eyebrow at me.

I don't know if she's going to give me a chance to speak or not, so I quickly say, "Does he restrain and degrade you every time you have sex, even though you don't want it? Does he slap you across the face and tell you you're a worthless slut, but then call it foreplay? Does he say, 'aw, come on, you know you like it rough. You know it's better that way?'"

Her color blanches, which only gives me the strength to continue. "And did you know that when he's humiliating and degrading you, he's recording it?"

Her hand, holding the phone, drops down to her side. She looks at him and then back at me.

"Julianna, I don't like you. Not at all. But realize that a leopard doesn't change his spots. Save yourself. Get out now before he does to you what he did to me."

Her eyes grow wide for a minute and then narrow, laser beam focus on me. Uh oh. This is not going to be good.

"So, you're Gloria. It's nice to see you with some clothes on. I'm used to seeing you ..." she looks me up and down. "Differently."

"Get out." Mrs. Keene says, marching in. Standing next to her is a guy in skinny jeans and a flannel, despite it being mid-June. "Julianne, you need to leave now."

Grayson stands up. "Mom, don't. A.J., you need to leave, but Julianna please don't go. We need to talk this through."

What?

Grayson looks at me and shakes his head. He mouths, "I'm sorry."

I don't need to hear anything else. I spin on my heel, my bare skin ripping with the friction. I don't care. My toes could be falling off and I wouldn't be able to feel them.

I never want to feel again.

"Gloria, wait!" Mrs. Keene comes running after me. "Please. Let me help you."

I stop, halfway down the gravelly driveway. I will not cry. I will not cry. *I will not cry.*

Dammit.

"Ria," she touches my arm and says softly, "*Gloria*, please. Come into the house. Let me take care of you. Your feet."

I look down to see a bloody mess. Once my eyes see them, my brain begins to process the pain, and then suddenly, I can barely walk. Tears spill, fat and hot, down my cheeks.

If Grayson were here—if he really *loved* me—he'd sweep me up in his arms and carry me into the house. But he's not because he's inside The Edison, begging Julianna to stay. All the proof I need that he doesn't love me because I am not worthy of love.

Then it hits me: if Julianna stays, undoubtedly Aaron will as well.

This town isn't big enough for the both of us.

Hell, this planet isn't big enough.

I finally manage to limp into the kitchen and fall into a chair. Mrs. Keene sets about with a towel and a bowl of water, washing my feet like Mary Magdalene did to Jesus in *Jesus Christ Superstar*.

Only now, I am the one not worthy to be in the company of someone like her. This day has gone to hell in a handbasket, and it's all my fault. If it hadn't been for me, this wouldn't have blown up. And definitely not in front of the reporter from *Backstage Magazine*.

I cover my face with my hands, cringing at what this coverage is going to do to The Edison.

It's all my fault.

"Gloria, it's okay," Mrs. Keene murmurs. "We will get this straightened out and make sure you are safe."

Every since I extended the olive branch and came up with the plan to help out Grayson, Mrs. Keene and I have found a peace with each other. I'm thankful for that, as well as her protection right now.

"From the ass kicking she was giving, I'm not sure she has to be the one to worry about being safe." The voice startles me. Oh shit, it's the reporter. I knew he'd seen everything, but I'd sort of hoped that he vanished or something.

But no. He's here. And true to his reporter nature, he's like a dog with a bone. "Linda, do you want to fill me in on what's going on? You don't seem upset that she was attacking one of the biggest directors on the Great White Way."

Biggest directors? He's made it? I probably would have known if I hadn't avoided mention of all things theater since it happened. This is so unfair. His life has become everything he's ever wanted while mine is in tatters.

"Why don't you go ask him?" Mrs. Keene answers. The reporter's mouth opens and then closes. "No, seriously. Go talk to him. See what he says. And then come back to us and we'll tell you why you will also want to kick him in the nuts."

I stifle a small giggle as the reporter leaves. "Mrs. Keene—"

"Linda. Call me Linda."

"Li ... Linda." I stumble over the words. "Why did you do that? You can't afford to piss off Aaron any more. Or have bad publicity. We need to fix this. *You* need to fix this, not make it worse."

"We need to worry about fixing you. That's our number one priority." Linda's words are meant to comfort but instead they chafe. Why isn't Grayson the one saying them? Oh right. Because he's chasing after *them*. They are what's important to him right now. That and saving The Edison.

"But what about The Edison?" I ask feebly. I don't care about The Damn Edison.

A look of pain shoots across her face. "I doubt there's much we can do now." Her gaze shifts out the window. "I ... I failed my parents. And grandparents. And Allen. It's on me."

Suddenly, the reporter sprints back into the kitchen, scraping a chair across the floor before sitting down on it backward. He extends his hand to me. "Carson Reuben, *Backstage Magazine*. But you already knew that."

Limply I shake his hand while nodding in agreement. "You're already back?"

"Mr. Michaels refused to speak with me."

Sounds like him. I don't even have the words to correctly identify the type of scum he is.

"So I'd like to hear your side of the story. And if I only have one side to publish, so be it." He gives me a knowing wink.

Holy shit, here it is. Suddenly, I'm very hungry for a dish called revenge. I hear it's best served cold.

Justice shall be mine.

Chapter 36: Grayson

Ria, the woman I love, is in pieces, and I'm over here trying to save a show.

But it's not just a show. It's three weeks of almost sold-out shows that we need to pay back the loan. To keep the theater. To keep our home.

If I have to cancel this show and refund the tickets ... we won't make it. My mom will lose everything. All I have to lose is Ria. In other words, my everything.

How do I choose between the two?

I have to get Julianna to stay and fulfill her commitment. I want that bastard off my property but I need her.

"Julianna, wait." I catch up to her in the front parking lot.

"Grayson, you cannot be serious. You cannot think A.J. and I will stay here and be treated like this. We should press charges."

That's all I'd need to drive the last nail in The Edison's coffin. I need to play this cool. She cannot get wind of my desperation, which I'm sure is radiating off me in waves.

Maybe it's just nervous sweat.

And where is the douche bag anyway? I glance around, relieved not to see him. If he were here, I'd rip his throat out.

"Listen, I think we need to take a breather and talk this through. Surely there's some sort of compromise we can come to. Let's go into town and get a drink at Biff's and talk."

Julianna shakes her head, giving new meaning to the word haughty. "Why should we? What's in it for us? You've humiliated us in front of everyone."

That gives me pause. "Excuse me?"

"How do you think A.J. is supposed to go back in there and face everyone? You attacked him and let your girlfriend assault him. How do you think that makes us look?"

I've heard enough. I'm about to launch into her when she continues. "But you know, Grayson, you and I go way back. I could *probably* be persuaded to stay."

There's no doubt she's laying a trap, yet still I walk right in. "On what terms?" I wouldn't put it past her to ask for a share of ownership or something ridiculous like that.

"We'll stay if *she* goes."

I burst out laughing at her utter ridiculousness.

"God, Julianna, you can't be serious. There's no way in hell this piece of garbage will ever set foot on my stage. And do you really think I'd toss Ria aside for you?"

At this point, A.J. walks up, sliding his phone in his pocket. I don't know where he's been hiding. I try to remember killing him would be bad.

"But I'm the only one who can do the show. Your choice. Us or her."

There is no choice. I don't hesitate one second. If Julianna cannot separate herself from this twatwaffle, then neither can I. I cannot stomach either of them one second longer, even if it means losing The Edison. While I love my mom and this place, there's no way in hell I can grovel or beg or tolerate the presence of these miscreants any longer.

"You know what, Julianna, the choice is easy. I don't want anything to do with you or him. He is the scum of the Earth. Actually, no. He's lower than that." A.J. looks at me, saying nothing. This pisses me off even more. "Don't you want to defend yourself? Don't you have something to say? You're not so dominant now that you let *her* be your mouthpiece."

He folds his arms across his chest, leaning against my car. I will never get his ass print off it. Maybe if I take a blow torch to it?

"I'm just waiting for the police to get here. I called them."

Shit.

That's probably the only reason why Julianna even engaged in conversation with me. She was never going to consider staying. She wanted to trap me. I shake my head, kicking at the gravel. "Man, you two are perfect for each other. Just go. Get out."

At that moment, the Hicklam Town Police pull up, in cruiser number one. There are only three cruisers in town. Odds are about one-hundred percent that I'm going to know the officer. Fingers crossed that it's my favorite one.

Bingo.

"Hullo, Grayson," booms Officer White. As in Drew White, Senior. Here's hoping that the fact that I'm best friends with his son carries some weight. "What seems to be the problem?"

Julianna jumps in, pointing a finger at me. "This man attacked my boyfriend."

Officer White slides his sunglasses down on the bridge of his nose to look them up and down. "I've never seen you before. Were you trespassing? A man has a right to protect his property."

Her hands fly to her hips. "No, we were not trespassing. He hired us to be in his show. We got here and then suddenly, he attacked A.J."

I shrug my shoulders, doing my best to look innocent. "I don't know what she means. We were rehearsing. That's all. You know, there's a very exciting scene, and it ends in murder. Very dramatic, but some people," I give a head tilt toward A.J. the twat, "have trouble with that sort of complex choreography. He came highly recommended. I didn't know he'd be so new to all of this."

A.J. jumps off of my car and swings at me. Luckily, he's not a born fighter, so I see it coming and duck in plenty of time. Officer White is not so lucky as A.J. clips him on the shoulder. Immediately, A.J. blanches.

"I wanted to hit this asshole, not you."

The prick doesn't even apologize.

Officer White looks at them. "I think you need to leave. Now. If you evacuate the premises immediately, I won't arrest you for assaulting an officer."

"But what about Grayson's assault?" Julianna stomps her foot.

"Ma'am, this man just assaulted an officer of the law. I'm tempted to haul both of you in right now. I suggest you leave before I do just that."

Extra points to Officer White for calling her 'ma'am' instead of 'miss.' Any insult to her self image is a good one.

Her mouth opens and then closes. She turns to me. "This isn't over, Grayson Keene. If you think you will *ever* get hired anywhere close to Broadway, you are sorely mistaken. You committed suicide today." She looks over my shoulder at the main theater building. "You can kiss all of this goodbye."

And with that she stomps off toward their rental car, parked haphazardly in the middle of the lot. I raise my eyebrow at A.J., who has yet to admit defeat. He looks me up and down. "It's too bad. I heard you actually had talent before you wasted it up here."

It's my turn to give him the same dismissive gaze. "Probably much like Gloria did before you destroyed her. At least at the end of the day, I can live with myself. I doubt you can say the same."

I don't wait for him to go. I turn to Officer White, thank him for his help, and head back into the theater.

The minute I walk in, I wish I had gone anywhere but here though. The cast and Henderson pepper me with questions.

"What the fuck, man?"

"What happened?"

"Why did you do that?"

"Where's Julianna?"

"Is she coming back?"

"Are we still going to have a show?"

I have no answers for anyone. "Guys, take ... five. Hell, take the afternoon. Help the crew with the set. Hopefully I'll have answers in the morning. Ten sharp."

Wearily, I push through the door and head over to the house. Today feels like it has been forty hours long.

And it's only going to get longer.

I don't know what I'm going to do. I don't know how I'm going to tell my mother we have to cancel *Chicago*. The only thing I'm certain of is that Julianna and A.J. will stop at nothing to ruin me. I'm not going to be able to find someone else to play Roxie. And I'll bet that anyone I call will be *suddenly unavailable*.

Blacklists suck.

So does losing your family's home and business.

But they all seem so superficial compared to what Ria's lost.

I can figure something out. I have to.

Entering the kitchen, my mother holds a finger up to her lips. "Shh. Gloria just went to go lay down. She's wiped out by all of this."

"Here?" I whisper. "Isn't she going back to her old flat?"

Mom shakes her head. "No, we thought it would be best if she stayed here in case she needed someone tonight. Her mother is on her way and will be here probably sometime in the middle of the night."

"She ... she called her mom?"

My mother just raises an eyebrow at me like I'm the dumbest nimrod on the face of the Earth. Which is not far off the mark. "This is bad, isn't it?" As if I need it spelled out for me. See previous note about being a dumb nimrod.

"Yes, Grayson, it's bad."

"Oh God, did we just undo everything she's worked so hard for?" I did this to her. And that realization is monumentally worse than knowing we're going to lose The Edison. So much worse.

I look around the kitchen. *My* kitchen. It's been the soul of this home since my grandmother was a child. Maybe we can financially swing it to keep the house, but it sits so close to the theater and dorms that I doubt a new owner would be tolerant of us here. That would be if the new owner didn't bulldoze the place and put a subdivision here. The thought makes me want to vomit.

I glance at my mother, who's puttering about, as if our world has not just ended. Does she know? Does she understand?

"Mom."

She finishes washing her mug, shaking the water off before turning it upside down on the dish rack. I've probably seen her do this a thousand times.

"Mom," I say, a little more forcefully. "Mom, we have to figure out ..."

"Grayson, keep your voice down. You don't want to wake Gloria. She needs to rest. This was hard on her."

"Mom," I hiss through my teeth. "Would you please sit down? We have to figure out what we're going to do."

She sighs, tossing the dishtowel on the counter before coming to sit opposite me. She crosses her arms and gives me her stern look. "What is so important that you have to take that impudent tone with me?"

"Mom, don't you understand? We have to cancel *Chicago*. We're going to have to refund all the tickets. Without that revenue, we won't be able to make the loan payments. We're going to lose The Edison."

I still don't understand how she doesn't get this.

"Don't be silly, Grayson. You were always so quick to jump to action without thinking things through."

Gee, I wonder where I got that trait from.

"I *have* thought this through. Hell, it's why I brought Julianna Rickey up here in the first place. You know I can't stand her. You know all the unreasonable demands she made and how unprofessional she was. We open in four days—four—and she's not fully run the show one time! We've never been this unprepared for a show before. And not that that even matters anymore; she's gone and won't be coming back."

Good riddance.

"Then what are you going to do?" Mom sits back and crosses her arms.

"We have to cancel and refund." Duh.

"Don't be ridiculous. We can't do that. We have to have a show."

I lean in, my eyebrows about to meet my hairline. "What are you smoking, Mom? We sort of need the main character to have the show."

"Don't talk to me in that patronizing tone, Grayson. Of course you do. Just cast someone else."

That's it. I jump to my feet, slamming my hands down on the table. "Who? Who exactly am I supposed to pull out of thin air to play this part? Julianna wouldn't let me cast an understudy. Now I know why. I bet she was trying to screw me over from the get go. No one knows the part. It's not like someone will just waltz into my kitchen who can sing and dance and act."

As soon as the words are out of my mouth, I know exactly what Mom is thinking. There's only one solution to save The Edison. To save my home.

Mom raises her eyebrow and nods knowingly.

But there's no way in hell I can ask her to do it.

Chapter 37: Gloria

The raised voices pull me out of my tenuous slumber. My eyes feel as if they are full of sand and my throat is raw. I lay there for a few minutes, willing the voices to quiet and the memories of the day to fade.

I wish that it was a bad dream.

I've wished that a lot over the past decade.

If there's one thing I've learned, it's that my wishes don't come true.

Slowly, I walk down the hall to see what all the fuss is about. My feet are bandaged and sore, but not as wounded as my heart.

Grayson and his mother are sitting at the kitchen table. With the dated look of the kitchen and their proximity, it looks like it could be a set from a 50s sitcom.

Except for the yelling.

"Mom, stop. It won't work and I'm through discussing it." He pushes his chair back, standing. "I can make a last-ditch appeal, but you have to accept the reality of the situation. It's done. We have to close."

"Grayson, don't be ridiculous. You know it's the right answer. It's so simple and perfect and—" she breaks off when she sees me. "Oh, hello, Gloria. We didn't wake you, did we? Grayson, I told you to keep your voice down."

"I ... uh ... I needed to get a drink of water. That's all. Go back to your ... discussion." I shuffle through the kitchen, holding my head down so my hair shields my face. I can't look at him.

"Discussion's done," Grayson practically growls. "It's finished, Mom. You need to accept it."

"What's finished?" My head pops up. I need to know what bad news he could possibly have that would have him this upset. I wish his concern was about me, but he's barely looked at me.

He probably can't bear to face me after he chased after Julianna and Aaron like that. And he won't need to. My mom and brother are on their way and we'll be leaving as soon as they get here. Mom called to tell me Gabe wouldn't let her drive alone. At least one of us can watch out for her.

Good-bye, Hicklam, you hell hole.

I don't want to look at him anyway. How can he tell me he loves me and then go after them like that? He left me alone while he chased after the person responsible for my pain and suffering. Grayson didn't even think of me.

In case I had any doubts, I don't belong here.

And to think, I was starting to see this as my home. I felt comfortable here. Maybe even like I could have a new beginning. But no, that was ripped away, and I was left standing there, naked and afraid. At least this time, it was only proverbially naked instead of actual naked.

"Nothing for you to worry about. Are you okay? How are you feeling?" Grayson tries to pull me into a hug. I don't think so. It's too late for comfort.

I put my hand up to stop him from coming any closer. I don't want him touching me again. Not after what he did. "How do you think I'm feeling?"

"Scared. Anxious. Upset. And from the way you kicked him in the johnson, I'd say super mad."

These are all accurate. But he left out the biggest one.

Betrayed.

The rational part of me realizes that he *probably* didn't know who Aaron was before he hired him. But the rational part of me is not actually in charge right now. Not to mention how he ran after Julianna. He begged her to stay. I know he did.

Saving the show—The Edison—is the most important thing to him. More important than me and my fragile self. I understand. I would make the same decision if I were him. Frankly, I can't believe he's put up with me for this long. I wouldn't put up with me if I didn't have to.

Who in their right mind would want someone this out of their mind? I must have been crazy to think that someone could love me as I am. I just wish he hadn't lied about loving me.

"I'm going to go lay back down. I'll try not to wake you when I leave."

Grayson takes a step toward me, but again I put my hands up. I wish I could let him close. I wish I could feel his arms around me, comforting and protecting me. I can never feel that again.

He freezes. "Ria, what do you mean 'leave?'"

"My mom and brother are on their way out. I'm going home. Back to Ohio."

He steps closer, ignoring my invisible wall and grasps my wrist. "I need to talk to you. Now. Outside." He pulls me after him. I stumble a bit on the back stairs and race to keep up with him as he's marching out toward the field. I tell myself that no matter what he says, I can't listen. He's only thinking about what he needs.

Once we finally get far enough away from any of the buildings for anyone to hear, he drops my wrist. "What do you mean you are leaving?"

"Did I stutter?" I jut my chin out in a feeble attempt to appear strong and determined. Maybe he won't see that I'm truly weak and wilted. "I'm going to stay down at the flat until they get here. I'll feel safer there."

"Ria, you can't leave," he pleads.

I put my hands on my hips. "Why not?" I brace myself, ready to hear him say that he needs me to work things here. For camp. To manage the property and maintenance.

He lifts his palms up, as if offering peace. "Because I love you."

I expected him to tell me why he needs Julianna. I didn't expect him to say that he loves me.

My knees buckle slightly. Why is he keeping up this charade? Does he think he can use it to manipulate me into staying?

"What?"

"I love you, Ria. I need you. I need you in my life. I can't imagine going a day without seeing you. Please don't leave me."

My brow tightens as I try to process this. "But what about Julianna? The Edison? Camp? The work I do here."

He shrugs, but it doesn't hide his defeat. "The Edison is a sunk ship. The rest is like the orchestra playing on the Titanic. It's not going to matter. The old girl is going down, but it doesn't matter. All that matters is that you're okay and safe." Pain radiates off him in waves.

Suddenly I doubt that he's manipulating me. He's as heartbroken as I am.

Oh, Grayson.

I take a step toward him and tentatively reach for his hand. "Don't say that. Ticket sales have been good. You'll make it."

Grayson looks at me, the anguish apparent in his eyes, now a deep green. "No, we won't. I have to cancel *Chicago*. We can't cover the loan repayment without that show. I'm going to take a bath on it."

"I ... I don't understand. Why are you cancelling?" The pit grows in my stomach. I don't want to hear the answer but need to nonetheless.

"It's hard to have a show without a lead actor and actress. I hear people really think that's important to the show, especially when they've paid to see a big name."

"But you went after her. Didn't you beg her to stay?"

He kicks at a rock in the grass. "For a split second, I started to. I asked her to talk. But then she went on about how I'd humiliated her and A.J. *Me*." He points to his chest. "And all I could think is what A.J. had done to you. And I knew, even if it meant losing everything, I could never stand to work with people like that. You're worth too much to me. Actually, you're worth too much. Period. There is no way I could ever have anything to do with him, knowing what he did to you. I'm glad you kicked him in the balls. I only wish you had been wearing steel-toe boots when you did it."

I return the small smile he gives me.

Grayson continues, "Not to mention, The Edison is a family business, built on hard work and integrity. My family's integrity. I was not about to sacrifice it or you."

Tears well in his eyes.

"But ... your show."

"It is what it is."

"You need them."

He steps in, taking my hands and pulling me to him. "I need you more."

None of this makes sense. What does he get out of this? "But if they go, you lose The Edison."

He looks away quickly, but not before I see the pain again. "Maybe it wasn't able to be saved."

I look down. "I felt—feel—that way about myself sometimes. A lot of the time."

He cups my chin in his hand, forcing me to look at him. "But you are worth it. Don't you see?"

"Not worth your family's whole life. Your legacy." I can't believe I'm going to say this. "You have to make them come back."

He blinks, his hand falling away. "What? I can't do business with people like that. Some people"—he tilts his head—"are worth it. They are not."

"But what are you going to do? Do you have another plan?"

Now it's his turn to look down, and if I didn't know better, I'd say he looks ... guilty?

"Grayson, what's your plan? Tell me."

He turns, looking toward the woods that run along the edge of the property. "I can't. It's a terrible idea, but the only thing we can come up with. So we're going to Plan B, which is to cancel."

"Plan A can't be that bad." I reach out, gently touching his hunched shoulder. This poor man is suffering because of me. Because he loves me.

He loves me. I'm starting to believe it. Maybe.

"Grayson? Look at me, please," I plead softly, my voice drifting off with the gentle evening breeze.

"I ... I have to go. I need to get down to help with the set."

"Is there anything else you can do?"

He shakes his head. "There's not enough time. Julianna and A.J. will do their best to ruin me, so I'll be lucky to get anyone up here ever again. It's done."

My chest is so tight, I can barely breathe. This time it's not panic; it's devastation. For me. For him. For this loss that's all my fault.

Because I love him and I'm hurting him, and this has all blown up because of me. I would give anything to stop his pain.

Chapter 38: Grayson

I am a coward.

I head toward the theater, anxious to get away from Ria. Anxious because I know the more time I spend with her, the more likely I'm going to hurt her.

More, that is.

I can't bear to see her crumple like that again. It was like watching a balloon deflate, except it was her soul. I will not be the one to hurt her like that again.

Even if it means losing everything I have.

Once inside the theater, we finally have the *Rent* set cleared, and then I dismiss everyone.

"What are we going to do, man?" Henderson sits down next to me on the edge of the stage.

"I don't want to talk about it."

"You have to. We have to come up with something. We have got to run this show at some point."

"What if we don't?"

"Gray, you can't mean it."

I sigh, burying my face in my hands. "I don't want to mean it. I don't know what else to do."

"We gotta get this show re-cast and fast."

"We open in three days. *Three days.* We've never run the show, and we don't have two out of the three leads. Even if people knew the show, it'd be nearly impossible to pull it off. Not to mention all the folks who are coming only to see Julianna Rickey."

Henderson pats my back. "I'm not saying it would be easy. But it's do-able. We have to get on social media, though, and spin this before Julianna and A.J. can."

"You know they're going to blackball me. It's going to be impossible to get anyone new up here, even if I could on this short notice. Let alone someone who knows the part and can pull it off in three days. Not gonna happen." I look at Henderson.

"Yeah, that's why your only option is to cast from within. I think you can do Billy, since you've pretty much been running it already. Braedyn can go back to Amos. He'll be fine. One problem solved."

"So who do we pull from the ensemble to be Roxie? Everyone who could do the part is in another role. If we start pulling people, it'll create a cascade. And while the girls in the ensemble are great, no one's ready for this part yet." I've been running all the permutations in my head. There isn't a solution from within. Henderson has got to see this.

"Gray, you know there's only one way."

I was hoping he wouldn't reach the only conclusion I'd come to. I was hoping he'd have some other idea. Instead, he has to go all Dr. Strange on me and tell me there's only one way to end this.

I hop off the front of the stage, holding my arms up. "Don't say it, man. I can't and I won't."

Henderson hops down after me. "Gray, you have to. She'll say yes. She's totally in love with you. She'll do it for you. She did it for you today."

He has no idea what it cost her. "Ria's never going to go on stage again. She can't. It'll kill her to try. I can't ask it of her. It's too much for her."

"But what about all of us? Have you thought about that?" Henderson's voice is beginning to rise. "I know you consider losing your family business and all but what about the *people* here? Did you think about us? All the kids who cut their teeth on this stage? The opportunities you give them. The experience. The family. This isn't just about the Keenes. It's about Hicklam. We're all part of the family here. And we all do whatever we need to to make this place work. The whole town. Hell, you pressed your high school buddies into service. You picked up a girl in a coffee shop and had her doing drywall and tile. The entire *town* depends on the income that this place helps generate. If The Edison goes under, the whole town does."

As if I needed any more fucking pressure.

Without answering, I storm out. I want to scream or hit someone. Maybe both.

Instead, and also because I've already been in one round of fisticuffs today, I run. I run down the hill and around the park. Over to the other side of town and back. When I don't have the energy to run anymore, I walk. And think. And try to come up with something—anything—but I keep coming back to the only answer.

Ria.

The problem and the solution all in one.

How can I ask her? It will tear her apart from the inside out. But if I don't, then I let everyone down. The entire town could go under. Mom and I will lose not only our business but our house. It's an impossible situation.

I have to do it.

And before I know it, I'm on Chapel Street, staring up at her flat. The lights are on, even though it's well after midnight, much like the first time I came here in the middle of the night. The first time we made love.

Now I stand down here, poised to destroy her. Not for me. If it were only me, I'd let it go. But it's my mom and our house and the town. Henderson was right. There are entire restaurants that open—and succeed—based on our theater schedule. Heidi kills it during the summer, between the cast and the cabaret, not to mention the increase in foot traffic through downtown, benefiting all the Mom and Pop stores.

It's the only way, I tell myself, over and over as my hand raises to knock on the door.

She opens it before my hand makes contact. Words—all the words I've practiced in my head—vanish as I stare at her face, ravaged by anguish and pain. Pain caused by me.

Pain that I'm about to make a million times worse.

She steps aside and I enter. Movement catches my eye. There are people here, sitting at her small table.

Thank God she isn't alone.

"Grayson, this is my mom, Gretchen, and my brother, Gabe. Mom, Gabe, this is Grayson."

In any other normal situation, I'd shake hands and make pleasantries.

This is not a normal situation. I shove my hands in my pockets and pace. I don't know what to say or how even to begin.

"Grayson, I'm so sorry. I know you can't forgive me, but I didn't mean for this to happen. I ..."

I glance over at her brother, who is staring at nothing on the table. He took up MMA as a way to cope with what his sister went through. Damn, I wish he had been here when A.J. showed up. Gabe clenches his hands into fists. Though with that rage directed at me, maybe he's not the guy I want to have around right now.

"Ria, can I talk to you? In private." I nod toward the bedroom door.

Once inside, I close the door. She sits down nervously on the end of the bed. I continue pacing.

"You must hate me," she says. "This ... it's all my fault. I know you can't forgive me. I don't blame you for hating me. I hate myself for it. I'm sorry."

Her words stop me cold, faster than a swift kick to the gut. "Hate you?"

"If I wasn't here, if it wasn't for me, you wouldn't be losing The Edison."

"If it wasn't for you, The Edison never would have opened this season," I clarify.

"You'd still have Julianna and Aaron and a show if it weren't for me."

I look down at my feet. She's right about that, but how can I make her see that I'm okay being on her side of the line during this?

"Ria, I don't want to work with people like that. I don't want to sell my soul just to succeed. And there's a chance it's not the end." I look at her hopefully, hoping this blow doesn't land as I expect it to. "It doesn't have to be over."

Her eyes grow wide. "You mean you can still do the show? But how?" The trust and expectation is evident on her face. I lean into the door, my head banging back. If only I could bang it hard enough to lose consciousness and not have to do what I'm about to do. But I can't.

It's time to deal my reluctant strike.

"If we don't have the show, The Edison will go under, which means most of the local businesses in town will eventually fold. It's not just us. It's everyone here. We have to have a show. And we have to sell tickets." I loathe what I'm doing to her.

Ria nods, her arms still pulled tightly around her body. How I wish I could hold her in my arms and ease her pain. Instead, I'm here to tear her apart from the inside out.

I take a deep breath and begin. "Henderson and I have looked at it from every angle. We have to try to save The Edison. And with only three days of rehearsal until opening, we are limited with what we can do. We've run every permutation in the cast, and there's no one who can play Roxie without starting a major cascade. We need someone who can step into the role at a moment's notice. Someone who knows the bones of the part already." I look down, unable to meet her gaze. "We need you to get up on that stage and perform. You are the only person who can save The Edison."

Chapter 39: Gloria

It's a good thing I'm sitting down. Otherwise, I'm one-hundred percent certain my legs would have given out.

I may be the one with actual mental health issues, but Grayson is out of his ever-lovin' mind. Me—on stage and performing?

There's no way in hell.

That's what it would be for me. Hell. And I can't believe Grayson is asking me to walk through it. As if I even could.

But it's not even that. It's the fact that he would ask. I thought he knew. I thought he understood. I thought he cared.

He doesn't. He's just out for himself.

Like Aaron.

I should have known better. I should have seen this coming.

"I ... I can't," I manage in a whisper.

Grayson sags into the door, sliding down to the ground. His legs flop in front of him as if he's a rag doll. He sits there, limp and unmoving.

Broken.

Broken by me.

Broken just like me.

Instinctually, I want to run to him. To comfort him. To reassure him. But I can't. Because I too am broken.

By Aaron and his betrayal, and now by Grayson.

I should have known. They're all alike.

My wounds are fresh and bleeding, ripped wide open today. God, was it only today? I glance at the clock, which tells me it's the middle of the night. I guess it was yesterday after all. Still a lot has changed in twenty-four hours.

"I wish I could, Grayson, but I can't. It's all my fault, so I know I should." Slowly, feeling as if my entire body is made of lead, I rise from the bed and take the six steps to where Grayson sits on the floor. As I approach, he pulls his knees in, hugging them to his chest. I mimic his position. Despite his betrayal, I'm still drawn to comfort him. I deserve this, since I'm obviously not smart enough to stay away.

But I can't. His pain is palpable and despite what he's done to me, I want to make his pain go away. Perhaps Aaron had me pegged correctly. I am a masochist after all.

There's only about six inches between us, but it may as well be a million miles. The pain is radiating off him in seismic waves, and there's nothing I can do.

"I'm sorry," I say. "I know you won't be able to forgive me for this. For ruining it all. I wish ... I wish more than anything it could be different."

That you could be different. That I could be different.

"Forgive you? *You*!" Grayson's suddenly on his feet, his voice rising, while I scramble to the corner, still not standing. "You don't see it, do you? How can you not—"

"Everything okay in here?" Gabe pushes open the door without waiting for an answer. He takes one look at me, cowering on the floor, before he grabs Grayson by the shirt and muscles him out the door.

I hear them yelling, exchanging words, but I can't process what they're saying. A door slams and then it's quiet. Mom comes in, quickly dropping down to my side.

"It's okay, Gloria. It'll all be okay." She's pulling me into her, whispering to me as she's done so many times. But this time, it's different. It's not panic or anxiety.

It's heartbreak.

Heartbreak for being taken advantage of, yet again. Of being betrayed by someone who claimed to love me, but was, in fact, using me. But as much as I tell myself that this is what happened here, I can't help but hurt for Grayson. He may not be enough for me, but that doesn't stop me from loving him.

Heartbreak for not being able to help Grayson. For not being what he needs me to be. For not being able to save The Edison or the local businesses that are sure to go under when The Edison folds. For not being worthy of his love.

But mostly, heartbreak for me. Because at the end of the day, Grayson's not the only one losing it all. And so my heart shatters for this thing that I loved so much, that I can never do again.

I'm losing my first love all over again.

I feel like I'm dying.

I put my head on my mom's shoulder and for the millionth time, cry myself to sleep. I don't know where she finds the strength for me, but I'm so lucky she does. My head drops down and I jerk awake. Gabe is picking me up.

"What are you doing?"

"Putting you on your bed, idiot. Mom's not comfortable on the floor. She's had a long day."

I want to thank him, because I know he too has had a long day because of me. But exhaustion yields to sleep before I can.

I wake up feeling nothing close to refreshed. More like I've been through the wringer. Mom's in my kitchen talking. As I shuffle out, I'm surprised to see Mrs. Keene—Linda—here.

"Hello?" I say, more of a question than a greeting. I squint at the clock above the stove. It's almost nine. I can't believe I slept that long. A whopping four hours, at least.

My mom stands up, ready to jump in and protect me. I wish I could say that she was overdoing it, but I did make her drive ten hours to be with me. But still. "Mom, I'm fine. Did you get any sleep? Where's Gabe?"

"He went to get coffee at that place you always talk about."

"Dean's Beans," I clarify. One of the many places I'm letting down by my massive inability to suck it up and get on stage.

"Gloria, may I please speak with you?" Linda stands up.

I nod, not at all anxious to hear what she has to say. Frankly, I don't need to hear it to know. She's going to accuse me, rightfully so, of being selfish. Of ruining Grayson's life. Of everything. And I'll have nothing to say in my defense because it's all true.

So instead of waiting to be attacked, I lead with my defense. "Linda, you don't need to tell me. I already know. But before you launch into me, I need you to hear one thing. I wish I could. I wish with all my heart that I could get up on that stage and sing and dance and act. One of the reasons that this *thing* hit me so hard was that it took my home, my passion, my *soul* from me. Being on stage is all I ever wanted. I can't even think about what I would do next because I can't imagine anything that doesn't involve theater. The loss of that nearly killed me. And I feel like it might again."

"I can relate. I have a child much like that," Linda says dryly.

"Do you know that from the night this happened until I was here, dry walling, *ten years later,* I haven't sung a note? And I used to sing. All the time."

"*All the time,*" chimes in my mother. "All the freakin' time."

Linda smiles slightly. "Again, I can relate."

"What Aaron and Marissa did to me stripped away my dignity, to say the least. It stripped away my confidence. My trust. But it also took my life. I've been totally lost since then. I'm just starting to find my way back. It's hard for me to trust, and then when I do ..." I trail off. Grayson's betrayal hurts. But in the light of morning, I'm processing a deeper loss. The knowledge that I can never truly go back to what I love doing. "I can't afford to lose me again."

Linda nods, tears filling her eyes. "I know, Gloria. It's okay. Really, it is. I understand."

I look down at the ground, at my feet that seem rooted into the floor. "Will Grayson ever understand? Does he know that I'd help him if I could?" I don't know why it matters, but it does.

My mom stands up and comes to me, wrapping me in her arms. I can't even begin to count the number of times she's done this for me. Drawing on her strength, I look at Linda. "Can you tell Grayson that? Please."

Linda stands up. "Grayson will be fine. He will land on his feet. He's got talent in spades and the world will see that."

I break free from my mom's protective hold. "But what about you? What will you do?"

Linda smiles sadly. "I'll figure it out too. It'll be an adjustment, for certain. But everything's been an adjustment for me the last few years. The Edison is part of me. It's my heritage and legacy. But it's also just a business. I found that out the hard way when Allen got sick and died. I love The Edison, but I'd trade it all in a heartbeat for one more day with him. But really, I'm thankful we spent the money we did on his treatment. It gave me days we wouldn't have had otherwise. If The Edison was the collateral, then I consider it money well-spent." She begins to head toward the door. "He was the love of my life. Everyone should be so lucky as to have what we did."

I thought maybe I could have it with her son. Why did he have to ask me to do this? Why did he put me in this terrible no-win position? Linda crosses toward the door and suddenly I know why he asked.

For his mother.

"But what will you do when The Edison goes under?" I ask eagerly. I hope she has a plan or something that will get her through.

She stops, one hand on the doorknob. "Who knows? Maybe I'll write a book about the textile industry in Hicklam, since no one else I know will be writing it." Linda gives me the smallest of smiles and looks around. "Maybe I'll see if the Andrewses have a place I can rent. It won't be that interesting since there's no wild sex parties going on, but I'll make due."

A laugh bubbles out, mixed with tears. This woman will never cease to puzzle me with her words and actions. It's clear she loves her son and her late husband. She may not have a good head for business, but she cares about people and that's worth admiring.

"Gloria," she adds, now half-way through the door, "Grayson will understand. He didn't want to ask you because he knew it would hurt you. He won't forgive you because there's nothing to forgive. I just hope he can forgive himself."

The door closes and she's gone. I look at my own mother. "Do you think that's right? How can there be nothing to forgive? This is all my fault."

My mom steps back, still holding onto my hands. "Gloria, when will you see? It's never been your fault. It sounds like this Julianna character was a bad seed from the start. She's in bed with the likes of Aaron, so she has terrible judgment. She refused to allow an understudy. She walked out on and missed rehearsals. There's a good chance she was planning on sticking it to Grayson, regardless of you. You just made it easier for them to screw him over."

"I've lost everything, Mom."

I look into her brown eyes, the same color as my own. I see the deep creases around them, made deeper by my own inability to cope with the results of my own actions. If ever given the chance to go back, I'd never allow myself to be seduced by Aaron. I wouldn't let myself be flattered by his attention. I'd say no when I wasn't comfortable with what he wanted to do. I take her hands in mine and hold on tight.

"I admire and am jealous of Linda. Her life is in the crapper, but at least she can say she has no regrets. She made a choice and chose love. So even though she's losing, she's not losing everything. She still has the important things."

My mom stares back at me. "Gloria, honey, when will you see that you haven't lost everything? The important things are all right here. You just have to take them. It's time to take that chance."

Chapter 40: Grayson

I roll over and check the clock. Holy shit, how did it get to be two in the afternoon?

Oh right, I didn't go to sleep until after six this morning and that sleeping pill I took probably helped with my complete and total lack of consciousness.

Too bad, I don't feel any more refreshed. On the contrary, I feel groggy and worn out. And like a man so down on his luck, he'll never get up again.

That's probably because I am.

I don't know how I'm going to break it to the cast that we are cancelling *Chicago*. That we can probably survive for the rest of the season, but that this will be the final season for The Edison.

That I failed them.

If only I hadn't put all my eggs in Julianna Rickey's basket.

If only I had managed finances better the past two years or not started the renovation.

If only I'd cast someone—anyone—else.

If only I hadn't had to rip Ria apart, asking her to do something I know she can't do.

If only I didn't hate myself for doing all these things.

Self-loathing never makes it any easier to get out of bed.

I take a shower, spending much longer in there than I should. I feel as if I'm moving through quicksand. Dread weighs on me, making it hard to move my limbs. What's normally a two minute walk from the house to the theater takes me triple that. I might as well be a dead man walking.

It's not like I have to hurry to get to rehearsal. There's nothing to rehearse.

So when the sounds of music waft out of the theater, meeting me on the path in, I'm confused. Dammit, Henderson. How can he be putting the cast through rehearsal right now? That's cruel.

I hear the piano. Maybe Josh is simply playing around. The finale number, "Hot Honey Rag" is one of those fun numbers piano players either detest or love. I would guess the latter for Josh, who's a skilled and accomplished pianist in his own right.

Then I hear the 'whoop' and laughter. Someone yells, "Shit." Another voice calls out, "Sugar two, three, four, five, six, seven, eight. Shimmy and strut in a circle."

What the hell?

I push open the door to the theater and it bangs hard against the wall. Josh stops playing and Marcelina and Ria freeze, mid-step. Marcelina holds her hand up, shielding against a light. "Gray, is that you? Where the hell you been? It's about time."

I step forward, stumbling down the aisle. Is this some kind of dream? "What ... what's going on here?"

Henderson calls out. "You're interrupting and you're late. So, nothing out of the ordinary." He walks up the aisle to meet me where I'm standing, as apparently my feet have lost all ability to work. He grasps my shoulders. "It's amazing, man. *She's* amazing. I'd heard a little, but I ... I had no idea."

I look around him where Kori, the choreographer, is going over a step with Ria and Marcelina. I look back to Henderson. "But I don't understand. Ria?"

Henderson shrugs. "She showed up promptly at ten and asked us to go over the show with her. I'd already told some of the cast the predicament. I've never seen a group work harder than they have today."

I glance over his shoulder. "But Ria?"

None of it makes sense.

He turns and watches her. Marcelina is a stronger dancer, but she also knows the dance better. It doesn't matter though. Ria has that natural stage presence that exudes out of every pore, making it impossible to tear your eyes away from her.

They finally get through the number, cartwheel and all, and laugh as they throw their arms around each other for the final pose. I'm still in awe.

Kori turns to me. "Gray, we have to work with you on your dance section for 'Razzle Dazzle'. You good on everything else?"

Shit, I'm going to have to dance. At least it's a small section and done in soft shoe. Easier to hide my flubs that way. Henderson turns around and walks toward the stage. "Great work, everyone. You've all put in a tremendous amount of work, but we have lots more to go. We open in"—he looks at his watch—"approximately fifty-two hours. No pressure. Take twenty for lunch and then we'll run from the top. Ria, use the book if you have to, but get off it as soon as you can."

She nods, quickly sitting down and yanking her shoes off. Wait—where did she get character shoes? What is happening here?

"Can I talk to you for a minute?" I walk over to her, a little more brusquely than intended. She stretches out her foot to reveal several bandages. I know I missed a lot this morning, but surely she hasn't been dancing so hard as to make her feet bleed in one day. "What happened?"

"I tore my feet up ... yesterday ..." she struggles to put a day to the most messed up, longest week ever. "Running up here barefoot. If only I'd known I'd be dancing in these demon shoes, I would have stopped to put my sneakers on first."

I cannot understand what she's saying. I look at her, cocking my head, trying to figure out if this is some sort of dream that I'll wake from any minute and still be as screwed as ever. I squint at her feet and then back up at her. "But I don't ..."

"Gray, we need you to work on this choreography. You showed up five hours late. You don't get a break," Kori calls.

Ria reaches out every so gently and places her hand on my arm. "You were out of options. And so was I. It was now or never."

Kori pulls me away and off to the rehearsal room and as much as I'd like to think about what the hell is happening here, I can't because I've got to learn a song and dance. Time to pull out the old razzle dazzle indeed.

I don't see Ria again until we're up on stage together. She's tired. Dragging. But singing her heart out. She's also limping.

"K, guys. Time for the press conference scene," Henderson calls. He's really stepped up as director. Thank God. I'm too behind the eight ball to be able to multi-task that much. I'm barely keeping up with lines. Ria's not the only one who's going to be studying the book for the next two days.

Two days. "Can we even pull this off?" Imminent defeat presses down on me. This is a mess. The entire cast turns to look at me. Oops. I didn't realize I said that out loud.

Ria looks down. I follow her gaze. She's changed into jazz shoes. Where did she get those? Her feet must be in agony, but she's still standing. Still dancing.

Hell, she's on stage.

For me.

I shake my head, letting the movement travel down my body, through my shoulders and trunk and arms and hands. I have got to pull myself together. There's not enough time to panic.

There's also not enough time to talk to Ria about all this. We're too busy running scenes, dances, learning lines, getting fitted for costumes. I've got to help Braedyn with his role. I've got to spin the social media. I've got to pray that the opening night audience doesn't walk out when they don't get Julianna Rickey.

Every single minute is accounted for until I collapse at my desk, well into the wee hours of the morning.

The next morning arrives too quickly and too abruptly with Henderson plopping a large coffee down on my desk. "Get up, man. You need to take a shower and get to rehearsal."

Bleary-eyed, I glance at my phone. "Shit, man. It's eight."

"Rehearsal starts at eight-thirty for you. You have a lot of work to do."

I look at him, dragging my hand down over my mouth. I feel like someone went to war inside my head, and I'm the definite loser. "What are we doing? Why are we even trying?"

"Because it's what you do. You throw your heart and soul into every performance. Everything. And you are saving this theater."

"I'm not saving it. It's all Ria." I still ... can't. "Did you talk to her? Is she okay? Why is she doing this?"

Henderson shrugs, standing. "She seemed okay with it yesterday. A little overwhelmed at times, but we're all there. She told the cast what happened with that d-bag A.J. and why she has trouble being in front of people. They were all great to her about it. It'll come together today. She knows it. You'll get there. Try and keep up with her." He winks before leaving.

A minute later, he pops his head back in. "Yeah, there is one thing."

Dread fills me. This can't be good.

"Ria wanted to know if she can have a few people come into the audience today during the dress rehearsal. She said it would help her if she could see some faces rather than empty seats."

She must be in agony and anguish going through this. The idea of getting up, performing for people, all for me. I'll bet my agony is only a fraction of what hers is, and it's still crippling. "Yeah, sure. Whatever she needs. Whatever she asks. Make sure she has it."

This time, Henderson leaves for good. I shake the mouse, waking my computer. As predicted, Julianna's all over social media, playing the victim. Fuck. I'm never going to get in front of this. So even if the show does go on, will anyone come to see it?

Chapter 41: Gloria

I've never seen Grayson this stressed before. He can barely look at me. Did I do the right thing, stepping in like this? My body, especially my feet, are telling me no. While I knew a lot of the show, there's still a great deal I'm trying to cram into my brain. I feel as if I'm trying to carry water in a strainer.

"Oh, sorry," the costumer says as she pokes me, stitching up the back of my costume. With me in it.

"No worries." I wish I could remember her name, but my brain is filled beyond capacity. I know it's important, but I'll learn it after I don't have to keep dialogue, direction, songs, and dances up in the foreground. "I'm just happy that I've been doing yoga faithfully. This costume ..." I look down, "wasn't made for me."

"When I'm done with it, you'll never know."

I only have two costumes for the entire show. A dress—super short and made of lace—that I wear with and without a suit coat. There's a finale costume, an itty-bitty dress, also with a coat, that matches the one Marcelina wears. I smile at the costumer. "I'm sure. You do beautiful work. All the costumes are great, and sheer fabric like this can be hard to work with."

Not to mention most of the costumes are revealing and if they aren't tailored for a perfect fit, someone in the front row is liable to be hit by a flying nipple. Not that this was ever a family show, but we don't want to be charged with indecent exposure either.

"You have a great figure. Easy to dress." She steps back and looks me up and down. "I'd say, everything about you is easy. You're good to go." She smiles at me.

"Thanks ..." Dammit, I really need to learn her name. I promise I will. "I'm anything but easy, but I appreciate the vote of confidence. I could use all I can get."

Henderson pokes his head in the room. I suck in a sharp breath. I'll have to get used to this, the constant activity and people. Not to mention having to change clothes on the side of the stage. It never bothered me before. Even the nude bodysuit I'm wearing under this costume doesn't help me feel less naked. "You ready, Ria?"

I nod, running my fingers over the microphone wire woven through my hair. Rather than fiddle with a wig, my hair is slicked back into a tight, sleek bun at the base of my neck. I have a feeling I'll have a massive headache from it later on tonight, though I may not even notice it. My feet, held captive in the torture devices otherwise known as character shoes, are already screaming, and we haven't even started the dress rehearsal yet.

"Places everyone!" Grayson yells.

As the ensemble and Marcelina take their positions on the stage, I feel Grayson behind me. Lightly, he puts his hands on my arms. For the briefest of moments, I sag back into him, forgetting all that's transpired between us since yesterday. He rests his chin on my shoulder. "Normally I can put my chin on your head. Why are you taller?"

I lift my foot straight out in front of me. "The shoes from hell."

"Ria, I don't even know what to say."

With the house lights dark and the spots on, the curtain opens as the band plays. Even though this is our dress rehearsal, it feels real. My heart speeds up, and I open my mouth in an attempt to get more air into my lungs. "Grayson—I don't know if I can do this."

He spins me around. "You can. You are amazing. I ... I will never be able to repay you for doing this for me." He leans in and kisses me lightly. "Now get out there and knock 'em dead. First up, killing Fred Casely."

I stumble a bit as I head out to strike my first pose. My mind is blank and I can't remember a single thing I have to do. I freeze, my old friend panic threatening to take over. But then I turn and see my mom in the audience. And Gabe. And Malachi. And Carson Reuben from *Backstage Magazine*.

I have to do this.

This is the final step in my recovery. Going through the treatment and counseling wasn't enough. I will never be healed—and whole—until I can reclaim the one thing in life that I wanted most.

The stage.

And if I don't do this, I won't be able to fully love myself, let alone anyone else.

Two hours later, I'm dripping with sweat and exhilaration. I don't know whether to collapse or shout from the rooftop.

I did it.

I got up on stage and made it through the entire show. There were a few bobbles here and there; a few flubbed lines and missed steps. But it doesn't matter.

I made it through.

I rush off the stage and out into the audience to find my mom. She's crying.

"God, Mom. Was it that bad?"

She purses her lips together and shakes her head. "You were great. I never thought I'd get the chance to see you up there again. I always told you I loved watching you perform. How wonderful you were. It's like you never stepped off the stage. You're better than ever."

Sheepishly I look down. "You have to say that. You're my mom."

Malachi steps forward, pulling me into a tight hug. "But I'm not and I don't have to say it. You're not even paying me to. And you were fantastic,

Gloria. I wish you'd come to me sooner, so we could have gotten you back up there sooner. The stage has been suffering in your absence." He steps back and looks at me. "How do you feel?"

Now that I'm not nervous about forgetting all my lines, the enormity of what just happened hits me. "I don't know. There's too much to process."

"You know where to find me when you need to talk." Malachi lets go of me and heads toward the exit.

When you need to talk. When, not if.

He knows it's going to take me a while to unpack all of this.

Carson Reuben just nods at me and smiles before turning to leave the theater. I hope I did the right thing in having him come here.

Grayson and Henderson are up on stage giving notes. I need to hear this, as I'm sure there are a list of corrections a mile long for me. I wave quickly to my support squad and head back, plopping down on the side of the stage. One by one, cast members peel off to go hang their costumes up.

I can't get up. I'm too tired to move. I just sit there on the stage, leaning back on my arms and my legs stuck out in front of me. Someone comes over and takes my mic off, leaving the back of my dress unzipped. I don't even flinch when they pull the tape off the back of my neck. I don't care. I should care, but I'm too drained. I close my eyes.

Drained of everything. Energy and feeling. I'm a void.

And then, suddenly, I don't feel so empty. I open my eyes to see Grayson sitting next to me.

"Hey," he says softly, nudging me with his shoulder. "Are you sleeping sitting up?"

"Maybe. I ... I'm trying to process all of this. I can't. Nothing's happening. It's like I overloaded the system and blew a fuse or something. I can't even get up."

"Then let me." Grayson gets to his feet and scoops me up as if I'm a bag of groceries. He has to be as tired as I am, so I don't know where he's finding the strength to do this. He brings me back to my dressing room and sets me down on the couch, where he proceeds to take off my shoes, carefully rubbing my feet before placing them on the ground, one at a time. Then, he pulls me to my feet. Still standing in front of me, he reaches around and slowly eases the zipper on the back of my dress all the way down. He eases the delicate fabric off my shoulders and lets it puddle down around my feet.

Grayson steps back and bends over, sweat staining the back of his white dress shirt, his undershirt showing through. He picks up my dress and hangs it on the hanger before returning to me. He eases my black tights down, careful not to rip them. He squats as he gets lower and I place my hand on his shoulder to steady myself as I lift first one foot out and then the other. He shakes out the tights and drapes them over the edge of the couch. I stand in front of him, clad only in a nude bodysuit.

His eyes meet mine as he slides a finger under one strap and then the other. I nod as he slides the straps down, pulling the leotard off. I lift a foot to step out and use my other foot to toss it across the room. I'm down to my bra and underwear.

His gaze travels down my body and then back up to my face. "I want to take these off."

I don't say anything. Not because I don't want to. Words are slamming at my brain too fast for me to make sense of. I glance toward my dressing room door which is shut but not locked. It's also not a private dressing room. Marcelina could come in here at any moment.

But also, I don't have the mental or physical strength to figure out what's going on.

"Grayson, I ..."

He turns around and picks up my T-shirt, sliding it over my head. He finds my shorts and hands them to me as well.

"Stay here," he tells me. "I'll be right back."

I sit down on the couch and wait, forming my words carefully in my head. Grayson returns, also in shorts and a T. He looks at the empty spot on the couch next to me but instead pulls up a chair to sit right in front of me. He takes my hands in his, looking down at them instead of my face. I need to say this before I lose courage. "I spent a large chunk of yesterday thinking about how I'd never be able to forgive you for this."

"I won't forgive myself either. You have to know that if there were any other wa—"

"Grayson, please let me get this out. I ...I'm not doing this for you."

He drops my hands, his head falling. His shoulders sag, not understanding what I'm saying.

"The other day was terrible. The worst. But only part of it was. Before Aaron showed up, I was having fun. I miss being on the stage more than anything. I was having a good time until ..." I shrug. "You know. And then I had a panic attack to end all panic attacks. Thank you, by the way, for getting me out of there and getting Malachi. It's what I needed."

"I didn't know what else to do. I had to protect you."

I nod, and this time I reach for one of his hands. "You did it exactly right. And thank you for trying to beat him up. It was stupid, but I appreciate the gesture. Plus, your ineptitude at fighting allowed me to get those crotch shots in, and I've been wanting to get those for years."

Grayson finally looks up and smiles very faintly.

"I know why you asked. I know that you would have done anything else, if there was any other option. I saw how much it hurt you to hurt me. But I'm not doing this for you. I can't do it for you."

His head snaps up. "Because you can't forgive me?"

I swallow. "No, because I had to do it for *me*. Not because I felt guilty or because you asked. But because I needed this to become whole again. As good as I was doing, I don't know that I could be fully recovered without this part of me. You asked what I'd go back to school for, what I'd do with my life. I couldn't answer because I didn't know. There was nothing I wanted *but* this. And I didn't think I could have it. But I'm going to. I'm going to take that chance and go for it."

His eyes brim with tears. Mine follow suit. "Then why can't you forgive me? You know I didn't want to ask. I didn't want to hurt you. I wanted to protect you and care for you and ..." he breaks off. After a moment he adds, pleading, "Why won't you forgive me?"

"Because there's nothing to forgive. We were both in terrible situations. I wanted to doubt you and to doubt your love for me, but even I couldn't. I could see how torn you were. But you didn't know that *I* needed this. Being with you was a risk for me. But throughout all of this, the biggest chance that I'm taking is on *me*. And maybe, I think maybe, I'm going to make it through with my two loves. The stage and you."

Grayson drops to his knees, burying his head in my lap. "God, Ria, I love you. You are my hero. You are the strongest person I know, and I will never ever be able to thank you for saving me."

Gently, I lift his chin and lower my forehead to meet his. "I'm pretty sure we saved each other."

Chapter 42: Grayson

"I don't understand, Mom. Check the numbers again."

She sighs. "Grayson, we are at eighty-percent tonight. Sold out for Friday, Saturday night, and the matinee on Sunday. Ninety-six percent for Saturday afternoon and eighty-two for Sunday night."

"But are they telling people it's not Julianna? I put it up on the website and social media. I don't want people upset."

"They know, Grayson. They're coming to support you. Us."

"Why though? We haven't been able to get numbers like this in years."

Mom sits back in her desk chair and looks at me. "Before all this went down with that woman, Gloria came to me and asked for help. We ... we called in a favor for you."

"Favor? What kind of favor? Mom, it doesn't help us to buy the tickets ourselves."

God, she has no sense for business.

She shakes her head and smiles. She clicks a few things on her mouse and then swivels her monitor around to face me. "This kind of favor. Read it."

A Star Is Born by Carson Reuben for Backstage Magazine

If you were planning on scoring tickets to see Julianna Rickey and A.J. Michaels in Chicago *at The Edison Theater in Hicklam, NY, this weekend, there's been a change of plans. You know what they say about things that sound too good to be true—they usually are. While you may have thought that paying only forty or fifty or even eighty dollars a ticket to see Julianna Rickey was a steal, I'm afraid it's not going to happen. So what's your next move? Call The Edison and ask for a refund? Anger and outrage on social media? Demand that Executive Producer, Director, and star Grayson Keene never work in this business again?*

If you listen to Julianna Rickey, you'll do those things.

But I'm here to tell you to do none of those things. Keep your tickets and go to see Chicago. *Tell your friends. Post your reviews on social media. Let me tell you why.*

The Edison Theater, located in Hicklam, NY, is about a two hour drive from New York City, and it's worth every moment of travel. The entire town caters to the theater going crowd, making it feel like a night on the town without the smog, people, and dirt. I had the privilege of attending a rehearsal and let me tell you, this cast raises the bar for how this show should be performed. Every single person in the cast has the potential to be a star on the Great White Way. Marcelina Rios is captivating as stage-star murderess Velma Kelly. She completely embodies the Fosse vision of choreography as if she was trained by Chita Rivera herself. Grayson Keene is sly and smooth as the lawyer to end all lawyers, Billy Flynn. He has that charisma that will have you drinking the Kool-Aid and rooting for the acquittal of his wannabe-celebrity client, Roxie Hart.

Now let's talk Roxie, which is the role Julianna Rickey was originally scheduled to play. This iconic role, originated by Gwen Verdon herself, and played by so many others including Ann Reinking, Bebe Neuwirth, Brooke Shields, and Brandy Norwood, now has a new icon, thanks to The Edison's newcomer, Ria Dinetti. You've never heard of Ria Dinetti before and for good reason. This story is perhaps even more captivating than the story of the musical itself.

Ria had a calling to the stage from a young age. Musical theater throughout her middle and high school years in both school and company productions tapped into this future star. She received a college scholarship as a musical theater major where her path to stardom was practically guaranteed.

But behind the stage lights there is darkness and that darkness often dwells in the hearts and souls of men and women. Darkness befell on Ria Dinetti as she entered into a relationship with a graduate student who subsequently recorded a sexual encounter without Ria's consent. His other romantic partner, jealous of the attention Ria was receiving while playing the role of Roxie Hart, leaked the video to a mass audience. Ria's career was over before it began as she became debilitated by crippling panic and PTSD as a result of this highly personal viral recording. Even Ria's consent in the video is dubious as her boyfriend binds and gags her while she is sleeping. Read into that what you will.

So in the decade since Ria suffered this attack of revenge porn, her former-boyfriend, none other than A.J. Michaels, has continued on, building his career and celebrity while Ria has struggled to hold a job and connections, and has spent most of her time in therapy and treatment trying to regain her mental health. Here in Hicklam, Ria found help from psychologist Malachi Andrews, using Eye-Movement Desensitization and Reprocessing therapy. EMDR is often used to treat vets for PTSD.

As Julianna Rickey and A.J. Michaels failed to show for scheduled rehearsals for Chicago, *Grayson Keene and Ria Dinetti were forced to step in to play those roles. It should be interesting to note that Julianna Rickey demanded that no one be cast as her understudy and was livid to find out that someone was helping the cast at rehearsals. This was confirmed by nearly all the members of the cast as well as the pit band, as Ms. Rickey declined all requests for interview and comment. Mr. Michaels also refused to comment.*

When Ms. Rickey and Mr. Michaels finally did appear for rehearsal and Ms. Dinetti realized who was scheduled to perform, chaos ensued. With just three days until opening night, Ms. Dinetti made the courageous decision to return to the stage in an attempt to save The Edison Theater.

The Edison has been family owned for four generations. Linda Keene, Grayson's mother, grew up on the property, in the house. Her grandparents, Aldrich and Beatrix Edison, opened the theater in the early 1900s, at the height of the textile milling industry in Hicklam. The Edison has survived through two world wars, The Great Depression, countless recessions, and transportation advances that no longer make going to New York City out of reach for the common man. But treatments for

Allen Keene's cancer wiped out the family savings and much-needed renovations on The Edison (including in the cast dormitories and the public bathrooms in the theater) have extended the Keene's beyond their means, and the only thing that will save them is a successful summer season near or at capacity.

Which is why the loss of Ms. Rickey and Mr. Michaels have the potential to devastate not only The Edison and the Keene family, but the whole economic survival of the sleepy town of Hicklam. Knowing the evidence surrounding Mr. Michael's character and Ms. Rickey's firm demand that an understudy not be cast, it is not a stretch to see that this was a recipe for disaster.

But what isn't a disaster is The Edison's performance of Chicago. *Though Grayson Keene and Ria Dinetti stepped in with only a moment's notice, you'll never know. If you have tickets, keep them. Come to the show. Stay for the coffeehouse cabaret. Enjoy a few hours in this quaint town. And be ready to have your socks knocked off by newcomer Ria Dinetti. Both she and Grayson Keene are talents to watch and root for.*

The theater world will lose a great venue if The Edison can't weather this storm. Take this chance to enjoy a night of entertainment, save the economy of a town, and help a star return to the stage where she belongs. Chicago *is playing now through July 5 at The Edison Theater. Please visit their website for tickets.*

I look up at my mother and then back at the screen. "She ... she put it all in there. It's out there for everyone who comes to see the show to know. People might try to find her."

Mom nods. "Quite courageous and also hence the further change in her name. I updated the programs and website already."

"I ... I have to find her." I glance at the clock on the wall. Call is in forty-five minutes.

Shit. There's something I need to do first.

I hop into my car and race to the downtown area. I smile and wave at people, hoping they understand my hurry as I rush into Feldman's Florist. "Oh, thank God it's you, Mrs. Feldman. You're the only one who can help me. I need a large bouquet of roses—two dozen at least."

"When for? Tomorrow?" She pulls out her pad to write down the order.

"No, I'm so sorry. I need them for tonight. Now. I know I should have thought of it earlier but ... well, things have been crazy up the hill."

"Anything for you Grayson, sweetie," she says as she turns to her cooler. "Give me a hot second and I'll wrap these up."

Tapping my fingers impatiently, I look around the shop. Weddings, funerals, and stupid men keep Mrs. Feldman in business generally, but she sees a spike during our season as the families of the cast often buy them flowers when they visit.

Another business that we're saving. That Ria's saving.

Mrs. Feldman hands me the large bouquet and swipes my card. "Thanks, Mrs. F. These are great."

She hands me my card back. "Next time, Grayson, give me a little bit of notice."

"I will, promise!" I call, hurrying out the door, the bell clinking and chiming as I push a little too hard.

I take the roads a bit too fast trying to get back to The Edison. As I skid slightly, I slam on the brakes and force myself to stop and breathe for a minute. This will all be useless if I die on the way there.

By the time I reach her dressing room, Ria is already mic'd and is sitting in front of her mirror, the mic pack sticking out of the back of her nude leotard. Her hair is slicked back, shining with product to keep even a strand from going awry over the next few hours. I see her face in the mirror, her eyes focusing immediately on the flowers.

"Are those for me?" she asks, whirling around. "Aren't you supposed to wait for the end of the show to give them to me?"

I extend the impressive bouquet toward her. "If you want, I'll bring them out to you then, but I didn't want to wait that long to give my girl flowers."

Her expression softens and she sighs ever so slightly. She looks like an angel, her face clean and shining.

"Grayson, that's so sweet." She looks at the bouquet. "Can you put them in water? I have to do makeup and I'm really out of practice. I ... I don't even really have any." Her voice is starting to shake, nerves creeping in.

"They'll last. Let me do your makeup."

"You?" she asks incredulously.

"Hang on," I say, dashing out of the room. I run around, collecting some supplies. Marcelina offers her large cache, and I get to work.

As I dot and daub, pressing and blotting, I shade in and fill in and smudge until Ria's clean, innocent features are nearly unrecognizable. She's now every bit the jaded, self-centered character she's about to play. In other words, nothing like herself. "Ticket sales are through the roof, you know." As soon as I say it, I want to kick myself. She doesn't need to think about playing to a packed house. "It's because of the article," I add quickly.

She shrugs, trying to keep her eyes downcast as I apply fake lashes. "That was the point."

"But, Ria, you told him ... everything."

Her eyes dart up, framed now in a heavy black fringe that makes her own mahogany seem luminescent. "I realized that was part of what was driving the fear. The thought that people *might find out*. I'm not particularly proud of the direction my sex life took while I was with him because it wasn't what I wanted. I let him use and manipulate me, and I need to do better for myself. But other than that, I was a victim. Of the recording and the emailing. If I had been robbed, I wouldn't feel ashamed that someone stole from me. Just because this was sexual in nature, I shouldn't be ashamed either. And it wasn't about sex for either Aaron or Marissa. It was about power and control and jealousy. So today, as long as I can not freak out in the meantime, I get that power back."

I grab her face and pull her in, kissing her long and hard. I let my mouth communicate all the things I cannot say. How proud I am of her. How special and strong she is. How lucky I am to have her in my life. How much I love her.

"Grayson, you're going to ruin that great makeup job you just did." Marcelina laughs. I hadn't even heard her come back in the room. "Let me finish her, while you get yourself ready."

I stand up and see that indeed, there is some smudging. Ria laughs. "You look good in my shade of lipstick."

I wipe my lips with my thumb, joining in her laughter, which is the sweetest sound on Earth, next to her singing. "Will you be okay?"

She nods. "Yes, I think so."

Henderson calls, "Ten minutes until curtain. Into costumes everyone!"

I turn back to her one last time, "Break a leg."

Ria looks at me as she slides her black dress off the hanger I put it on last night. "Grayson, I love you too."

Epilogue: Gloria

As I turn my cartwheel for the eighteenth time on stage in front of a live audience, I bite my lip to hold back the tears. This time, however, they aren't tears of fear and pain. They are tears of joy. Marcelina and I strike our final pose, arms around each other, and the audience erupts into thunderous applause.

People are instantly on their feet. Marcelina reaches her right arm across my front and pulls me into a deep hug. Soon, we're enveloped by most of the cast. I don't know what they're doing, as we need to clear the stage for bows to begin. Then, over the din, I hear Grayson's voice.

"Ladies and gentlemen, please! A moment! We'll take our bows in a minute because every single person in this cast deserves your applause and adoration. I just have to tell you why."

The audience quiets and he takes center stage.

"I want to thank you all for coming. A few weeks ago, we weren't sure this show was going to happen. As I'm sure you've heard, the two leads we had hired for this show did not make The Edison a priority, missing rehearsals and finally walking out.

Every single person here on this stage worked their asses off to make sure that this show still happened. This cast and crew are amazing. Absolutely and truly amazing."

Grayson steps aside for a minute, raising his hand to us and the audience applauds again. After a moment, he continues.

"What makes The Edison so special is that it's part of this community. And when it was in danger of not opening or cancelling a show, this town stepped up. We are all family here, and we hope that each and everyone of you will continue to be a part of our family. So we need to extend a big thank you to each and every one of you in the audience, many of whom put your faith in a company of unknowns, even though you'd planned on seeing a big star. I think we gave you many stars here tonight."

The audience applauds again. I feel my eyes filling with tears. I love each and every person here. They welcomed me in, supported me, embraced me, and protected me. They have become family, and none more than Grayson Keene.

He continues, "But there's one person up here that I need to extend a special thanks to. She came up here months ago, looking for a job. I promptly put her to work and the first thing she did was drywall. Then came painting and tiling. If you enjoyed your experience in the bathroom and the toilet didn't tip when you sat down, you have Ria Dinetti to thank. But then, she kept working. Kept doing. She took over our kids' camp, which started this past week. And when our lead left us in the lurch, Ria stepped in to make sure The Edison had a fighting chance to stay open. Ria, come here."

I step forward, letting go of Marcelina's hand, which I didn't even realize I'd been grasping tightly. I see all of the faces in the crowd and take a deep breath. I have to remind myself again that I am safe. This might always be my first instinct, but I never imagined I'd have this all again.

He takes my hands. "Ladies and gentleman, this talented actress, along with the support of my cast and crew, is why we are still here and The Edison isn't going anywhere. So I hope you'll be back to see us again this summer and in the summers to follow. Now let's let the cast appropriately bow."

Grayson pulls me off to the wings while the ensemble take their bows. "Ria, I ... this is all because of you."

I have one eye on him and one eye on the stage. Braedyn's out there now. Then it'll be Marcelina's turn and then Grayson's. "You have to get out there."

"But there's ..."

"Go!" I push him out, furrowing my brow as he looks back. Marcelina takes her turn and then it's me. The place erupts and the cheers are deafening. I take my bow, blown away at the difference between that last night in college and now. The same role. The same songs and the same lines. Boyfriend in the cast. But now, it's all different.

It's home.

The curtain falls for the last time and Grayson pulls me into him. "I was going to do this in front of the audience, but then I thought you might not like all those people seeing."

I don't know what he's up to. "Yes, you know that's an issue for me."

"So I'm going to do it now. Gloria, I hate the road that put you here in Hicklam. I hate the suffering and pain and anguish it's caused. But I am so happy that you ended up here, even if my awesomely funny joke was too much for you on day one."

"It was a terrible joke, and you knew it."

"I've never been a believer in fate, but for some reasons, our paths not only crossed but quickly became intermingled and one. For years, all I wanted was to go out and succeed and to be a star. This summer has taught me that all I need is right here in Hicklam. I have the stage, I have my family legacy. I have friends who are more like family. But it won't mean anything if I don't have you. Gloria, will you stay here with me?"

I'm not sure where he's going with this. "You know I'm here for the rest of the summer. I've got camp and their show and I figure you can find something else for me to do."

"No, Gloria. Ria. I want you to stay here. For good. Let's do this together. Let's get married and have babies and have the next generation to keep this thing that means so much to us going for our kids." He drops to one knee. "Marry me, Ria."

I'm stunned for a minute. But there's no fear. No anxiety. No panic. Only the feeling of absolute peace. This is where I'm meant to be. Right here, with Grayson.

"Yes," I nod, tears springing forth. He jumps to his feet, pulling me into him and kissing me. "Oh, Ria, I love you."

As I kiss Grayson back, I know how much I love him too. I also know that the road through hell was worth this reward. All I had to do was take a chance.

THE END

ACKNOWLEDGMENTS

To the lovely and incomparable Heather Novak for helping me work through my first ideations of what this novel would look like, as well as making me accountable for putting words on paper.

To the Romance Binders for inviting me to the 85k90 book and that awesome spread sheet where I had to put a number down for each day. Without that accountability, I wouldn't have pushed to get this novel done, especially in the face of a global pandemic.

My editors are simply the best and a global pandemic will not stop them from balancing day jobs and fixing my words. Thank you Bria Quinlan for pushing me to be better with each word. Thank you Tami Lund for putting everything else aside and just getting it done. This book is so much better because of you both.

To my Friday night Zoom Crew (we really need a better name than that): I don't know how I'd have survived this long through publishing without each and every one of you. Becky, Aven, Melissa, Erin, Laura, and Whitney, thank you for lifting me up.

To my real-life support team of Michele, Patrick, Jake, Sophia, Mom, and Dad: There's no way this would happen without you.

To the Mac-Hadyn Theatre: Thank you for so many seasons and so many performances. I'm confident your curtain will rise again. The show must go on!

ABOUT THE AUTHOR

Telling stories of resilient women, Kathryn R. Biel hails from Upstate New York where her most important role is being mom and wife to an incredibly understanding family who don't mind fetching coffee and living in a dusty house. In addition to being Chief Home Officer and Director of Child Development of the Biel household, she works as a school-based physical therapist. She attended Boston University and received her Doctorate in Physical Therapy from The Sage Colleges. After years of writing countless letters of medical necessity for wheelchairs, finding increasingly creative ways to encourage insurance companies to fund her client's needs, and writing entertaining annual Christmas letters, she decided to take a shot at writing the kind of novel that she likes to read. Kathryn is the author of twelve women's fiction, romantic comedy, contemporary romance, and chick lit works, including the award-winning books, *Live for This* and *Made for Me*. Please follow Kathryn on her website, http://www.kathrynrbiel.com and sign up for her newsletter.

Stand Alone Books:
Good Intentions
Hold Her Down
I'm Still Here
Jump, Jive, and Wail
Killing Me Softly
Live for This
Once in a Lifetime
Paradise by the Dashboard Light
Take a Chance on Me

A New Beginnings Series:
Completions and Connections: A New Beginnings Novella
Made for Me
New Attitude
Queen of Hearts

The UnBRCAble Women Series
Ready for Whatever
Seize the Day

If you've enjoyed this book, please help the author out by leaving a review on your favorite retailer and Goodreads. A few minutes of your time makes a huge difference to an indie author!

Made in the USA
Middletown, DE
02 June 2020

96551505R00239